WORLD OF

GREED

ARK II

For more information
Visit: Website: www.michaelhooper.com.au
Facebook Page: facebook.com/michaelhoopertheark
Instagram Page: @michaelhoopertheark

Book design concepts by Michael Hooper.
Book cover by GET COVERS

Website by Raz Marcovich
At Purplelink - purplelink.com.au

Paperback ISBN: 978-0-6455690-4-9

ACKNOWLEDGEMENTS

DEDICATED TO Georgina Hooper, the heart, spine and soul of my book of life. Thank you to all my friends and family for the support and help to get this book completed. SPECIAL THANKS Wayne Firns, Ian Timperley and Kate Hall and Claudia Williams, without you I would never have had the courage to move forward with this project.

CONTENTS

CHAPTER 1

SNAKE HUNTERS

"Let me make this unequivocally clear to the world, the United States did not make any acts of aggression towards the People's Republic of China; I will not back down to threats by the Chinese President, and I will protect the United States, its assets and allies with all the means at my disposal. China has to allow the UN and WHO investigators into their country and cease all military build-ups on their borders immediately!"

"There you have it, the strongest words yet from President Edwin in the build-up of tensions between the United States, Russia, and China. The smoking gun evidence is that China is behind the Covid MAN outbreak. Was this a declaration of war? And is there truth behind the unconfirmed report that there has been activity in Chinese nuclear silos? Are we heading towards the war to end all wars? Stay tuned for hourly updates on this growing concern. This is Tanya Chelmer with CNN signing off."

"Cut. Geez, Troy, is this real? Look, my hands are shaking. I can barely hold the mic. Just put the camera in the van for now. Let's go down the road. I need a drink."

****

Meanwhile, in Altaskivi Estonia

"Fuck," Ji-tae Jin slams his fist on the table. Immediately regretting the action with the company in the room.

"What is your problem, Water Tiger? A calm but inquisitive voice came from behind.

Ji-tae Jin, The Water Tiger, had to think quickly as to not give away his thoughts too much. He regretted these impulsive bursts he has been having since his failure to kill the American president and the Australian SAS captain. Failure was eating at him like nothing in his life has ever done before.

"I expected the man to show some balls and go after his enemy. Not just keep the rhetoric going," Jin answered.

"He is just playing the game as expected. Anyway, we will know when he's going to do something before he announces it. All is as it should be. Best we check all the chemicals are here. If we die, I don't want it to be because of someone else's mistake."

****

While at a dock in Kotka Finland

Apart from a few night birds and gentle waves splashing against the shore, there was a creepy silence as the team went about securing their gear. The snow covered everything as the temperature dropped well below zero.

"I can't feel my nuts."

"Why did your hands fall off?" Steel teased Smith.

"No! I meant it's so cold; I can't feel them," Smith added.

"I can't argue with you, Smith; it's been a while since I've been in this kind of weather," 2 Planks said as he joined in the conversation.

Smith started looking around warily. "Has anyone seen the movie The Fog?"

"Don't start your shit Smith" 2 Planks snapped over the comms.

"Quiet! I think the boat is coming. Remember, no conversation on the boat; we don't know who's listening or watching." So commanded the group leader of this Australian Special Forces team. "Remember, we're Recon. We will observe and report on what we find, remember the rules of engagement, protect the integrity of the intel and then only fire back to protect your life or each other."

"Roger," the team replied.

This team composed of five members, Team leader Captain Mike Madden (codename: Sherlock), Second in command Sargent Sebastian Morrison (codename: 2 Planks), Zikmund Chvalat (codename: Smith, Medic/rifleman), Katelyn Gouw (codename: Steel, Medic/hand to hand specialist), Thomas Ash (codename: Jedi, sniper/Tech and Communication).

The air was so still a vapour of fog covered the water here in Kotka, like a scene from so many Dracula movies from the 60's. It didn't move; it was just there, because there wasn't any breeze. The

Finland gulf temperatures are at their lowest for over 78 years. Once everyone had stopped talking, everything seemed to go deftly quiet, not a sound that soldiers like to hear; it's usually a warning that something is amiss. They all felt it; their instincts told them to be prepared. If they had looked at each other, they would have noticed they all had their hands on their secondary weapons.

The tiny chugs of the little steamboat grew louder as it made its way to the docks. A crewman jumped off the boat and tied off to the old timber docks as the boat came alongside. As Sherlock looked at the captain, he wondered who was older, the boat or the captain. He looked like the Old salty sea captains you see in movies, big white beards, solid and robust but with the weathered face of someone who had lived through four men's lifetimes.

The protocol of the arrangement was to only speak if absolutely necessary. The sea captain waved for Sherlock to come up to the helm. As Sherlock approached, the sea captain stuck out his hand. "I know the protocol, but I thought this was information you might want to know. I noticed on the trip here that ice was forming on the shallow sections of the shores. It has been a while since I have been to the area we are travelling. But I remember there were a lot of shallow shores near the drop-off. So, I may not be able to drop you off at the exact spot."

"That is ok, Captain. Anywhere near that shore will be fine; we can hike the rest of the way," Sherlock assured him.

"Well, I hope you came prepared. The forecast is for fine weather during the day, but the night temps will drop another 3 degrees lower if that's even possible."

"We might have to ice skate back to the boat," Sherlock joked.

"Ha, you might have to son, you might have to," the sea captain laughed as he slapped Sherlock on the shoulder.

The gear was moved onto the tug quickly, and they were heading off again within seconds. Into the fog, the fog that doesn't move. As the tug moved out into the Finland Gulf, the mist grew higher until it engulfed the tiny boat. 'Great, now we just have to sit here for an hour in the fog, can't see, can't speak, hate this mission already,' Smith thought.

They made good time across the gulf, no traffic; it seems like this boat, and its passengers were the only ones stupid enough to be out in this weather. The team was lucky. The jetty was out far enough for the tug to tie off; the frozen shoreline hadn't come out this far.

They disembarked with their gear quickly. The sea captain came up to Sherlock as he was handing equipment over the side to his team. "I'll await your call then," he says to Sherlock.

"Yes, we will let you know. It's a 3-day max, but we might have to be picked up urgently," Sherlock informed the sea captain.

"I was told no daytime pickups. Is that still the case?"

"Yes, we will have to survive till night if something happens," Sherlock informed him.

"Ok, remember it will be half an hour from when you call to when I get here, so plan that in as well," the sea captain explains.

"Roger that," responded Sherlock, and on that, the men shook hands, and Sherlock disembarked from the boat.

In less than a minute, the tug was gone, off into the fog like it had never been here.

The team removed their Primary weapons from their kits, loaded and were ready to move within seconds.

"You know the drill, Steel, you're on point … get us there, move out."

Even after the death of Deen (codename: Quassy) in their last mission, Sherlock still didn't hesitate with commands, but there were still lingering doubts when he gave orders. He is sure they will pass in time and swore that he will learn everything he can from that loss, so it doesn't happen again. 'Now he's hunting the terrorist whose team killed Deen and attempted to assassinate the US president. They then came for his family in their own home, but he can't make it personal. But it doesn't get any more personal. For the team's lives, he will be the team leader and get this job done. I am Recon. We will gather the Intel and then act,' Sherlock thought to himself.

Steel checked her GPS and headed off, leading the team. They fanned out in an arrowhead formation. Steel was their tip, and the rest of the group was the penetrating force. The air was still, but the fog was only 12 inches off the ground on land, which made navigation slow. A three-quarter moon illuminated the endless white of the snow-covered ground and trees. If you were a child, you would believe this is where Santa Claus lived and not where the evilest, dead-hearted human being that lived on the earth was last seen.

The thick covering of snow slowed the trek, but easy is not something this team is used to, and they soon reached point A on their mission. Ahead they were looking at an island covered with snow in the middle of a frozen Lake; this was point B, the observation point. This is where the team will split up. Sherlock and 2 Planks travelled by inflatable dingy to the small isle to set up a recording observation point. Team 2, comprising Jedi, Steel, and Smith, set up a sniper point on a slight rise 200 meters to the north. Jedi was the team's new sniper after the death of their teammate Quassy in the last mission. Where they helped rescue the President of the United States from a terrorist attack at the ARK. Jedi would do all sniping with Steel and Smith protecting his arse, also being on the mainland to help Sherlock and 2 Planks with cover fire if they're spotted and need to make a hasty retreat.

2 Planks was setting up their observation post with the snow camouflage cover, as Sherlock was setting up the telescopic recording devices needed to spot the Water Tiger if he was at this location. While at camp 2, Steel and Smith had found their spots to cover Jedi and Camp 1.

After 20 minutes, they were all set now for the surveillance of the Altaskivi/Balmoral castle in the county of Tartu, Estonia. The 17th century building looked magnificent in the snow. It was copied from the royal residence in Balmoral, Scotland. The castle has gone through many rebuilds in its time, but the latest started 2 months ago when engineers weren't happy with some structural work done 15 years ago, so they closed it until they could renovate it again.

To the surprise of the current owners, the Russian government declared it a piece of local history of the region and offered to pay for the rebuild; not wanting to look a gift horse in the mouth, they accepted. Now evidence of the Water Tiger (the world's number one wanted terrorist) being here causes concerns.

"Are you going to tell us now what you've been carrying in that big bag this whole trip?" Smith asked Jedi.

"I wanted to keep it a secret; she needs to make her own entrance," Jedi responded.

"SHE?" asked Smith startled, "Did you bring a girly bot with you... that's just creepy, not to mention against army regs," Smith joked.

"So, says the guy who has a robot Frankenstein doing his housework at home," Steel interrupted, laughing.

"Franky was a gift, and he doesn't do my washing anymore; he just answers the door," Smith informed them.

"I know I'm going to regret asking this," said 2 Planks over the mic. "But why doesn't Franky do your laundry anymore?"

"Because he saw me hit the washing machine once and thought that's what he had to do, I stopped him washing after I replaced the third machine," Smith said shamefully.

The laughs and snickers could be heard over the mic as they all had a good laugh at Smiths' expense.

"It's not funny, those things are expensive, and the warranty wouldn't cover the damage," Smith added.

Another burst of laughter over the comms brought the captain back online. "Focus, let's get this done and go home. Jedi, tell them what's in your bag of tricks."

As Jedi opened the bag, he lifted what looked like a big turkey, unplucked. He reached for a mini console in the bag and started hitting some buttons. Smith watched as the turkey unfolded from his position, with a head rising from its feathered chest to legs extending from underneath it. "I would like to introduce you to the latest team member, Scree," Jedi said in a proud, fatherly voice.

"Oh My God, you brought a turkey!" Smith bellowed through his mic.

"It's not a turkey, you turkey, it's an Eagle!" Steel said, amazed. "And a big one at that," she added.

Just then, Scree took off and flew into the air. As the team watched; even Jedi, who had trained with the robotic bird, were all amazed at just how real it looked and flew.

"What can it do?" asked Steel

"She's equipped with HD vision recording, night vision, and thermal vision. In addition, she has ultrasound pic ups, twice the range of our normal mics. For me, she has wind readings, temperatures gauges for my sniper calls." Jedi said proudly.

"Holy shit," 2 Planks said over the comms, amazed.

Smith injected himself into the conversation again. "Can it make hot chocolate? I could go a hot cuppa right now."

"Hahaha, yep, me too," added Steel.

"I'll bring it up at the next meeting," Jedi responded.

"Ok, work time now, kiddies. Let's keep the chatter down. Jedi let her loose. Remember the plan, a survey from further out, circling the premises, then work your way in. Make sure you keep in mind the training of what the eagle would normally do." Sherlock had set the scene and requested the team focus on the job at hand.

Scree had another helpful skill: she could tag soldiers outside with her visuals, and then they came up on both Sherlocks and Jedi's monitors to track precisely where any soldier was at any time. So, it was convenient when you were sneaking around all the time.

The first 3 hours of daylight were busy tracking everyone coming and going. Getting visual readings from Scree and then analysing the pictures. Sherlock studied the images with 2 Planks. "Heavily guarded for a castle rebuild, don't you think? Maybe they found the Ark of the covenant in there," 2 Planks jests.

"By the rigs and weapons, most of them are Russian and a few soldiers for hire as well. What's the count so far?"

"We've seen 22 different soldiers and 12 additional staff or technicians by the look of their clothes. The suits some of them have on scare me; they look biological," 2 Planks said.

"Yes, I thought the same thing, but no Water Tiger yet."

Another 2 hours passed with only a few more new contacts; 2 Planks was grateful for the new goggles Art Damani gave them for this work in the snow, not to mention the new thermals; these were way better than the standard army issue. Everyone was checking their gear; Scurrying through the snow like a white badger, Smith found a better spot to cover both positions from. He didn't like staying in the one spot for long, in this cold he felt better keeping his circulation moving. Scree was resting in a tree at the edge of her vision range when suddenly, "New contact, he fits the configurations of the Water Tiger. What do you want me to do, Sherlock?"

"Send Scree out circling around till we get facial recognition," Sherlock ordered

"Roger," Jedi replied

Jedi grabbed the controls and let Scree loose, just circling up high like Eagles do, then slowly swooping down to a different altitude, circling for food. On her dive to the lower level, she got close enough to do stills and video of the unknown figure exiting the Altaskivi castle through the front main entrance. As the figure turned and made his way around the side of the castle, he appeared to look up at the eagle flying overhead. He had a few looks at Scree enough to make Jedi uncomfortable, so he started moving Scree further away from the castle to make it appear he was not just flying over the same area.

"It's him! Facial recognition is through; we have the target, get as much footage as you can of him and where he goes," Sherlock ordered.

"Boss, look at what he's doing; it's weird," Jedi said.

Sherlock hopped onto his monitor, and here was The Water Tiger, standing at the edge of the lake staring straight across at where Sherlock and 2 Planks were camped.

"Shit, he seems to be staring straight at us," 2 Planks said warily.

"Sherlock, through the scope, it looks like he is holding something on his chest; it looks like a mobile phone," Jedi informed him.

"What? Send Scree up for a better look, Jedi," Sherlock said.

"Roger that,"

Jedi set Scree loose in the sky, soaring gracefully just like a real Brown Eagle; she started circling like she had been doing spying on all the guards, but this time as soon as The Water Tiger saw Scree in the air, he kept looking at her.

"He's starting to freak me out, Sherlock. Does he know it's not real?" Jedi puzzled. "He's in range, yes, it's a phone, and now he's holding it further away from his chest. I think he wants me to see the phone!"

"Zoom in and see what you get," Sherlock asked

"Got it!" Jedi called over the comms.

Then, while everyone was still stunned by the fact that the Water Tiger had made them, the hackles on their necks started rising again as the Water Tiger did something that no one saw coming; he made a hand jester to the side of his head and his mouth.

"Did he just tell us to call him?" Jedi said.

"What the fuck" Smith yelled over the comms.

"Yep, he sure did," replied Sherlock.

Earlier that day

Sam had freshened up before exiting the Azteck private jet before it touched down on the private airfield of the ARK. Even with all its luxury, 18 hours on a plane with two teenagers is draining. The overcast day didn't overshadow the generous, sunny smile of Art Damani, CEO of Azteck industries.

"Mrs. Madden, so lovely to finally meet you," Art Damani calls out from the bottom of the flight steps. As Sam Madden, a striking redhead, makes her way down the stairs of the plane with her two sons.

"Call me Sam, Art. With all that has gone on in recent months, we're practically family," she said. Samantha Madden is the wife of Australian Special Forces Captain Mike Madden.

As they all reach the tarmac, Sam introduces her two boys. "Art this is Aidan, and this is Oliver"

"Let's see if I get this right, Aidan. Your 12 and your call sign is Yoda, and your Oliver, your 14, and your call sign is Point Break. How'd I do?"

"Spot on," Aidan says. "How did you know all that? We haven't met before?"

"It's my job to know everything!" Art tells Aidan

The young lads' eyes lit up. "Everything?"

"Everything," Art repeated in a mysterious voice.

"Whoo awesome, you can help me with my exams coming up; I'm sure you have the tech to find out what's on the exam sheet."

"Hahahaha, I probably do, young man, I probably do," Art said, laughing.

"I'm sure Mr. Damani isn't going to help you cheat on your exam, Adi," Sam said in a firm voice.

"It's not cheating, mum; knowledge is power!" Aidan said in an evil genius voice.

Oliver clips Aidan over the back of the head, evoking an "OWW" from Aidan, "Stop being an idiot," Oliver says

"Oliver, don't hit your brother; use your words," Sam informs him.

"Sorry mum, Aidan… you're an idiot."

"Oliver!"

"Ahhh, Duffus?" Oliver enquires to his mother.

Sam sighs and slumps her shoulders. "Sorry, Art, it's been a long flight for these two."

"All good. I can see that these two would do anything for the other, even if they pretend otherwise. Come; I have prepared your rooms for you to relax before I give you the grand tour. Welcome to the ARK." Art greeted them warmly. Sam was right, Art thought; Even though they hadn't met before, they felt like family. Having Sam and the family here gave Art a sense of peace. Since their home was attacked by the monster her husband is tracking now, he felt better having her under the ARK's protection.

CHAPTER 2

THE SURPRISE

The click-clack of computer keys being hit wasn't even noticed by Art Damani as he checked the latest Intel on his laptop. He was in the Hub with Lexi Eldridge and Doby Heinlinker, his two master programmers and hackers.

Art went over the latest reports from Captain Mike Madden's Australian Special Forces team before sending them to Colonel Jim Briggs's their commanding officer. This passing of knowledge is because the team is using new tech from AZTECK Industries, developed to ensure their communications won't be hijacked. It was a field test, and if successful, it could be another selling point to interested military groups, or maybe AZTECK will keep it for themselves.

Art heard footsteps coming down the hall from the elevator. Before he could turn, there was a knock at the door. "Mrs. Madden, you don't have to knock your family here," Art said.

"Well, I'll keep knocking till you call me Sam," Sam offered in a take it or leave it deal.

"Hmm, fair trade. Where's the boys?" Art replied happily.

"Taking a nap. Can you believe it? Two teenage boys taking a nap in the afternoon like pre-schoolers…. I love it! The flight and the tour around the park wore them out. I haven't seen them so excited for a long time." Sam informed Art.

"Good timing; I was just sending the latest report to Jim Briggs," Art told her.

"So, what's happening? Have they found the Water Tiger yet?" Sam enquired.

"No, nothing in the last report, but something is definitely going on in the castle. It is supposed to just be a renovating job, but there are over two dozen armed security there, mostly Russian. Also, there were technicians there in Bio suits."

"Well, that certainly doesn't sound good. Are Mike and the team safe?" Sam asked, concerned.

"Yes, they're fine. Mike's job is to spot and record, they don't...."

"Unscheduled message coming through," Doby shouted out. "Hang on, it's still coming through. What? ... This can't be right."

"What is it, Doby? Tell us, what does it say?" Art asked, concerned.

"It says, spotted Water Tiger. He made us and signalled that he wants us to call him and sent a phone number," Doby repeated, still not believing what he just read out.

"What the ..." Lexi said out loud.

"Yeah, what she said," Sam agreed.

Art was trying to envision what Mike's train of thought would be at this moment. Is it a delay to entrap the team? Or is this totally different?

"And that is all that was in the message, Doby?"

"Yes, that's everything," Doby replied.

"So, Mike hasn't decided yet on whether to contact him... we will just have to wait and see," Art said, concerned.

"Sam, are the boys fine in the room?" Art enquired.

"Yes, they're fine. I left a note beside Oliver's phone to say where I'm going." Sam said.

"Good, when they get up, we will take them on some of the fun parts of the Ark," Art said.

"There's more?" Sam said, surprised.

"Yes, some people are dying to meet you all," Art said proudly.

"Who?" Sam enquired.

"Tyson and the Major," Art said.

Sam laughed, "The monster maker and the Legend of the Ark, I can't wait to meet them. I have heard so much about them. When Mike told me about the monsters helping to fight the mercenaries to protect the Ark. I thought he may have taken a head knock in the battle. Robot monsters, robot Panthers and Tigers, it sounded like a Mike Hooper novel." Sam let out another laugh. It was a joyful, infectious laugh as everyone in the room joined in.

"Yes, then he told me about Deen and all the other soldiers and security killed in the battle. I had a feeling about Deen; no one mentioned him when they got back; it weighed deeply on them all. Mike couldn't even bring himself to say anything yet. And you, Art, how are you dealing with it? I heard how you saved Katelyn twice. First, coming to the rescue at the baboon enclosure and saving her from the mercenaries, I didn't think that lady would need rescuing from anything," Sam stated.

"Me too… sorry, just a fan" Lexi jumped into the conversation.

"Me, I have been too busy with the rebuild and the upgrades to think about it during the day… but at night, they all come back, not haunting me but forever reminding me of the mistake I made," Art said solemnly.

"Maybe you should talk to someone about it, Art," Sam said, concerned.

"Yes, you're right. I should… Do you prefer tea or coffee?" Art enquired cheekily.

"Me? If we are going to talk about all that happened, we would need a bottle of vodka," Sam said, joking.

Lexi jumped into the conversation again, "Me too… sorry, a fan of that too".

"That's my girl, wild women, and booze," Doby threw into the conversation jokingly.

"Gee, I love it when you say I'm your girl! It makes me so hot, Asslicker," Lexi licked her lips and made a wild cat growl.

"Down kitty. We have guests," Doby said in his neutral business voice.

"You think a sultry redhead like Sam, who is married to a hot super-soldier, doesn't know about sex?" Lexi said, teasing.

"Oh My God, Lexi, show some decorum," Doby yelled, embarrassed.

Sam and Art started laughing, but Sam could feel her cheeks blushing wildly. These two were precisely as Mike had described them, and Lexi was as hot as Zikmund kept going on and on about. The jokes were a momentary distraction because their partners were just made by a psychopath. 'Waiting sucks,' Sam thought.

CHAPTER 3

THE ARMAGEDDON PROTOCOLS

The Whitehouse Bee-hive was alive as usual. The worker bees buzzed around, trying to get the work done handed down by the supervisors. The Chief of Staff of the

Whitehouse was on the constant move here; there was always something to do, and as soon as you've done it, there would be a call to do another job or tear down the last job you did, such is the life in politics.

Chief of staff Linwood Cashdon was one of the most efficient Chief of Staff the Whitehouse had ever seen. Great with planning, a quick thinker, always seemed to have the next move already planned. However, Cashdon was always in your face, which doesn't always go down well with the staff; he was impatient with how fast the system works in the Whitehouse. He may follow procedures, but he didn't like how long they took to implement his commands.

As the bees flew around the domain of the President bee, scurrying from one room to the next, happy to go about their given chores. There was always one thing that puts them on edge, makes the hair stand up on the back of their necks... The ding of the elevator bell. It's a momentary pause, a freeze-frame. Everyone pauses to see who'll disembark from the lift. Sometimes it's just another worker bee, and the freeze-frame ends, and everybody just continues in the flow of what they were doing. But sometimes, it's something worse; they're

Described as the Monster Trucks, barrelling they're way over staff who dare cross their path. Some call them the evil Titans, as they have no time for the worker bees, because they are below them so much that they only notice them when they trample over one going from the elevator to the Oval Office. Then, only because they have dirtied their shoes in the trampling. But on occasions they stop, help the bee to their feet in a kind jester ... and then they have them fired. Such is the life of politics; therefore, the freeze-frame is all about self-preservation.

Today, there was a ding, and the elevator doors became the gates of Hell as the Three Evil Titans came out together. First, there was Damien Spelling, CIA Chief Director, then 4-star General Hagart, Minister of Defence and the Armed forces. Then there was Linwood Cashdon, Chief of Staff of the Whitehouse and the President's right-hand man. As they boomed out of the elevator like rampaging bulls, it was an incredible sight to see… from a distance. The power, the fury that these Titans of men exuberated from them, the CIA Chief, a 4-star general, both over six feet tall and the power that seemed to glow around them… then there was Cashdon, he was like a little penguin waddling behind barely five feet with thick sole shoes, but he also glowed with power, shuffling down the corridor, saying, your fired, and you're fired.

As they come to the door of the Oval Office, the new Secret Service officer by the name of Jamieson opened the door as they made him aware of the meeting with the President. Willy Jamieson hired after the slaughter of Secret Service officers at the ARK to protect the President. When the Water Tiger and a horde of mercenaries ambushed and slaughtered them. Only with the help of Special Forces Captain Mike Madden team, Art Damani, and the staff of the ARK rescued the President and saved the ARK from destruction.

The three Titans entered the Oval Office and were greeted warmly by the President.

"Good morning, gentlemen, please be seated. So, what has happened that all of you needed this emergency meeting this morning?"

"Well, Mr. President, I brought General Hagart and Director Spelling to give you as much information as possible. There has been a fresh outbreak of covid in a small village outside Lüderitz in Namibia." the Chief of staff explained.

"That doesn't seem to be big news. So, I'm assuming there's more to it," the President queried.

"Yes, Mr. President, the World Health Organization is on the scene. They're saying it's a totally new strain. The early reports say it has a death ratio of ten times all the other strains; this one is lethal. Its death toll worldwide would make the bubonic plague seem like a summer cold," Cashdon informed him.

"My God! We will have to keep a close eye on this one, but why you both are here gentlemen?" the President referring to Spelling and Hagart.

"Well, Mr. President, Mr. Cashdon asked me to look into any sources in the area for more info. The ground report came back that it just appeared out of nowhere, ground zero, and the village infected within 48 hours, the entire village," said Director Spelling.

"And you general, why are you here?" asked the President.

"Well, sir, we are extremely concerned about this; if this virus gets out and makes it to the United States, I feel the country will have major civil strife, looting of the likes the country has ever seen. This virus can shut down countries and send us back to the stone ages." The General said gravely.

"That seems a little far-fetched general," the President said, surprised.

"Not at all," Cashdon interjected, "we would lose a third of the country's skilled labour in the 3 months it would take to spread through the states. Industries would shut down; the economy would crash within 12 months. This has the power to change the world politically; there will be countries out to take advantage of the situation and at home. Don't forget the administration's poor response to covid-19 and the drastic results that happened there." Cashdon was pushing the point across.

"Yes, I see your point, so what is it you want me to do?" the President asked.

"We all agreed we should start prepping the Armageddon protocol," Cashdon said.

"Jesus, Linwood, that is just a theory Protocol, the taking over of all essential services by the military, was always a last-ditch invasion stratagem," the President stated.

"We are being invaded, and the invaders will kill over a third of the nation, Mr. President, and we will sit in the dark burning candles if the stores have any left." Tanner pressed.

"Ok fine, work on the protocol and see what we need to prep. Keep me posted on what WHO finds in that village. Then, Linwood, consult legal and see where we stand with

Marshal Law and how to implement it; and pray to God, they can contain this. We will also need to know how to lock down the country tight if the need arises. So, gentlemen, you have 2 days to come up with a viable plan that I can take to congress; that will be all." the President stood up and shook their hands.

"Let's hope God blesses America," he added.

"He always has Mr. President," Director Spelling added.

As they reached the elevator, the Chief of staff turned to address the two men.

"General, I will need to know what the forces are going to need before everything is in short supply. Director, can your people on the ground keep monitoring the situation in Namibia so we can get a heads up if WHO can't contain it?"

"Yes, that's possible," the director replied.

"Ok, gentlemen, we will talk soon," the Chief of staff finished, and he turned and walked back to his office.

CHAPTER 4

RAPTOR REVELS

There was a contrasting situation going on. The picturesque night aura of a golden lite castle. The calming fields of snow and moonlight on the frozen lake. Then there was the other. The turmoil running through the minds of the SAS special unit. 'Do we run, since our covers are blown?' Nerves on edge, but....

Everyone was quiet as to let Sherlock access the situation. 'Stay and possibly be penned in and trapped here, but why would he go to all that trouble? He looked like he was trying to hide his phone from the castle,' Sherlock thought.

"We're packing up camps; get your gear rolled up ready to move," Sherlock instructed over the comms.

"Brilliant move, boss. We shouldn't trust that fucker," Smith added.

"We're not, but I am going to ring him," Sherlock informed them.

"What! Why would you trust anything that guy says? Just let Jedi put one in his head, and let's go home," Smith stated.

"One, we are not assassins, we are recon, two, we haven't heard from the base. Three, you're not in charge!"

"Roger that, Sherlock," Smith said, realising he had overstepped.

"Steel, Smith, further your perimeter. Jedi, send me the number you saw on his phone and get Scree in the air; if anything, even looks like moving in our direction, nail it. 2 Planks and I are returning to the mainland after the call." Sherlock had issued the orders, and everyone went about their roles.

Jedi sent the number, and Sherlock dialled it on the new comm set Azteck had supplied. It rang three times as Jedi saw on the scope that the Water Tiger put it on hands-free and started walking. Finally, the Water Tiger answered, "It took you long enough to find me; I left enough clues?"

Sherlock kept his cool and kept it business-like. "We have you in our scope; surrender now, or I will order your death."

"If you wanted to shoot me, you would have done it by now. I sent for you; I left clues for your friend Damani to track me, knowing you'd show up. I don't have time now to talk; I'm due back in. Northern end of the lake, 9pm, just you and I will tell you everything," the Water Tiger stated.

"Trusting you is not an option; why would I want to hear what you have to say?" Sherlock remained strong.

"You like to play the hero and save the day; come tonight, and you might help stop a World War." He hung up his phone and started walking back towards the castle. Jedi looked through the scope; he had a perfect shot but not the order.

Sherlock and 2 Planks grabbed their gear and made their way to the inflatable raft to go back to the mainland; after scraping over the frozen water's edge, they greeted the rest of the team.

"What did he want?" asked Steel.

"He wants to meet me alone at 9 at the northern edge of the lake," Sherlock told them.

"Not a chance," Steel and 2 Planks said in unison.

"Come on, boss, that sounds like a trap," Smith added.

Jedi didn't say anything; he just watched Sherlock. "There's more to it, isn't there? You know I will have you covered with a shot. You have already decided to go meet him; what else did he say?" Jedi asked.

"He said he had information to give me to help stop a World War," Sherlock said.

"What? Any World War would be started by him. Piece of shit he is," 2 Planks snarled.

"Jedi, send the info back to base. Tell them there will be a special transmission coming after 9."

"Roger that," Jedi answered.

The team has the utmost confidence in their team leader; he has a sixth sense they have witnessed regularly on countless missions over the past years. He keeps them alive and always has their backs... but there was a hesitant sentiment that Sherlock 'had lost the plot' on this one.

While back at the ARK

The outburst came like the thundering sound of a 100mm cannon on a battleship. With just as much force and intent.

"NO WAY! You send a message and tell him HIS WIFE! Says to get his arse back on the boat and come home." Sam said furiously, "Your, not typing Doby?" Sam said, surprised.

Doby looked at Sam sympathetically. "I don't think Mike would appreciate the message; he wouldn't do anything he hasn't thought out first. Sorry Sam."

"Doby is right, Sam. Mike will do the right thing; he wouldn't go meet him if he didn't believe there was some truth to what he was saying. Plus, he has a great team watching his back." Art assured her.

"Yes, I know you're right, but we all know how soulless that animal is," Sam said dejectedly.

Just then, Art and Sam heard the ding from the elevator. They heard what sounded like the running of the bulls in Spain. Art knew the boys were coming and was thankful for the break in the tension. Sam was worried, and so she should be; they all were. Their friends and family were going to meet with a psychopath.

Sam changed her frown to a smile just before she heard the call from the door "MUM" as two galloping teenagers flew into her arms.

"Mum, Oliver snores just like you," Aidan said excitedly.

"Who told you I snore?" Sam questioned firmly.

"Dad," Aidan said like it was nothing.

"And I don't snore, Duffus!" Oliver said to correct this incorrect statement.

"And where did YOU get that word from, young man?" Sam questioned Oliver.

"Uncle Seb, he said it was a sign of respect for those who don't deserve any; it's a military secret," Oliver informed her.

Sam dropped her chin on her chest and looked down at Oliver. "Reeeally," Lexi let off a snicker to this Abbott and Costello routine.

"Well, I think it's time to go see some more cool things before more military secrets come out." Art said.

"Let's go visit Tyson, The Monster Maker," Art said in a mysterious voice, which the boys didn't think was very spooky.

"AWESOME!" the boys yelled in unison.

"I think he has something special for you to try."

The boys turned and bolted to the elevator. "Come on, mum," they shouted.

They all arrived at Tyson's workshop, and the boys shook his hand with their best MAN shake that their dad had taught them. The quick tour got the boys all excited again, with Tyson showing them the animal robotics he was working on. The little chimpanzee was freaky, but cool. Then the excitement level peaked as they got introduced to the Wolfman robot.

They headed out to the console area;

"Boys, I need your help; I need someone to help me road-test something new. Do you both know how to use one of these?" Tyson showed them a PlayStation gaming controller.

The look on Sam's face as she rolled her eyes said it all, that the boys had PlayStation consoles.

"Know them; their hands are glued to them, 6 hours a day," Sam offered the information, with an 'are you kidding,' tone.

Tyson went to the computer console, hit a few keys, and up popped a screen.

"Cool, a game," Oliver said.

"Ah yeah, a game… of sorts; who wants to go first?" Tyson asked.

"Let Aidan go first; that way, he won't complain," Oliver said in his big brother voice.

"Cool!" Aidan jumped in the seat in front of the screen.

"Ok, Aidan, now remember this is a live simulator; when the creature comes on the screen, it can't do slow-motion karate kicks; it can only do what it could do in real life, ok?" Tyson instructed.

"Got it; what is the creature?" Aidan asked excitedly.

"Hit F2 on the keys," Tyson said.

Aidan hit F2 and up popped a view of what looked like a jungle, from the first-person perspective of the creature.

"If you want to see what he is, hit shift/z."

Aidan hit the keys, and the creature went to 3rd person view. "Cool, it's a raptor." On the screen, Aidan was now controlling a raptor from the Jurassic era. But, unbeknown to Aidan, he was actually controlling one of Tyson's and Art's new toys, raptor guards.

"Move him around and see what he can do." Tyson urged. Like a true professional of the PlayStation world, Aidan hit each button to see what they did and then started doing combos of buttons to see what happens. The raptor flew through the jungle with ease, speed, and with the dexterity of the person's fingers controlling him.

"Outstanding graphics, Mr. Damani. Are you going into games?" Oliver asked.

"Well, sort of Oliver, we are actually already in game ware but under a different company." A person came on screen; he looked like a gardener pushing a wheelbarrow full of leaves and branches.

Aidan chased the man to see what happens. As the gardener turned to see what the noise was behind him, he let out a girly scream and started running.

Aidan hit the buttons that make the raptor use his call voice, terrifying the man even more. Tyson was exceedingly awe-stricken by his latest innovation. The manoeuvrability of the raptor exceeded even his optimistic projections. Letting the boys do the trial was a stroke of genius. The fact they don't know it's real having Aidan trying movements Tyson may not have tried in a standard test. Although chasing the grounds person probably wouldn't have been on his list of tests.

Aidan and Oliver started laughing as the man jumped a fence to safety, still screaming. Art leaned over to Tyson. "There's another lawsuit,"

"Yep," Tyson replied. Sam overheard the comment and elbowed Art in the ribs and mouthed the words 'Is this real?'. Art nodded, and Sam had a horrified look on her face. Art just waved his hand with a 'don't worry about it look.'

"Aidan, test out his speed. Hold L! and keep hitting the run button," Tyson informed him. Aidan hit the buttons, and off the raptor ran, going faster and faster as he topped at 48 kph. "Turn left here, on that path" Aidan hit the keys and lightly manoeuvred the controls, and the raptor turned the 90 degrees with ease and grace. Aidan kept following the path, jumping and snapping the vicious jaws of the creature. As the trail wand up this mountain, Oliver spoke out, "Hey, isn't that the path around ARK mountain? COOL! You made a game about the Ark; that's brilliant now kids are going to see first-hand what it's really like, your brilliant Mr. Damani," Oliver said. Art and Tyson looked at each with a 'why didn't we think of that expression?' In the back of Art's mind, he has already started marketing and costings, no time to waste.

"Look, we're coming up to the Hub entrance, and it's opened". As Aidan slowed the raptor, he slowly crept into the Hub, and there, sitting with his back to the doorway, was Doby; Lexi was on the other side, facing the raptor. Lexi looked but didn't react to the creature as Aidan slowly crept in. "Wow, the resolution is unbelievable; they look so real," Oliver said. Sam, Art, and Tyson clenched their teeth.

Then, suddenly, the character that was Lexi said, "Is this a friend of yours, Doby?" As Doby turned around, he let out a huge girly scream, "EEEEEK." As he tried to get up and run, but fell back into his computer chair and went sailing across the Hub floor. While screaming and sailing across the Hub floor, Doby's milkshake flew out of his hand and landed on his monitor.

"Sorry, guys," Tyson said over a headset he was wearing. He had to turn off the sound as Doby started throwing expletives and finger jesters to the raptor's screen.

"Holy Shit! That was real; you made a raptor, awesome," Oliver blurted.

"Language, young man," Sam corrected firmly.

"Sorry, mum," Oliver replied.

"Can we see it, Tyson?" Aidan asked.

"I don't know, Aidan, they're pretty scary," Tyson teased.

Oliver laughed, a big tough boy laugh, "Nah, they're not that scary." Unbeknown to Oliver, Tyson had a controller in his hand and was manoeuvring a second raptor through the lab door behind him. Aidan could see the raptor coming and thought to play along.

"I don't know, Oli; they looked pretty scary to me," Aidan said.

"Nah, did you see Doby though, and his big girly scream" as Oliver started laughing, Tyson moved the raptor beside him. "EEEEEK" Oliver let out a girly scream and jumped halfway across the room in one stride. 'Very impressive' Art thought. As everyone was laughing, except Oliver.

Sam said, "what was that about a girly scream?",

"Hilarious," Oliver said, sulking.

"Well, tomorrow boys, you get to ride with the Major. The legend of the ARK, and do a trial run of the raptors," Art informed them.

"Cool," the boys replied; Oliver's sulky face changed quickly with the news.

"Well, the rest of the night is yours, Madden family. I expect you will join us at 9 tonight, Sam?" Art enquired.

"OH, I'll be there," Sam said firmly.

"What's on at 9, mum?" Aidan enquired.

"Oh, we're just hoping to get some more info from dad, that's all," Sam and Art tried to put on their best poker faces.

CHAPTER 5

TO TRUST A LIAR?

"Everyone in place?" Sherlock asked.

"Roger" was the team's response.

'Picture perfect' was the thought going through Sherlock's mind. 'This looks like a scene from a calendar from the most beautiful places in the world.' He looked around, and the crystal-clear night, the reflection from the three-quarter moon, glistens off the snow all around him. The decorative coloured lights of the Alatskivi Castle shone on the snow-covered lawns around the building. Some of the lights glimmer reached the lake's sparkling waters, and they lit up the area like Santa's sleigh. Yet, here I lay in the freezing cold snow waiting for a psychopath to tell me about the next world war and Armageddon. 'What's wrong with this picture' he thought again. 'I am,' was his response.

"Target approaching, he's a half an hour early," Jedi informed them, even though they all already knew.

The Water Tiger sauntered to the lake's edge on the south end and slowly made his way north. He pretended to be checking areas and shining his flashlight around as if he were on patrol. He made his way to the North to a darkened nest of trees at the tip of the lake where the area was heavily wooded. He knew the Australian would be there with his team to take him down.

Mike stepped out from the shadow of a large birch tree. Smith and Steel also made themselves slightly visible to give the impression he had nowhere to go. "Why aren't you dead?" Mike asked.

"I nearly was because of your wife, and I'm not dead now because you are curious, and you sensed I was telling the truth; you have good instincts, Captain." The Water Tiger said.

The air was charged between the two; you could practically see it bouncing off the shimmering snow around them. After their last two encounters, they had a history together where the Water Tiger tried to kill the President of the United States at the ARK. Mike and his team intervened and foiled the attempt. Both men lost a close friend and team member. But it was the Water Tiger, No.1 on the world's most wanted terrorist list that lost his cool and made an attempt at revenge on Mike and his family at their home in Bryon Bay, Australia. Once again, the Water Tiger's attempt failed, and they left him bleeding out on the beach after being shot 3 times by Mike's wife. Mike and the team tracked him here with the help of their friend Art Damani, Billionaire and creator of the ARK.

"I assume you are on a fake border check and only have minutes at hand, so you have those minutes to convince me whether you will return to the castle!" Mike stated firmly.

"Don't get pushy, Captain; I sent for you! Not the other way around," the Water Tiger said in a matter-of-fact tone of voice.

"What?" Mike said, stunned.

"I let Damani track me, knowing he'd send you and your team, the righteous soldier, to bring me in. I've been watching for signs for days; you were slow getting here. Oh, tell the new boy in your team, he picked the wrong eagle; there are no brown eagles in this area. No one else would have known the difference except me. The eagle is very impressive, a toy from Damani, I assume. Yes, I know who is in your team and what they do; my employers have contacts like Damani." he said once again in a calm voice.

"So, you did your homework, but your time and lifespan are running out," Mike stated firmly again.

"My death or disappearance would only start the process running faster; The same people that hired me for the attempt on the American President have hired me again. I believe that mission was linked to this one, so your intervention has changed the timetable. They are planning something biological, just what I don't know. The technicians are sworn to secrecy, but some fear me and have told me about minor features of it. Whatever it is, it is highly contagious. There are several sites hidden worldwide, which they will ask me to secure at some stage. This group of people is planning an attack on China, hoping to start a war, and the proceeds of the war will be a defeated China and new borders as they divvy up the country." Water Tiger said in a somewhat emotional voice.

"Rubbish! No one can take on China; they're a world power now with a military to rival the United States; no one would be stupid enough to do it because China would have no qualms in fighting back. So, who is this country that you reckon is going to attack them?" Mike demanded.

"Not A, country but multiple countries joined... the United States and Russia are the two dominant forces behind it," he said.

"What, you can't be serious. You want me to believe that the United States and Russia will use a biological weapon in China and start a war so they can defeat China and take over their country? What proof do you have of this nonsense?" Mike demanded.

"I am the proof, captain; there is the proof," the Water Tiger pointed to the castle.

"The President of the United States would never allow this," Mike informed him.

"I don't know who are the key chess pieces, but they have to be very high with their leaders' ears, and before you think of taking this castle down, if you did, they would use the others to speed up the process." the Water Tiger informed him.

"Well, that leaves two unanswered questions. First, why are you helping us when you're the master of world chaos? And what did you want from us?" Mike stated firmly as he looked the Water Tiger straight in the eyes to see if he was telling the truth.

"Why am I helping you? I'm not; I'm helping myself. Surely you don't just point your gun and shoot people or sneak up on them and call in a drone strike. Do you know, captain, why and what you are fighting for? I do. We are the same, just on different sides of an invisible line in the dirt. On one side, I am a psychopathic terrorist, and on the other side, I'm a national hero fighting for a country's freedom to make its own choices. Why am I helping? Suppose China goes to war with the United States and Russia, how long before China's allies step in. In that case, Nth Korea will attack a distracted United States and attack South Korea, Japan, and Taiwan will step in, Australia and England, where will Indonesia stand in this."

"Europe could erupt because Russia has its own enemies and won't care about any alliance with the USA. Captain, if a world power goes to war, the world goes to war, if three world powers go to war, how far away is a nuclear war? We all have lives, captain, even psychopathic terrorists. And why you? You have a moral compass, and my friends don't, plus you are now friends with the most extensive spy network in the world, AZTECK. I assume you don't know what your friend Art Damani is capable of? The people that supply my funding are only afraid of one person, Art Damani." The Water Tiger went silent.

"Proof, we will need some kind of evidence to go on, and there's the question...?" Mike went silent.

"Can you trust me?" the Water Tiger finished Mike's sentence. "I don't have any smoking gun, as you call it, yet, but I will give you something towards trust to ease your mind. I joined in a conversation when I heard Art Damani's name come up. His enemy has pulled some strings and he will be indited to the United Nations committee to answer questions about his dealings with the World Heritage Committee and how he got his land grant through. It's to distract him and damage his brand." Once again, Water Tiger went silent to see what Captain Madden had to say.

Mike stuck out his hand and handed Water Tiger his unique 2-way phone tracker Art Damani gave them. If only he could see the look on Smith and Steel's face when he did it. Shock! Was a vast understatement. Strangely enough, Jedi was listening to the entire conversation through Scree and had even taken his finger off the trigger. He, like Mike, believed the Water Tiger was telling the truth, as far-fetched as the story seemed.

"Two days. You have two days to find us something to prove this. This phone can't be tracked and is always secure. Two days, then I'll burn this place to the ground," Mike told him.

The Water Tiger took the phone, turned, and left just like that.

2 Planks, Smith and Steel, all converged on Sherlock's position. Jedi held his position with Scree, checking there was no other activity around and their position was not compromised. As they moved in on Sherlock, all was quiet, as no one was sure how to broach the subject of, you just gave a terrorist a secure communication device. Except for Smith, he always had words to say, whether they were right or wrong.

"Are you mad! You just gave a secure line to the world's most wanted terrorist; what were you thinking!" Smith ranted.

"I must admit Sherlock, I've never doubted a decision you've ever made, till now," 2 Planks agreed with Smith.

"He was telling the truth," Sherlock said cool-headed.

"You bought that dribble about the USA and Russia plotting together against China?" Steel asked Sherlock. "I don't know if what he is saying is true, but he believes it, which is worth investigating," Sherlock informed them. Suddenly, a voice came from behind.

"I agree with Sherlock; Water Tiger was telling the truth," Jedi said as he was approaching with his sniper rifle slung over his shoulder.

"What would you know?" Smith challenged Jedi.

"I just do; he believes what he thinks is going on is real, plus, add to the fact Water Tiger made himself a target by contacting us," he said calmly. Just then, Sherlock had a flashback of Quassy's dying last words, "he is you, Mike," meaning Jedi. "Jedi..." Sherlock started to ask Jedi something.

"Yes, the area is clear, and Scree is still doing patrol," Jedi finished Sherlock's sentence. Now Sherlock was just getting shivers up his spine, creepy.

"Ah, great. We will set positions for a quick exit. Jedi, send through a message. We need Art to bring Colonel Briggs to the Ark. All we have learned is too big to send through as a message, plus if it's true, we now don't know who we can trust. They're to let us know when he has arrived. Also, let them know we are secure for now, and we will evacuate in two days." Sherlock finished

"Roger," Jedi answered.

"Smith, no, I'm not mad. Set up a perimeter in case we get betrayed. We wait and see if Water Tiger comes up with anything tangible in the next two days, then we send Colonel Briggs all the info we have collected, and we will do, as we are ordered, roger that?"

"Roger Sherlock," 2 Planks said for them all.

Once again, the night was deftly quiet, night birds, the occasional squeak of snow crushed underfoot as Smith moved positions through the night, an occasional cough from guards as they did their patrols around the castle. Yep, the night was the quietest Sherlock has ever remembered from his team.

The following day, Scree was patrolling. They all did perimeter walks to stretch and stay alert, but hardly a word was spoken... until "SHIT!" Sherlock said over the comms.

"You don't get to say shit, Sherlock. We say shit, and then you say, it's all right, we can blah blah blah... but you don't get to say, shit." 2 Planks said in a smug voice.

"I've never said blah blah blah in my entire career ... you have to be a Colonel or higher rank to blah blah blah," Sherlock said, mocking 2 Planks comment.

"Jedi, send a message. Number 1 comm compromised. If it can't be isolated, no further communications till back at base, unless in an emergency."

"Roger," Jedi responded.

"Your right... That was an OH SHIT moment," 2 Planks said, digging at Sherlock again.

"Must be old age," Steel added.

"Or the cold, because I still can't feel my...",

"Smith, if you mention your nuts again, so help me God, when they finally drop again, I will cut them off," Steel jumped in on Smith's comment. This bought a round of laughs on the comms.

"Boss, do you really buy that story the Water Tiger was selling?" 2 Planks asked.

"No, not hook, line and sinker, BUT everything he said and has done has led to something big going on, and remember with his reputation, you wouldn't lie to him if you wanted to stay alive, that is." Sherlock answered.

"That's a good point," Smith agreed.

Once again, the comms went silent. The area turned into this winter wonderland, white glistening snow, an ice-covered lake, clear crystal skies, and this beautiful castle in the foreground. One would expect to see Santa Claus tending reindeers or elves frolicking in the snow-covered grounds, but no. Here wandering the grounds were 6-foot Russian mercenaries and not an elf in site, most likely mowed down by semi-automatic machine gun fire, Smith thought.

"What...? Jedi is Scree in the air?" Steel asked over the comms.

"No, he's down recharging; why, do you see something?" Jedi responded.

"..." Steel

"Steel report," Sherlock requested.

"All clear... I think. I just had the feeling I'm being watched," Steel responded.

Steel definitely had a sense of something. The hairs on her arm were standing up, and it wasn't from the cold.

"Women's intuition," Smith joked.

"Any intuition is better than none," Sherlock responded. "Everyone check your six; Smith, do you have eyes on Steel?"

"Yeah, boss, nothing. Maybe Jedi's checking out Steel's ass again," Smith joked.

"Stay on your game, everyone," Sherlock ordered.

A voice came over the comms; it gave everyone the creeps hearing the Water Tiger voice over their comms. "Captain, are you there?"

"Roger that," Sherlock responded.

"I don't have your smoking gun yet, but here is some information which could be helpful. First, the person who was my contact for the attack on the President and the Ark is the same contact for here. I believe he is connected to ILLUMIUN Corp. He may not be on their payroll, but he definitely works for them. His name is Fredrick Nessler."

"Second, a technician said to me they are working on a virus and that the other sites are working on a cure or a vaccine to help prevent catching it. They knew nothing about what it was being used for. Only Nessler seems to be privy to this information. He has hinted that there will be a visit from one of their inner circle this afternoon. So, I suggest getting your bird ready. I still have no word about who the Kremlin and the Whitehouse contacts are. Out."

The comms went silent.

"Chatty fellow, isn't he?" 2 Planks joked.

"Jedi, is Scree ready?" Sherlock asked.

"In 10, he will be at full capacity and can stay up for 1 ½ hour and another 30 minutes on Solar if the skies stay clear," Jedi informed him.

"Ok, be ready to send him up when the moment arises," Sherlock instructed.

"There it is again!" Steel said over comms. Once again, Steel had that perception of being watched. 'If it is a sixth sense, then show me what the hell is watching me,' she thought.

"Cracking under pressure, Steel, feeling ghosts, hahaha," Smith joked.

"2 Planks do a perimeter," Sherlock ordered.

"Roger," 2 Planks replied.

2 Planks set off immediately to do a semi-circle around the team. He has known Steel for 4 years now and knows she isn't one to say things for the hell of it. So, he kept a watchful eye and checked out everything that even remotely looked suspicious, with his finger on the trigger the whole time. Moving, stopping, looking through his scope, nothing so far. He was approximately 30 meters

behind Steel's vantage point; as he came out into the open, he checked the area cautiously to not get spotted and shot.

Apprehension was mounting, but there was nothing; as he crept forward, suddenly something jumped in front of him, and 2 Planks snapped his rifle up to fire. He couldn't see anything, just the snow being thrown everywhere. Moving his rifle side to side, bewilderment and infuriation built in him.

"Shit, shit, shit! Something's in the snow. But I can't see it." 2 Planks said, annoyed.

He kept trying to get a bearing on something to shoot, but he couldn't see anything. Then, suddenly, a pair of green eyes lit up in front of him, and 2 planks fell back, startled, losing his balance, and landed on his arse in the bitter cold snow. Still keeping control of his weapon and pointing it in front of him, he still couldn't find anything to shoot.

Hearing 2 Planks call out, a startled Steel swung around and came to aid. Then, pointing her weapon, as she looked over and saw nothing but snow being thrown up, something in her instincts made her call out, "LOKI!" Immediately on command, hearing her masters voice, Loki a black panther and one of the robotic prototypes of AZTECK's animal range came out of camo mode and appeared in front of 2 Planks. Turning and bounding off to his master like a puppy, left alone for the day. Loki ran to Steel and started bouncing around her in excitement. "Settle down," Steel instructed him, and on command, he sat immediately and was waiting for a command.

"Jesus, Loki, you gave me a heart attack. I'll never get used to that cloaking device." 2 Planks said.

Just then, Loki turned to where 2 Planks was getting up out of the snow and let out a low growl; just then, Steel saw another pair of green eyes light up on their own. Steel looked over and said in a very unsure voice, "Thor?" Just then, Thor, a Bengal tiger, appeared, the partner of Loki. He appeared in front of 2 Planks and startled him, sending him flat on his arse again. Thor bounced off to Steel, wagging his big tail like a puppy as well. "When did you get camo, boy?" Steel said to Thor. "We will have to talk to daddy about keeping secrets," she said.

"Is that the last of them?" 2 Planks asked before he tried to stand up again.

"Yep, I think so. That would explain the feeling of being watched." Steel answered.

"What's the commotion?" Sherlock asked.

"Loki and Thor are here," 2 Planks says.

"Did you know about this, Steel?" Sherlock asked.

"No, not a clue," she answered.

"Keep Loki and Thor hidden. We don't want them to give our position away." Sherlock ordered.

"Trust me, boss, they have better camo than us; maybe we should get Mr. Damani to make us suits from their hair?" 2 Planks stated.

"Good idea. I'll bring that up when we get back," Jedi said.

Steel went back into her position, as did 2 Planks, "Boys" Steel called. Just then, Loki came and laid down beside Steel, and Thor took up a defensive position 5 meters behind Steel, facing out behind her, watching her six. Steel looked back at Thor and realised Art had sent them to protect her. 'a sweet jester, but something Art should have shared,' she thought. "Boys Camo," and with that, the boys disappeared; you would only know they were there if you knew they were there.

As the team watched for the next 2 hours, there seemed to be a lull. It was Steel's turn to be on patrol, and the boys were also watching everything around her. Just then, Three Black Jeeps came down the entrance road, just as a call came across the comms. "Something's happening," Water Tiger called over the comms.

"Jedi get Scree up; I want pics of everyone in those cars," Sherlock commanded.

"Roger."

Scree took to the skies with his usual screech, as he took to a higher altitude first to home in on the car in question. Next, he started circling, making his way to the front of the castle with his usual eagle-like manner, trying to attract as little attention as possible. Finally, he reached his position to film the cars in question.

"Can you get down a little closer so we can get good visuals and sounds on the people getting out of the cars? We might be lucky enough to catch some names." Sherlock said.

"Dropping," Jedi responded.

As usual, the security team got out the first of the cars and formed a perimeter. "This person must be the real deal to have this amount of security, Sherlock."

"Exactly, get as much footage as possible," Sherlock said.

Scree started circling lower; Jedi noticed someone race out of the front entrance of the castle and ran straight to Fredrick Nessler, leaning over to speak in his ear; the Water Tiger was standing right next to him as all hell seemed to break loose. Nessler started yelling commands as the security team rushed the newcomer through the front doors.

Suddenly, the entire event played through the special forces comms sets; Water Tiger must have retrieved the comm from his pocket and was playing the entire event for them. Then, keeping it concealed in his palm, he issued orders, so Mike's team knew what was happening and how to respond.

"What have they found, Fredrick?" Water Tiger asked.

"They don't know; they have picked up an electronic emitter within range of the castle," Nessler said.

"Ok, I will handle this; get your guest inside while I find out what this is." Water Tiger commanded.

"That is Prince Mashhur, 3rd of Saudi. He is very touchy about his title; try not to speak down to him; we need his family." Nessler said.

"It shall be done, teams 1 to 3, do a sweeping circular radius of 1 km, report any findings, if someone is here, they will probably use the river so start there, use the quads as they may come in handy, over. Nessler, join the prince; we cannot afford to lose you either." Water Tiger commanded.

"Yes, ok," Nessler agreed.

After Nessler was inside and all the security was about their business, he called again. "You have roughly 5 minutes to clear more than a kilometre. Go, and take the bird with you," Water Tiger growled through the comm.

Sherlock moved into full gear. "Smith, you're with me; we'll head south. The rest of you head east to evac 5," Sherlock ordered.

"Sherlock, I have the boys, permission to evac where they came in?" Steel requested.

"Where's that?" Sherlock asked.

"I don't know, but they do," Steel responded.

"Roger that, you know the drill Steel. Ok, everybody out, NOW!"

CHAPTER 6

RHINO BUMPER CARS

"This is going to be cool," Aidan said.

"Be respectful and do as you are told; this is not a playground. There are a lot of dangers out there in the ARK game park."

"Yeees Muuum," the boys said in unison, adding their own drama to their voices.

"They will behave, Mrs. Madden, I will make sure of it" the Major smiled a vast evil grin and pulled out his machete. Oliver just stood there frozen, and Aidan looked like he was going to pass out as he saw the chips out of the blade of the Majors machete. Their dad gave Aidan and Oliver bedside stories of the Major and the battle for the ARK. This is where he got his reputation as the 'Legend of the ARK.'

"Stand up straight men, no slouching," the Major barked.

"They are only boys, Major," Sam said.

"Not today, Mrs. Madden; today, they are members of the ARK regiment." The Major held out his hand, and one of his officers handed him two uniforms. The boys' eyes lit up, and so did Sam's. Sam assumed Art had a hand in this, getting the boys their own uniforms, but later that day found out that it was all the Major's doing, and his mother, who sewed up the hats and uniforms to fit. The boys put on their hats and shirts and stood to attention.

"Right, do you swear to protect all animals in the ARK with your life?" the Major asked, reciting an oath.

"We do!" Oliver and Aidan shouted.

"Do you swear to keep your bunks made and rooms clean while in the service of the ARK regiment?" the Major asked.

"We do!"

"You are both sworn in, congratulations," the Major acknowledged. "Now go with sergeant Maji, and he will take you to the transport," The Major turned to look at Sam with a huge cheesy grin, "I will look after them, Sam," he said.

"You better, or I will make your last war here look like a tea party," Sam said, trying to sound brutal but failing terribly. The Major offered a hearty laugh and headed out to the truck.

Once he got there, he saw the boys sitting in the back seat, sitting perfectly still, with the two Raptor guards in the back of the truck with their heads just behind the boys. He let out a huge deep laugh and said, "To section 12, Sergeant".

"Sir, I think someone needs you," the sergeant says as he looks in the rear-view mirror.

The Major looks around and saw a member of the joint WWF and WAP ARK team running up from behind and waving his arms frantically.

"Sorry, Major, I missed you inside. These are the new instructions for today. Some animals were moved through last night to make way for Dan to leave early today."

"Where is Dan off too in a hurry?" the Major asked.

"They moved up his schedule on the Javan rhino's. Indonesia is backtracking on the deal. So, they sent Dan to get them out before they can find some legal premise to get out of the contract."

"Ok. I have another question?"

"Yes, what's that Major?"

"Why did your team call yourselves the Mosh pit?"

The animal welfare officer let out a laugh. "Well, because they threw in four members of the WWF, four members of the WAP and six members of the ARK, and said now work together. We all work in different styles and different agendas, but it's working because we have the same end goal, the animals. Like a dance floor in a mosh pit."

"Oh, I see now. Just like the ARK really. So many people, one goal. Well, thank you. We must be off now."

"Major, one last thing. Dan asked if you could check on the new rhino enclosure and make sure that the workers know that not being ready on time will not be acceptable."

"Ahh, so Dan wants me to use my charm." The Major said with a huge smile.

"Well, actually, he said for you to make sure you have your machete with you." The officer laughed.

"Yes, that could work too." The Major said, laughing.

"Have a good day, Major."

"And to you. Keep up the good work. Sergeant, section 12 please."

The day was a balmy 32 degrees centigrade after a quick blustery storm blew through last night. The storm gave a fresh new washed feel to the jungle, heightening the smell and colours of the flowers and other fauna on the drive to sector 12. Sector 12 was the new additions section, where they monitor new additions and keep regular checks on their health, especially their mental health. It can be very stressful for the animals, flown halfway around the world to live in an entirely new area.

As they approached the gates to the release area, Oliver couldn't help but think that Mr. Damani liked Jurassic Park movies, as the gateways all had that same style of framework. Jurassic Park was one of his dads 'old farts' movies; he didn't mind the Warriors or Zulu movies, though. As they drove through the gates, something niggled at Oliver; what was it? Something was wrong, something out of place, but he couldn't put his finger on it. Everything seemed fine; the Major didn't seem distressed or distracted; ahead, there was a group of men around a truck, and they were backing it up to what looked like a cattle ramp, where they loaded and unloaded cattle into trucks, but this was no cow. In the back of the truck, he could see the back of something that looked... black?

"What's in their Major?" Oliver asked.

"An endangered animal, my boy, a young Javan Rhino," the Major responded.

"WOW," the boys reacted together.

"We are going to watch as they load him into the ramp and send him into sector 12."

"Sector 12 is the area where they watch the newbies, isn't it?" asked Aidan

"Correct Aidan, the vets will keep a close eye on him for the next 2 weeks before they start to inter-grade him into his new home and introduce him to new friends."

"They use the hawks and eagles to keep a video track of him 24/7 and monitor his vitals," Aidan said proudly.

"Correct again. You have been doing your homework, I see," the Major said proudly.

"I think this stuff is cool; I want to work here when I get older," Aidan said with pride.

"Aren't you going to be a Special Forces soldier like your dad?" the Major said, puzzled.

"No, I think I want to be like you and lead a team of soldiers protecting the animals," Aidan said.

"Good choice, my boy, the pays better, and you don't get shot at as much… most of the time," the Major pondered, thinking of the battle here to save the American President. "And you, Oliver, what's your plans?"

"Follow dad and save the world," Oliver said in an easy 'do it before breakfast,' voice.

The Major chuckled. "Yep, just like your dad."

Just then, the animal transport started backing towards the ramps; the Javan Rhino seemed subdued, 'probably tranquilised,' Oliver thought. The ARK staff began undoing the latches on the back of the truck. For safety reasons, they always kept one latch unopened till the truck was up against the ramp. Oliver had that gnawing feeling again but still couldn't put his finger on it. Just then, there was a roar from the young rhino. 'Definitely not drugged anymore,' Oliver thought. The beast was upset; you could hear the pain in his roars. He bucked and kicked and was getting very agitated. One man there was a vet and ran to the front of the truck to get the tranquiliser gun to sedate him.

Oliver and Aidan were fascinated, scared, and sympathetic to the rhino all at one time. You don't see things like this at Byron Bay. Just then, the Rhino's frustration peaked, and with one massive kick, the back of the truck flew open with an enormous crash. The force of the door flying back sent two of the ARK staff hurtling through the air. It knocked one out cold; the other was having difficulties getting to his feet as one arm hung limp at his side. The man on the other side of the truck decided to not chance his luck and climbed to get on top of the vehicle, just as the Javan Rhino made his move for escape.

The Major and sergeant Maji leaped from the truck to aid the injured workers. "Stay in the truck," the Major yelled to the boys over his shoulder. Just then, a face came on the screen comms in the truck; it was Doby.

"What's going on? Why isn't anyone answering their comms?"

"Doby, it's us. The rhino is loose, and there are men badly injured here; send an ambulance."

"Where's the Major?"

"He and sergeant Maji are helping the injured men."

"Where's the rhino?"

"Doing circles trying to find a way out," Oliver said.

"Stay in that truck and don't move; help is on the way." Doby told Oliver.

"The gate! Shit!" Oliver said, anguished.

"What about the gate?" Doby asked.

"The gate to ARK mountain is open; they didn't shut it," Oliver said. That's what was bugging him; he knew the gate should be closed behind them. His instincts were telling him something was wrong.

"SHIT!" Doby screamed.

Just then, Tyson came on the comms; "boys under the seats are two controllers for the raptors; they would have enough strength to close the gate. I will send the control of the raptors to you, work together to push the gate closed." Before he finished his sentence, Aidan was under the seat, grabbing the container. When he opened it, yep, two PlayStation controllers; 'this day just got a lot better,' Aidan thought. The boys knelt on the back seat and waited for the lights to come on the controllers. Green light, GO!

The boys got their raptors to shuffle out of the van and started them running towards the gate. Once there, Aidan said, "head down and push."

"Ok," Oliver replied. The two raptors attracted the attention of the rhino and also the open gate. He made his move and charged towards the entrance.

"He's seen the open gate, PUSH!" the boy's fingers flew on the controls, trying to get as much out of the raptors as possible. The gate was moving too slow; the boys didn't think it would shut in time as the Rhino got closer and closer. Oliver thought, 'rhino on the loose,' just then, the gate swung shut in front of the rhino. Having no time to stop, he hit the skids on the soft soil and smashed into the gate. The force of the impact sat the Rhino on his arse. He sat there on his bum, shaking the stars out of his head.

"Great work, guys!" Tyson and Doby yelled over the comms. Unbeknown to them, their mother was standing behind Doby and Tyson, biting her nails, as she knew they had just locked themselves inside a cage with an angry, rampaging rhino.

"Now, just stay put till help arrives," Doby said.

The boys watched as the rhino continuously charged the fence, trying to escape. "He's going to hurt himself ramming the fence all the time," Aidan said. The boys looked over and saw the vet was on top of the truck now, too.

"Let's see if we can wear him out by getting him to chase the raptors," Oliver said.

"COOL!" was Aidan replied.

The boys got the raptors moving, heading towards the rhino, but as the raptors started off, they caught the eye of the young rhino, and he took off to meet them in battle. Unfortunately, the boy's timing wasn't great as they ran the raptors across the front of the AZTECK truck they were sitting in.

"Turn, Turn!" Oliver shouted as the rhino just missed the back of the vehicle by inches. Sam watched this on the screen in the Hub and nearly passed out.

"HOLY SHIT!" Aidan screamed, "I nearly pissed my pants," he added. The vulgar talk snapped Sam out of her giddiness.

"Aidan Madden, watch your mouth!" came bellowing across the comm. Aidan slumped down in his chair, knowing his mother was watching.

Lexi, this whole time, was watching everything and everyone in the Hub and saying nothing. Loving how Sam was so concerned that her children nearly got smashed by a rhino but still had time to berate them for swearing. 'Is this what motherhood is like? ...I can't wait!'

"Your better on the controls. Move in and ram his butt, but don't hurt him. For God's sake, don't let him catch you; Mum and Dad can't afford to replace one of these things," Oliver said.

"Gotcha," Aidan moved up at a trot and rammed the rhino in the butt with his raptor's head. The response from the rhino was a look of "OH, you didn't just do that." The rhino swung around on Aidan with a speed the boys didn't know possible, only Aidan's reflexes avoided the horn of the rhino ripping the side of his raptor off, Aidan did a side flip which he wasn't sure the raptor could do, but he had enough strength and balance to perform it.

"Run, Aidan, RUN" Oliver yelled, even though he was kneeling right beside him. 'Just another Saturday night in the lounge room' the boys thought. Just then, Tyson came on the comms; he noticed the raptors were running to the rhino.

"Boys... what are you doing?"

"The rhino was going to hurt himself, so we're going to tire him out," Oliver replied.

Just then, Art Damani entered the Hub.

"Ok, update," he said.

"Well, rhino escapes, men are injured, an ambulance is on route. The gate was left open. The boys and the Major are there. The boys used the raptors to shut the gate in time to prevent an escape; now... they're chasing the rhino with the raptors to tire him out." Tyson said reluctantly.

"Ok, let me get this straight. We managed to get two boys trapped inside a cage with a furious rhino, and now they're chasing this angry rhino with two-million-dollar robot raptors. Is this correct?" Art said with a serious face.

"Ah... yes," Doby said

Art leaned down to the comms with that serious face. Everyone in the room was grimacing at what he was going to say to the boys. He pushed the comm button.

"GO MY BOYS!" he yelled excitedly, the look of shock on everyone's face in the room as he cheered on the boys.

"Is that you, Uncle Art?" Aidan asked.

"Yes, my boy," Art replied; just then, in the background, Lexi let out a squeal and fell backward on her chair, landing on her back.

"What was that?" Oliver asked.

"Lexi just fell backward in her chair, laughing," Art replied.

"Is she wearing that short black skirt again?" Oliver asked.

Doby replies, "Yes, she is"

"Bet, that's not very lady-like," Oliver says.

"OLIVER MADDEN! I'll wash your mouth out with soap," Sam yelled from behind.

Doby looks back at Lexi, still lying on her back, cackling, "No, it's not Oliver. She's just laying on her back, feet in the air, laughing like an old drunk."

The boys looked at each other... paused, then broke out laughing loudly together. "Oli, watch out!" Aidan yelled. Oliver had lost concentration, and the rhino had caught up; just in time, he made the same flip manoeuvre Aidan had made earlier to avoid contact. "He's slowing," Aidan says.

"I have an idea; run to the gate that goes into sector 12," Aidan suggested. The boys ran their raptors towards the gate and stopped about 10 meters away. The rhino had had enough of this running game and started trotting towards the raptors by this time. He slowed his approach to a walk when he got to them and just started nuzzling against them.

"He doesn't see us as a threat," Aidan says.

"Major, can you open the side gate to let the rhino in?" Oliver yells.

"Ok," he yells back.

The Major makes his way to the side gate carefully and opens it, monitoring the rhino at the same time. The boys walked their raptors into the sector 12 compound, and behind them, the rhino trots calmly through the gate. As the boys walk the raptors out of sector 12, the rhino made his way to a water basin for refreshments. Finally, the Major and Maji made their way to the gate to let the ambulance in for the injured workers.

"Great work, boys, come on back in the ice-cream sundaes are on me," Art said.

"Awesome, we have to ask the Major though; we are on duty," Oliver says

"That's fine; soldiers have to eat too," the Major said with his enormous big smile.

CHAPTER 7

THE CHASE

The picturesque surroundings of the Altaskivi Castle suddenly disappeared; everything around the team became an obstacle or a threat. There was blood in the water and the sharks were circling. It has only happened once before; the team being spotted. It was 5yrs ago before Steel had joined the team. Since then, Mike has made a point of constantly training the team for this day.

But as Smith was thinking, 'this shit just got real.'

"Ok, let's move," Sherlock said as they all started at a run on their elective courses. Five minutes isn't much time to get a head start, on foot, in the snow. Smith led the way, with Sherlock close behind. Sherlock thought they may have to ditch their gear before they entered the town of Altaskivi if they even made it that far. The team first, then the mission. The team is off and running and is excellent at stealth and evasion. We have to get the info back; without the enemy knowing we were here; we can't get caught! Sherlock looked at his GPS, 5.2 kilometres to the town, but the team briefings showed there was a 2-kilometre open paddock area before they reached the town. Nowhere to hide.

Jedi programmed Scree to meet them 2 kilometres ahead. It would be safe there and they could pack him up to take back. There is valuable information on his drive that must survive this trip. 2 Planks let Jedi take the lead. Being taller, he would have better visuals from behind, plus he hates to lead, and even though Jedi is only new to the team, he has confidence in himself and his own decisions. Ploughing through this snow was a dead giveaway, leaving tracks a blind man could see, but we can't worry about that now, 'we just can't get caught or shot... shot would be bad' 2 planks thought. Remembering his last mission to save the American president, where he got caught and should have died if it wasn't for coming across a fellow Aussie, who decided NOT to shoot him. Keep running; GPS says we're nearly a kilometre away.

Steel paced well with Thor and Loki; they seemed to know what speed they had to go to get out of range and how far she could push herself. Steel assumed Loki was monitoring her vitals. As they took off, Steel asked Loki to take them back to where they were dropped off; she knew Art would only drop them off somewhere safe. Coordinates came upon her GPS, 20 kilometres away. 'Wow, a brisk walk ahead,' but I got to keep moving.

Setting a good pace, Smith and Sherlock both felt the tension in the situation affecting their stamina. Staying near the trees momentarily, they looked for the best way to move across the openness of the fields. There was an old half-collapsed shed in the back of one field, long grass around it, and no crops growing in the area.

"There's our place to stash our gear." Sherlock said, pointing,

"Roger that," Smith replied.

Then, just as they were about to jump the barbed wire fence, a call came across Smith's comms. "If you have broken up into three groups, my teams have found your tracks and are close in pursuit. I will do what I can; DON'T get caught!"

"Shit!" both men replied. "

"We have to run to that fence post, hurtle it into the paddock, run and stash our gear and get back to this same spot," Sherlock informed Smith.

"What, why?" Smith questioned.

"We need them to believe we continued on from here, or they will find our gear, now MOVE!"

Smith took off with a bolt and ran to the fence post, placed a hand on it, flung himself as far as he could into the paddock, and made his way towards the old shed. Sherlock was hot on his heels, as he knew time was of the essence.

As they reached the hut.

"Ditch the camo, put on your alternate jacket and hat, and grab your survival bag." Sherlock ordered, even though Smith was already in tune and changing dress. Subterfuge was part of their training and routine; the team had to know languages, they had to carry alternate clothing to suit the regions of their missions, to blend in for their assignments and in case of emergency, and this was an emergency.

Colder but lighter, the two men reversed, back to the tracks where they left off and continued at pace towards town. They used up some energy reserves to cut through paddocks to slow the men down in pursuit; every second counted. They could hear quad bikes nearby but didn't know if that was their pursuers.

Reaching what would count as the outer suburbs with houses lining streets, they assessed their surroundings and made their way to the centre of town where it would be more populated, then suddenly, over their comm came;

"Team 2 to base over,"

"Base here,"

"We have spotted two males running into town, possible intruders,"

"Team, are you armed?",

"Yes, of course, base,"

"Base to team 2, one member to stay outside town limits with gear and bikes, two members pursue on foot, small arms, over."

"Base, we don't understand,"

"Do as commanded! This is a stealth operation; you can't be seen. Challenge my orders, and I will deal with you personally when you return!"

"Roger base proceeding with direction."

"What was that?" Smith asked, confused.

"Water Tiger had his comm open to give us a heads up," Sherlock said.

"I don't know. I still don't trust him. I'm waiting for the sucker punch," Smith said uneasily.

"I know what you mean; for now, it's keeping us alive. Two mercs on our arse, with pistols." Sherlock said.

"Fair fight," Smith added.

"NO, we have to evade; if we kill them, they will know they have been compromised," Sherlock said while still running.

"You take all the fun out of missions; what if they shoot at us?" Smith said, seeking an answer to retaliate.

"Duck," Sherlock said with a note of frustration in his voice.

The two Special Forces men weaved and kept running till they could find a scenario where they could disappear; turning one corner, their lungs were burning from the pace they were running, but stopping now wasn't an option. Ahead, they could hear music. Smith could see there were a lot of cars parked along the streets. Sherlock sensed they may have found an opportunity to mingle with a crowd. When they turned the corner of the next block,

Sherlock had a look over his shoulder and saw who he thought were the two mercs chasing them; they had a 200-metre lead on them; not much, but it will have to do. As Sherlock and Smith continued, the music got louder, and the number of people grew rapidly; something was just ahead, a large crowd gathered in the one area. "Let's go; our chance to disappear could be just ahead," Sherlock said.

"Gotcha, have we got time to stop for a beer, or even a hot chocolate?" Smith jokingly asked.

"God, I wish, but I'd be happy just to stay alive at this moment," Sherlock responded.

"Yeah, that works for me, too." The men slowed their approach as they reached people standing around on the sidewalk. No need to attract further attention. As the men turned the corner, Sherlock said, "Perfect."

The open mall area of Altaskivi was in full festival mode. The Altaskivi Utopia Winter Festival is a day for the residents to come together to be different and still be together as a town. The Utopia festival encourages new ideas to be shared for the community, new dress, new food, new music with a blend of the old with the new. It is a 3-day experience with the Monday, a local public holiday. A colourful event: people wearing new style clothing, some with masks or hats. The open mall area lined with stalls selling new style clothing, much of which was aimed at the younger generation but taken on board by the older generation to bridge the gap between their ages and show a sign of togetherness.

The festive crowd was abuzz with over 500 people, sampling the food, drinks, and music. The day was filmed by the local TV network Casti 3GB, filming from one rooftop. The sounds in the air are dizzying as they mix all the different styles playing at once from other areas. Three young men travelled around the crowd playing piano accordions rigged with techno devices, mixing old music with new; they played everything from the Beatles, new wave, and the latest techno dance as they wandered through the delighted crowd.

As Sherlock and Smith rounded the corner, it was like entering a new Utopia. The waves of sounds and smells hit them like running into a wall, with their lungs burning, sucking in breaths; it was overwhelming.

"Stay focused, Zikmund; we can't lose focus here," Sherlock said, concerned, knowing how this ambience feels on his sensors; he knew it would affect Smith the same. Sherlock's use of his Christian name snapped him out of the daze that was engulfing him. Sherlock never uses his Christian name, ever. The stakes were grave, and they had a job to do.

The joyful crowd formed a chain behind the three men with the accordions as they played the Beatles hit, 'Let it be.' Smith and Sherlock shuffled their way east through the crowd. They needed to go north but wanted to be seen heading east before disappearing and heading north. Finally, the two mercs reached the edge of the crowd in the mall. "How are we going to find them in this crowd?" one merc asked.

"I am NOT going to lose them," the other said as he pulled his pistol from its holster and raised it above his head. The other merc looked on in horror and was too slow to react before his team member raised his hand and fired three shots in the air. Altaskivi is close to the border with Russia, and the sound of gunshots are very familiar to them.

Screams and panic gripped the immediate crowd around them.

"What are you doing? We were not to create an awareness of ourselves. The Water Tiger will have us shot for this."

"No, he will praise me for getting the job done, and we say that they shot at us and started the panic. People ran away screaming. The mercenary, looking for a promotion, raised the gun over his head and shot again in the air. The remaining of the crowd hit the ground with their hands over their heads. Only about ten remained standing; two of those were Sherlock and Smith.

"Guess we should have ducked," Smith said in a joking voice, avoiding the fact that their lives were in immediate danger.

As the television station crewman swung their camera to the gunman, screams of panic filled the air.

"We have to get away from this crowd before these people get hurt; follow me," Sherlock turned and bolted for the nearest building corner to give them protection. Two more shots rang out; as Sherlock and Smith turned the corner, one bullet hit the wall beside Smith. "RUN, they're not bad shots!" Smith yelled. The two mercenaries took off after them as they ran through the crowd of scared festival-goers. All this caught on LIVE tv, courtesy of CASTI 3 GB.

****

The atmosphere in the Hub was cheery, but there was an element of anxiousness underlying the mood. Everyone was waiting for a signal from the team on organising their pickup and that everyone was safe. Sam had come up to check in to see if they had heard anything. She knew Art would tell her immediately if there was contact, but being around their friends from the ARK gave her a measure of peace. While Art, Lexi, and Doby were chatting at the console area, Oliver was watching tv on the monitor, while Aidan was teaching Ab how to play flick football on the conference table, Ab was astounded that in this age of technology, playing with a bit of stick on a table as an imaginary Rugby League field was so entertaining. Just then;

"Mum," Oliver said

"Yes, honey," Sam replied.

"Dad's special forces, right?"

"Yes, honey,"

"And his job is to remain secret and make sure nobody knows who he is, right?" Oliver quizzed. Now everyone in the Hub had turned towards Oliver.

"Then why is he being shot at on television?"

"WHAT!" was everyone's immediate reply.

Art replied first, "Quickly get the tv on the main screens."

Ab and Aidan jumped beside to watch what Oliver was looking at as the tv news report came up on the wall of monitors. They were looking at a CNN news flash.

"Hello, this is Kylie Tamilson from the CNN newsroom; we are just receiving LIVE footage of a shooting in the town of Altaskivi in Estonia. I must warn viewers some of these images, viewers may find disturbing."

Two men opened fire at the peaceful festival during the Utopia Winter carnival. We have no information on how many injured or killed at this stage, as this is playing out live through our sister network CASTI 3GB in Estonia. Usually, bringing the town together, it has erupted in gunfire as scores of people, including many women and children.

Sam was the first to say anything. "Oh My God." The picture of her husband and friend, filmed while being shot at during the festival.

"We now have live footage from a mobile phone of one of 3GBs staff as he follows from a rooftop, filming the gunman." Kylie from CNN continued.

As they watched the footage, Art Damani planned an intervention. "Right, give me the headset, put me through to the retrieval teams. Doby, get me on that reporter's phone, NOW!"

"Art, if we do that, we are letting people know that we have that kind of technology. We could be traced!" Doby said, worried.

"Do what you have to do; you have 1 minute, then I want to be speaking to the person on that phone."

Doby and Lexi spun in their chairs and started hitting the keys.

"Doby, you do the southern hemisphere, and I'll do the northern hemisphere," Lexi said.

"Ok, great idea." The pair frantically punched away on keys, setting up signals worldwide to bounce their signal off to avoid detection. Governments can get away with doing this kind of manoeuvre and call it National security, but to actually infiltrate a signal phone shouldn't be possible unless your AZTECK.

Two minutes later, one minute more than Art wanted, Doby had the number.

The young man on the phone filming these events unfold was trying to keep his head down as he had his hand over the edge of the building, trying to film the assailants. Yonter Felder was 21 and working as a camera assistant for extra cash and Uni credits for his Arts degree with the Estonia University in Loksa. Scared shitless, but realising this was a big event unfolding in front of him, his enthusiasm for filming took over his common sense and survival mechanisms.

Yonter transverses the rooftops using chimneys and advertising signage to keep himself hidden. As he looked down the streets and laneways, he lost the men doing the shooting. But he also lost the men they were shooting at. Just then, two figures turned a corner up ahead, and Yonter dived behind a sign advertising a new Nestlé yogurt. He watched as the two figures entered a storage area beside a local clothing store. Just then, his phone rang. Yonter divided on the ground, grabbing it to answer before being heard. Luckily for Art Damani, Yonter answered his phone.

****

12 kilometres away

"Going good boys, we're 2 kilometres away," Steel says to Loki and Thor. Just as Steel was about to cross a dirt road, Thor jumps in front of her to prevent her proceeding and emits a low growl.

"What is it, boy? Do you hear something?"

Just then a voice speaks out, coming through Thor … a human voice.

"Get on the ground," it said.

Steel was stunned. She didn't know Thor had a voice regulator, and the shock slowed her reactions to a standstill.

"Get on the ground," the voice said again.

This time Steel recognising the voice emitting from Thor.

"Lexi?"

"YES, now get on the ground, NOW!"

Steel did as commanded and hit the ground quickly. Seconds later, she felt Thor and Loki hop over the top of her and saw their fur go into cloak mode. Moments later, she heard the engines of two quad bikes approaching. Knowing she can't allow herself to be captured and doesn't want to die before her wedding to a billionaire, she slides her hand down to her side to one of her knives.

As the bikes approached, they slowed and nearly stopped right opposite of where Steel was laying underneath the great cats.

"I've lost the tracks; can you see anything?"

"No, not a thing,"

"Should we go on? We have come out twice as far as what was ordered?"

"No, but let's go back and see if we have missed anything."

The bikes turned and made their way back the way they came. Steel lay there till Thor and Loki deemed it was safe. As she got to her feet, Steel spoke to Thor.

"Lexi, are you there?"

"Yep, all safe now, girlfriend." Lexi's voice said.

"First, do you know just how creepy it is to have your voice come at of Thor's mouth. Second, thanks for the save."

"You're welcome,"

"How long have you been able to track me through the boys?"

"Art had it set up before you left, but had never field tested it until now."

"How are the others doing?"

"We've heard nothing from Jedi and 2 Planks, so we assume they're doing fine, ..."

"Smith and Sherlock?"

"..., well, theirs is a work in progress. Art has organised pick up, so get your butt to the drop-off zone, girlfriend. We'll look after the others. Loki will lead, and Thor can protect your rear."

"You mean you'll be watching my rear?"

"... I would never!"

Loki took off across the dirt road and Steel followed with Thor in the rear. As they crossed the road into the bushland. Thor came up behind Steel and let out a growl, and started purring. Immediately, Steel put her free hand over her buttocks to block Thor and Lexi's view. Steel could hear a voice from behind, "spoil sport"

****

"Hello?"

"Yonter, how would you like to make a lot of money?" Art said to the young man.

"Sorry, I don't have time for a sales call; I'm trying to film something important, by...." Art cut off Yonter before he could finish.

"I know you are filming the shooting at the Utopia festival."

"How'd you know that? Who is this?" The young man's hackles on the back of his neck stood up.

"Who I am doesn't matter. Do you have transport with you?" Art asked.

"Yes, a trail bike."

"Fantastic! How much is it to buy a new one?" Art asked.

"Around $15,000."

"I'll give you $30,000 to get your bike to the men that are being shot at."

"Yeah, right, who is this" the young man demanded.

"You have 30 seconds to check your bank account, GO!"

Yonter's fingers were all thumbs as he tried to bring up his app on his phone. "HOLY SHIT!" The young film artist hadn't seen this kind of money in his whole life.

"Ok, I know where they're hiding; they're in a warehouse."

"Ok, Yonter, don't be seen by the shooters; they will kill you or worse if they see you with the other two." Art informed him.

"Fucking Hell, serious!" the young man said, worried.

"Ok, Yonter, I'll put in enough money for a year's Uni tuition also for you, now GO!"

"How do you know this stuff about me?" the young man asked, confused.

"GO!" Art said, frustrated.

"Young people these days," Art said to Sam, who was standing there in a state of shock.

Yonter Felder grabbed his 250cc Suzuki trail bike and rolled it to the warehouse door; luckily, it wasn't far away; he wanted to get this over with before getting shot.

Art had called Smith's comm to tell him the bike was on the way. Not long after the call, there was a knock on the door. Sherlock moved to the side of the door and drew his sidearm.

"Who is it?" he called,

"A friend with a bike," Yonter called back.

"Thank you, now run before you're seen here, GO!" Yonter took off as fast as his legs would carry him.

Sherlock and Smith had changed clothes in the warehouse and left all their survival cash to pay for the items they took. They exited the door carefully and hopped on the motorbike; Sherlock drove while Smith sat on the back as the passenger. Sherlock was fluent with riding bikes as he frequently took the boys and 2 Planks on hiking trips when back at home, which didn't seem a lot lately.

Sherlock had mapped his route on his GPS and memorised it to memory. Straight out north 300 meters, left, first right, left onto the town exit road, 15klms east till the road ends and becomes a national forest, 11 kilometres to LZ. Sherlock took off but not at any great speed; he just wanted to look like two guys on a bike, not two special forces guys escaping the scene.

As they turned the corner, the two mercenaries also did the same. "Unit 3, suspects on a motorbike now, bring up the quads 400 meters up the road." said the merc that did all the shooting.

"Copy," came the voice over their comm. The two mercs ran down the main access street as a quad was waiting for them there, and they saw the other member of their team running back to his quad. "Let's go," One merc said as they jumped on the bike with a wheel stand. They shot off up the road to finish these two.

Sherlock had other things to consider while he had a 500-meter lead on the mercs. 'How organised are the police here? Are there roadblocks ahead?' Sherlock and Smith had proper papers and identification that would hold up to scrutiny, but these guys chasing are a bit gun-happy.

"We have company, 400 meters and closing. Time to open up," Smith said; luckily, the local police were slow on their roadblocks, and it was an open run with no bystanders.

"Hang on," Sherlock said as he opened the throttle. The smaller powered bike took a second or two to pick up speed and slowly pulled ahead. It wasn't long before the chasers realised, they had opened the throttle and pulled away, so they did the same.

"They're coming up again faster, still 3 kilometres to go to the dirt tracks," Smith informed Sherlock.

"It's time for some Smith camouflage," Sherlock said

Smith leaned forward over Sherlock's shoulder, "What the fuck is Smith camouflage?"

"Stir them up, act like a young smart-ass," Sherlock said.

"I take offence to that," Smith stated firmly.

"Get offended later; give it to them."

"If I get shot in the arse, I want a purple heart," Smith said jokingly.

"I'll get Sam to put a band-aid on it," Sherlock returned

"Seriously!" Smith said, astounded.

"NO" was the flat return.

Smith slowly stood up on the seat, hands-on Sherlock's shoulders for balance. Sherlock maintained their speed while balancing the bike, with Smith moving so much. True to form, Smith started wiggling his arse at their pursuers.

"What the fuck," the merc riding passenger said. As he looked ahead, he couldn't believe his eyes; the passenger on the bike they were chasing was pulling down his pants and now slapping his arse.

"Cheeky Motherfucker, do you want me to shoot that kid?" he asked the driver. "No, we need them alive to find out what they know," the driver said as he throttled back to get even closer.

"You didn't just chuck a brown eye at them, did you?" Sherlock asked, while still staying focused on the ride.

"Yep, that should give them nightmares for a few months, ... or not, here they come again," Smith said in a 'Get us out of here voice.'

"One kilometre left, hang on; hopefully, we'll lose them on the tracks. We're more manoeuvrable; if not, we'll ditch and go bush," Sherlock said, so Smith knew what options were coming.

"Roger that."

Now both quads were in striking distance, waiting for them to slow down when the road ended. "Be ready; shoot out their wheels when they slow down." The merc driver said.

As they approached the final 50 metres, the shooter on the quad steadied his shot as the driver slowed down; he was ready, ready, ready. "They're not slowing," he yelled.

In the last 50 metres, Sherlock had already assessed his options. There was no room to ride straight into the tracks from the road; you had to push the bike in. Stop and run wasn't an option as they would be on them as soon as they stopped. Only one option left. A mound of dirt was 10 metres to the left. It didn't look high enough to jump over the national forest fence, but it was all they had. Sherlock had to swerve as late as possible, so they didn't know what they were trying and still kept up their speed. The dirt had to be hard enough and high enough to clear the fence or close enough to jump. 'A lot of ifs,' Sherlock thought.

At the last minute, Sherlock changed direction but maintained speed. Heading for the mound of dirt, it had the right effect. It caught the mercs off guard, and they came to a screeching halt at the park opening. "Get ready to jump," Sherlock yelled as they hit the mound at 70 km/hour, "Ahhh shit" they both screamed as the bike flew up in the air, only just making it, as their back tyre rolled across the top rail of the park fence. The seasoned SAS soldiers hit the ground with a God Almighty thud, bashing the bike seat up in Smith's famous frozen balls. They went skidding as Sherlock fought to gain control before they became a 'wet spot' on a tree. Gaining control, Sherlock sent them up a hill, swerving amongst trees that he thought the bike could just fit through. Upon reaching the crest of the hill, approximately 100 meters from the park gate opening.

Smith calls out, "Can we hoof it from here? I need to run out an injury,"

"Yeah, sure, probably a better idea, less sound for them to follow us." Sherlock answered.

As the pair dismounted the bike, they left it in the open to be found, making it look like kids trying to get away. The mercs followed on foot and eventually found the bike, but by that time,

Sherlock and Smith were a kilometre away, and the mercenaries returned to base empty-handed. Sherlock stopped for a moment, so they could regain some condition; he contacted the Hub to ask for an evac, where he was told it had already been sent and that a backup team was on site. 'Back-up team, what back-up team? Did Art send some of the Major's men to secure the LZ, overkill, but he must have thought it was better this way?'

Sherlock and Smith talked about all they have learned from the Water Tiger; on this mission, Smith constantly reminded Sherlock not to take anything at face value with that madman. Sherlock knew this, but sometimes it doesn't hurt to be reminded.

Tensions were easing as their heart rates were getting back to normal. But they were only to be replaced with a concern for the safety of the other teammates. They were professionals, but they were family.

Smith and Sherlock made their way through the shrub; it didn't look like anyone had come through this way for years or ever. Only 400 metres to the LZ, Smith heard it first and sensed it. They were being followed. Their first thought was Water Tiger had double-crossed them and had deliberately split them up to make it easier to take them down. Then they heard it and partly saw it, a White timber wolf, and where's there is one wolf, there's always more. Only 300 metres to the LZ, Sherlock decided to not use any firearms to give away their position, especially so close to the LZ, so they formed a carriage stance. Sherlock was behind Smith and put his right hand on Smith's left shoulder. He had his knife in his left hand, Smith in the front had his knife in his right hand. Smith could keep watch front on and to the right, while Sherlock could keep watch left and behind; they just walked normally to the LZ, watching, knowing the wolves were tracking them.

They hit the clearing 70 metres from the LZ and saw the pilot casually sitting on the edge of the chopper, watching them walk in.

"Hey, glad you made it," the pilot called to them.

"Yeah, hey, I thought Art said he sent a backup team with you?" Sherlock said as he was looking around for said backup.

"He did," as he pointed inside the chopper. Suddenly, a young girl appeared from inside the helicopter and crouched in the doorway beside the pilot.

"Hi," she said in the sweetest young girl's voice imaginable.

Sherlock and Smith stood there, stunned. "What is she going to do, cutesy them to death?" Smith said, confused. The girl started hitting keys on a tablet, then suddenly behind them growled the wolf. It made Smith jump a little. "Ok, yes, an impressive robot, but hardly back up," Smith said, unconvinced. The young lady looked at him sneakily and hit one button; she stood there proud with an 'Oh, yeah!' look about her as four more wolves appeared from nowhere out of camo mode. One was only a few feet away from Smith, making him jump again.

"Ok, I stand corrected," Smith said uneasily. "Ok, are they like Loki, all friendly and stuff?" Smith asked the young lady.

"No," was the flat answer. "These are pure robotic; they do exactly what I say... so don't piss me off," she said, staring at Smith.

"Hey, I'm cool with that. Nice doggies," Smith said, trying to act relaxed and calm.

Sherlock was standing there unflinchingly.

"How long have you been following us... miss?" Sherlock said, asking for an introduction.

"Jensen, Rosi Jensen, sorry I should have introduced myself, but I had to show your friend here, NOT to judge a book by their CUTESY," she said to Smith.

"Just call me Rosi; everyone does. Oh, and I've been tracking you for about a kilometre, Sherlock."

"Impressive, and you know our call signs. We only picked one up at 400 metres," Sherlock said.

"Yes, I know. That's when I let you know he was there." Rosi replied, "I'm Tyson's assistant."

"Rosi, do you know where the others are?" Sherlock asked.

"Best guess, 2 Planks and Jedi are heading here, now, and Art's girlfriend went rogue, her GPS is playing up, and she is bleeping in and out, but from what they have told me, she wasn't heading here," Rosi said.

"Why wouldn't she head here?" Smith asked Sherlock.

"She's not going rogue; she headed to the drop-off zone of Loki and Thor. Everything's a plan." Sherlock said.

Suddenly, the wolves all took off together, heading north. Rosi looked at her tablet and said, "Seems the other guys are heading in" 1 kilometre out.

Not soon after, Jedi came jogging into the clearing, followed by 2 Planks. "Come on, you two, we have to go get Steel," as the two men picked up the pace. The pilot called out, "where are we heading?" without answering, Sherlock grabbed Smith's comm, "Base, can you send the coordinates to where you dropped off Loki and Thor, to the pilot please"

"Roger that," came Doby's voice over the comms.

"Ahh yeah, good thinking, boss," 2 Planks said.

"That's why they pay you the big bucks," Rosi said chirpily.

"Rosi, you probably get paid more than me," Sherlock said.

"Serious, that sucks; you need to talk to your employer, dude," Rosi said seriously, which made the team burst out laughing; Rosi joined in, even though she didn't know what the joke was.

The chopper flew 36 kilometres north and came in for a landing in a clearing. Sitting there calmly on a tree log with Loki and Thor on either side of her was Steel. As the chopper landed, Sherlock came jogging over to her, Steel's only words were, "You're late,"

"Smith made us stop for a hot water bottle for his ..."

"Don't say it!" Steel laughed and got up. "Come on, boys, let's go home to daddy."

Sitting huddled together, Steel, 2 Planks, and Sherlock looked at each other.

"Did we pull it off?" Steel asked.

"I'm not sure. We haven't heard from Water Tiger. You guys made it back without an incident, but Smith and I were involved in a shootout in the middle of a festival that was being telecast through the news worldwide. I'm not sure if they made our faces."

"I would say so if Art came to the rescue like you said." 2 Planks added.

"We'll have to wait and see. Hopefully Water Tiger comes to our rescue... God I can't believe I just said that."

It was a scenic ride to Finland to a private airfield Art Damani had bought and replenished. Then a flight home to the ARK. Everyone introduced themselves to Rosi. Rosi seemed to have a bestie crush on Katelyn, and Katelyn was impressed with Rosi and the wolves she helped build. The fact astounded Katelyn, Thor and Loki treated her like they did with her and Art; they loved Rosi, fascinating.

Other connections were flying around the plane. Thomas and Rosi looked at each other but tried not to be seen doing it. Seb elbowed Mike in the side; he nodded his head towards the two, and Mike nodded back. It was like sitting in high school again watching two kids with a school crush. "I wonder when they'll start passing notes to each other," Mike said to Seb, laughing.

"Be nice, you too," Katelyn said, listening in on their conversation.

CHAPTER 8

FAILURE IS NOT ACCEPTABLE

The Altaskivi Castle, in all its years of radiance, has hosted balls and important meetings of state. From royalty to presidents. It has hosted nothing like this.

"Communication... commands ...following the plan... knowing your part, these are paramount for a successful mission. You are trained professionals." Water Tiger signalled for the guard at the door to open it; three-armed security team members came in, each with a hooded person with their hands bound, being led in.

The air in the room was so thick with tension you could have cut it with a knife. Two men stood off to one corner of the room, motionless, expressionless. One was Fredrick Nessler, the caretaker/administrator of this clandestine facility. The other Prince Mashur, 3rd of Saudi Arabia, one financier of this plan for worldwide chaos.

They made the three hooded men kneel in front of all the security personnel at this facility. Water Tiger nodded to the armed men. They took their hoods off; the prisoners had been gagged. The look of terror in their eyes as they knew that their time was short.

"Nobody, put a rifle in your hand and said go do what you want. You were all briefed on what your roles and perimeters are... yet, here we are. These three men took it on themselves to make their own rules and jeopardise the entire mission. The caretaker's connections have covered us, or we might have all been sharing the fate of these three."

Water Tiger grabbed the first man, brought him to his feet, and took off his gag. He addressed the man.

"Why didn't you stop this man from disobeying orders?"

"I did, I did. He wouldn't listen. He acted before I could stop him," he blurted out, terrified.

"Did you follow him after he disobeyed my orders?" Water Tiger asked calmly.

"... Yes, but only to monitor hi..." before he could finish his sentence, the Water Tiger pulled out his sidearm and shot the man in the back of the head. Bones and pieces of brains went sprawling onto the floor in front of the security men. They didn't flinch because to flinch meant you didn't have the stomach for this kind of work. "Liar," Water Tiger said as he put his pistol away in its holster.

He bent down and pulled the gag off the second man. "Why did you fire in the festival's crowd and give away our secrecy?"

"I didn't Water Tiger. It was the people we chased that fired on us, but we valiantly kept chase, though under fire."

"LIAR!" Water Tiger dropped on the man like an anvil falling from the sky; he smashed into the man's collarbone, hitting it so hard the shattered bone was driven into the man's shoulder. The man emitted a blood-curdling scream that no horror movie could ever reproduce; no one could act this much in pain, only live it. As the man kept screaming, the Water Tiger placed a mobile phone in front of him, showing him the news footage of him firing into the crowd of the festival. They showed footage on the screen behind him for the others to see. As he knelt there and tried to compose him and stop his screaming, the Water Tiger paused... "Never lie to me, anyone, ever."

He knelt down beside the man and showed him the mobile phone again; the man's eyes widened as big as an owl; his pupil dilated with the visions in front of him as the Water Tiger flicked from one screen to the next. The man emitted another scream, this one louder, more blood curdling; it was the sound of a soul and a heart being torn from a person's body simultaneously. The scream made the Saudi Prince jump and made many mercenaries restless in their position. They also had to bite their tongues as to not make a sound. Finally, the images from the phone came up on the screen. People lying dead on the floor riddled with bullets, the man's family, parents, wife, and children all slaughtered for his mistake. He shoved the phone in front of the man again, forcing him to look, and as he did, the Water Tiger drove his knife up in through the base of the skull into the man's brain; his eyes widened as the last thing he saw was his slaughtered family. He pulled the knife from his head and let him fall to the floor.

He pulled the last guard to his feet and took off his gag.

"Why did you not prevent this?"

"I was not with them; I was guarding the equipment at the main road," the 3rd guard said firmly.

"What could you have done?" Water Tiger asked calmly. "Nothing..." the man paused and didn't finish his sentence. "I should have prevented them from entering the town, called off the pursuit since there was no evidence to say that either man was not just from the town. In the final pursuit, just before we lost the people we were tracking, the men behaved in a manner that they were just pranksters out for a joy ride. In hindsight, I should have also called in straight away that there were gunshots to give you time to organise a cover story." The man finally went quiet.

Water Tiger looked out into the crowd of security guards. "This is how you analyse, know your role, think ahead, think of the big picture... know your part. This man I have been looking at for a while as a new lieutenant for my team." The man turned and looked at the screen behind him.

"No, I have not killed your family," Water Tiger said to the man as he put his hand on his shoulder. Some in the crowd breathed a sigh of relief, including the prince, that they would spare this man; he wouldn't kill a lieutenant that hadn't even been involved. However, the man quickly knelt, bowing his head, and just as quickly, the Water Tiger drew his pistol and shot the man in the back of the head. This made the prince visibly jump, including some guards.

"He was going to be my lieutenant, skilled, loyal... but he knew the price of failure... now there are no more excuses." The Water Tiger finished coldly.

He turned and walked towards Nessler and the Prince. The prince was looking past him at the dead men on the floor.

"Do you disapprove of my methods?" he addressed the prince.

"Very barbaric," the prince responded, with a quiver in his voice.

"You plan on releasing a disease into a country and then waging war on them... and YOU call me barbaric... your highness."

CHAPTER 9

HOME COMING

Not even the weather could dampen the hearts of the loved one's waiting. Mike and the team exited the plane on the runway at the ARK's private airstrip. The boys, Oliver and Aidan, weren't waiting; they bolted up the stairs to the plane's door as it opened. Welcoming Steel first with a double bear hug. On the spur of the moment, Katelyn lifted the boys over her head, like crowd surfing, to Zikmund, who greeted each boy and then passed them on to Seb, who welcomed and tickled each boy and then passed them on to Mike. Mike received the biggest dad hugs ever, but Oliver looked up with fearful eyes and said, "Where's Thomas?"

"He's in the back with Rosi, wh..." before he could finish his sentence, the boys had bolted off into the back of the plane and nearly crash tackled Thomas to the ground. They got introduced to Rosi and then turned and ran for the door again. Mike appreciated the show of affection from the boys for his return, but noticed that the cheerfulness was covering something else. He later found out that the boys had seen him on tv and saw firsthand the reality of their dad's job; both boys refused to leave the HUB till they knew their dad was safe at the LZ.

Hugs and shakes all around from everyone and a special guest on the tarmac also waiting to greet them back, Colonel Jim Briggs, their C.O.

"Good to see you, sir," Mike greeted.

"You too, Mike, good to see you all back safely," the replied.

"We need to talk, sir," Mike said gravely.

"I assumed so; otherwise, you wouldn't have sent for me to be here. First, get squared off with the family, and that's an order,"

"But sir," Mike protested,

"That's an order captain, go look after my god son's," the Colonel said firmly.

"Yes, sir." Mike had to pry Katelyn off of Art; her grip was so tight.

"Half hour, square your gear off, 2-hour break, meet in the HUB at 1800 hours," Mike addressed his team.

"Yes, sir," was the response.

After getting his gear put away, it took two hot chocolates and a swim in the heated pool with his family to catch up with all that had happened since he had left. First the wearisome flight here. Then the extraordinary tour of the Ark, Aidan telling the story of how Oliver nearly pissed his pants when the raptor came up behind him in Tyson's office. Then the story of how they were recruited by the Major, Legend of the ARK. Then they were trapped in a park area with a rampaging rhino and how their truck nearly got taken out. Then they saved the day by using raptors to herd the rhino in his cage.

Mike looked at the boys with amazement at how long and how fast they could talk without taking a breath. The last part of the story about the rhino and using raptors, he took as a boy's story, till he looked at Sam and saw the worried look on her face and her nodding her head. Mike's face went blank.

Then Oliver said, "Then we saw you on tv..." before Oliver could say more,

Mike cut in. "Then I came home safe and challenged my raptor guiding sons to a pizza-eating contest, YEAH!" Mike yelled, lightening the mood.

"Awesome, mum will lose; she eats like a mouse," Oliver joked.

"And you eat like a mouse plague," she returned. Mike and the family went off to feed their faces before the debrief.

Thomas was with Rosi, being shown her work with Tyson. Seb was sleeping, as he did on the whole flight back. Zikmund was checking his bids on items online. Katelyn and Art would need to be pried off each other again, and also Lexi and Doby, who took this time before the debrief to 'get freaky,' Lexi calls it. This down moment would be needed. The world was about to turn in the opposite direction at the debriefing.

They all gathered in the HUB conference room because it was the most secure building in the ARK, and what was about to be said couldn't be heard by anyone else. Mike and his SAS team were in attendance: Col. Jim Briggs, Art Damani, Ab Thoyana, Lexi Eldridge, Doby Heinlinker.

"I asked for you all here to hear the proceedings of our venture and the world-shattering news that was handed to us." Mike started.

"Before you go any further, I assume this news is of important military consequence, so I suggest we keep it in house, in the military." Col Briggs said.

"Yeah, that would be right. Keep it behind closed military doors, so you can keep it hush-hush," Lexi jumped in angrily.

"Young lady, we have protocols for a reason to protect people and keep the enemy from knowing what we know." Col Briggs said brashly.

"Settle Lexi, play nice. Colonel, normally that would be so, but we weren't on a military mission, so technically, the information belongs to Mr. Damani. I invited you here because you are the only one in the military that I actually trust, and shortly, you will see, WE are all WE have." Mike said.

"My apologies, Mike, Lexi, old habits. Please continue Mike," Col Briggs said.

"The mission was to track Water Tiger and bring him in if we found him. We found him, or more likely, he sent for us." Mike said.

"What!" Art and Col Briggs said.

"Yes, he said he deliberately left himself open enough for Art to track him there and for us to follow. He approached us when we got there. He wants our help to stop a conspiracy that he has been drawn into." Mike continued.

"And that's when you told him to stick it in his ass, and you shot him," Lexi said confidently.

Mike looked at Lexi. "No, I said we'd help."

"What?" Art and Col Briggs said together again.

"Water Tiger is involved in a scheme that will start a major war, possibly a Third World War. I didn't have the occasion or the inclination to say no. It involves major players, Russia, the Saudis... and America. If it's real, it's being played at the highest levels, and we don't know who to trust." Mike stated.

"Do we trust the word of a terrorist?" Ab said, sitting back, soaking it all in. No, they all mumbled and agreed.

"The intelligence he gave us was convincing; I believed he was telling the truth. So far from what he has worked out, because he is only being used for security, he's had to dig things out himself to find more without drawing suspicion. They plan a biological attack on China. Then America and Russia join forces and start a war with China, then divvy up the country's assets afterward."

"He is right, this Water Tiger. It would start a global conflict, the allies on both sides would join in to protect each other's interests. But China alone, with their foreign policies and leadership, if backed into a corner with war, it would become nuclear." Ab said austerely.

"Ok, immense mind-boggling story, but unfortunately plausible in the right conditions. Where's the smoking ..." Mike finished Col Briggs's sentence.

"Smoking gun, yes, that's what I said, but HE is the smoking gun. He is protecting a bio lab set up by the Russians at the bottom of the Altaskivi Castle; he is also the guy who came into MY house and tried to kill me. You wouldn't think he'd invite me if he had others to turn to. The last piece of info to prove his loyalty, he said that people from Illumiun Corp have bribed members of the UN council to vote on issuing a summons to AZTECK to show cause for their transactions with the World Heritage Committee. He said the caretaker for the hit on the American president and Azteck, plus the Bio lab in Estonia, was a Fredrick Nessler. Does the name ring a bell, Art?"

"Yes, it does," Art said gravely; he gave the nod to Ab, who left the room immediately. Seems it was time to lawyer up. "Yes, he is their hatchet man; we all have one, I have several." Art joked. "We should take this threat as being real; he wouldn't know his name if they weren't involved together. Nessler is a spectre to most; he doesn't exist." Art said gravely.

"So, what's our next move?" Doby joined the exchange. "How do we contact him? We don't know who he's with?"

"He will have to contact us, and we will have to find out who the players are," Mike said decisively.

"First, we have to shut down that lab," Col. Briggs said.

"We can't; that will tip them off that we are on to their operations; we better have everything prepped. Water Tiger could contact us, and we need to move then. He said there are three labs that they have asked him to secure. He gave Zik and I a heads up when we were on the run." Mike continued.

"Yeah, and that wasn't creepy at all," Zikmund said. But, Zikmund also noticed Mike shorten his Christian name, 'does that mean we're getting closer or that we are all doomed?' he thought.

"We need more people on this, no offence Art, I know your tech goes everywhere, and I know I wasn't the only one to notice you pulled a single phone from nowhere to help Mike and Smith, but there still has to be more eyes on the incoming info. We have a lead to start, but we need infrastructure and bums on seats." Seb said wisely.

"I have infrastructure all over the world, my boy, but you are right. We need computing power, people, to cut through the red tape." Art agreed.

"Oh, I know who may help," Doby said, and everyone turned to him. Doby turned and looked at Lexi. Then the penny dropped.

"Oh no, no way, I'm dead, remember," she said to Doby

"Maybe it's time to pull a Lazarus," Doby returned.

"Sorry, you've lost me," Katelyn said. "You're dead; what does that mean?" she continued.

Art stepped in. "Please let me explain; Lexi was rescued from a potential prison sentence and given a new life here. The only ones who know are the people in this room and her mother, who now lives with Doby's mother under AZTECK care. Lexi used to be a member of Anonymous."

"The cyber hackers?" Katelyn said.

"Cyber vigilantes," Lexi corrected.

"When were you going to tell me this, girlfriend? How were you going to sign my wedding certificate?" Katelyn said, huffy and pissed.

"We have more things to worry about. Is it possible they'd help Lexi?" Mike asked.

"No… maybe, I don't know; I haven't been in contact since I left. So, they would think I'm dead too," Lexi argued.

"We have to try, Lexi; they are the kind of people we need right now," Mike implored.

"I will certainly do my best," Lexi said, deflated.

"Well, our leads are the Nessler, Prince Mashhur, and anything that comes and goes from that castle."

"We're got the castle; we can be up and running in 48hrs," Doby said.

"Be careful; they have tech; they detected Scree when he got too close," Mike informed them.

"We need some heavy hitters in the spy ring, Col. Briggs?"

"Yes, I know someone that could help with Prince Mashur," he said.

"I might know someone also, BIG hitter," Art offered.

"Can they be trusted?" Mike asked.

"Oh, this one would love to have a word with me," Art said cryptically.

CHAPTER 10

COPY CATS

Tyson and Rosi were hard at work. Putting the finishing touches on a Grauer gorilla robot that was being sent into an area set aside for several incoming gorilla families. They stopped at the same time and lifted their heads. There was a thundering of hooves outside that was getting closer.

"Here they come," Rosi said, smiling.

Just then, Oliver and Aidan crash through the doorway.

"We got your message," Oliver said through puffing breaths.

"So, I see," Tyson said coyly.

"You said you have a mission for us." Aidan said with just enough breath to articulate.

"We'll leave this for a moment, Rosi, and get the boys on their secret mission."

"Secret mission!" the boys said in unison.

"Yes, a secret mission," Rosi said in a hushed voice.

"Aidan, Question. Why don't the workers get scared while Loki and Thor are walking around in the ARK?" Tyson asked in his best schoolteacher's voice.

"Because they know their robots and that we program them not to hurt anyone."

"Correct!"

"What would make the staff scared of Thor and Loki?" Tyson kept up his 20 questions.

"If one of them bit the head off of one of the staff," Oliver said, wanting to join the lesson.

"Yes, there's that." Tyson said, shaking his head.

"Aidan?"

"If they started acting strange. Different from their normal behaviour."

"Exactly, good work. Now, we have reopened Thor and Loki's AI back up to full capacity and we want you boys to take them outside with the Major and road test them. I have an eagle on standby to record everything they do, so we can review it later."

"Will they listen to us?" Oliver asked.

"Yes, they will be reassigned to you both. So, keep control of them."

"SWEET" Aidan yelled.

"Tyson, didn't the last time their AIs were fully open. Thor ripped a leg of a terrorist and brought it back to Art and Katelyn?"

"Um, Ahh, well yes, that's true, but we aren't under attack, so you should be right." Tyson said, struggling to sound confident that the same wouldn't happen again.

The boys went through the process of getting themselves set up to control the cats. As Thor and Loki came through the lab door, fully charged.

"Now, just speak normal English, no slang or gangster talk, just plain English."

"Got it Tyson" Aidan says.

"Follow us," Aidan says as they exited the door.

Heading down to the docks to meet up with the Major, the cats were more inquisitive. Their heads were turning all the time, taking in everything. People in the elevator, people eating in the food mall, people addressing them by their names. A lot of new data, but some of it is very familiar.

"Ah, here's my soldiers of the month," the Major says in his cheerful booming voice.

"Is there such a thing as a soldier of the month?" Oliver asks.

"No, I couldn't do it. It wouldn't be fair to the others... you boys would win it every month." the Major said bellowing with laughter that would make Santa Claus jealous.

The cats were ordered to jump in the back of the ARK transport, usually assigned to the raptor patrols. Once again, Thor and Loki were looking at everything, processing it all. Later on, studying the eagle video footage, Tyson believed Loki may have been having déjà vu episodes. Remembering bits of data lost when he was shot and killed by terrorists protecting Art and the ARK.

The Major saw ahead another ARK transport and decided this was as good a place as any to let the cats loose.

"Ok, boys, get the cats out and let's see what they get up to." The Major says.

"Roger that, Major," Oliver responds.

The boys and the Major looked around and couldn't find any staff near the vehicle.

"Thor, find them," Aidan commands, pointing to the abandoned vehicle.

Thor, equipped with high tech visual and scent detectors, jumped onto the vehicle and started scanning. He lifts his head, sniffing the air ... then he was off and running.

"Woo Thor, wait up" Aidan yelled as they all took off chasing him.

"He's following this path. He's got their scent," Oliver yells.

Then suddenly a voice rings out up ahead. "Thor, is that you? Are you here Art?"

"No, it's us Dan. Where are you?" the Major calls out.

"Up here, Major," Dan calls out from up a tree.

"What are you doing up there?" the Major calls while looking at Dan and one of his staff hanging onto a branch up a tree.

"Her," Dan calls out while pointing off to his left.

30 metres away was Buttercup, the friendly white rhino. Well, friendly to most, but seemingly not to Dan and his staff.

"She's all PMS today, cranky old tart."

Just then, as if she understood every word Dan was saying, Buttercup charged at the tree and pulled up 10 metres short, huffing, puffing and scratching the ground with her large hoofs.

"See! I'd appreciate it, Major, if you could move her on, so I can get down and continue my work."

"No worries, Dan, we're onto it."

"Aidan, can you get Loki too …" the Major's voice stopped mid-sentence as his eyes were transfixed on something. The boys followed the Major's line of sight, which led them to Loki. He was already in motion, heading towards Buttercup.

The scene was being played out in slow motion as Loki sleeked her way towards Buttercup in a slow, great cat like way. Loki's head was low but looking forward, she had Buttercups' attention now. Both animals were eyeing each other up. It was time to show dominance. Buttercup lunged forward and hit the brakes, thrashing up dirt and grass, huffing and snorting, showing her immense power and in so telling the cat to back off!

Everyone was transfixed by the challenge. The boys were loving the show; it was a lot better live than on tv. Now, their eyes were on Loki, he has been challenged. How will he respond? Strangely enough, Thor wasn't reacting to the entire episode. He sat there calmly, watching his brother challenge this monstrous beast.

Loki stopped, roared … then started scratching and snorting, copying Buttercups' moves. What? Was the reaction from animal and humans alike. Buttercup took a few steps back and was swinging her head from side to side, trying to figure out why this cat wasn't acting like a cat. Loki, making the moment even more confusing, started swinging his head from side to side, copying Buttercup.

Buttercup lost her patience for the cat and charged, as did Loki. A moment of common sense was lost on all watching as a five-million-dollar robotic cat charged at an endangered white rhino. That there are only two left in the world.

Charging on a collision course to settle this challenge, the two mighty beasts went head-to-head. Moments before impact, Loki leaped in the air, jumped on Buttercup's back, then sprung off gracefully, landing on the ground with perpetual grace. Buttercup hit the skids and swung her body around, throwing up dirt and grass. As she looked at the cat, it was prancing around, showing off as if it had out smarted, the white rhino.

Buttercup was pissed now. Snorting and letting out her own roar, she charged at the black cat again. Once again, the moment was caught by all the humans watching and still no one thought to stop the collision. Once again, the beasts charged, one with furious intent and the other with a cocky self-assuredness. The beasts were only metres apart and Loki's new opened up AI consciousness, learnt a new lesson. Don't use the same trick twice. Loki leaped in the air to land on Buttercups' back, but Buttercup was not being fooled twice. As Loki leaped, Buttercup thrust her head and horn up and caught Loki between the back legs and sent the black cat flying through the air. Loki landed ungracefully, bouncing off the ground hard and landing sprawled in a large prickle bush.

The major and the boys burst out laughing at the sight of Loki laid out in the bush. What made the scene more hilarious was Thor had his head down and a paw across his eyes, as if he was ashamed to look. Meanwhile Buttercup, having felt she made her point, huffed, stuck her head in the air and trotted off calmly to have a drink in a nearby creek.

"Well, I've been a ranger for over 20 years and I've never seen a sight like that before." Dan said as he climbed down the tree.

"Me neither," the Major agreed.

"It will be interesting to see what uncle Art has to say about it." Oliver says.

"Why is that?"

Pointing to the sky above, at an eagle looping overhead. "Because he filmed the whole thing."

"SHIT!" Dan and the Major said in unison.

CHAPTER 11

ANNOYING LITTLE SHIT

Damien Spelling was a master craftsman spy; he earned his position as the director of the CIA from the grassroots up. Recruited through an advertisement in the local newspaper. He passed with the highest aptitude test scores of all that sat on the entrance examination that whole year. He caught the eye of the head spook that day for having a particular skill, being perfectly plain. Damien was of average height, average looks with average features, nothing that would stand out or make him noticeable. 35 years in the field through Europe, caught twice, escaped once, and tortured twice before they offered him a unit leadership which has paved his way to the top as Director of the CIA. A complex man with the enemy, he has dealt with the Cold War, the New Russia, China, and numerous would-be terrorist groups, but none annoyed him more than Art Damani, CEO from AZTECK. After their last encounter when the president was nearly assassinated at the ARK, Damani gave Spelling a foretaste of real spying power. The CIA engineers still can only guess how he did it.

The weekends offer some respite to the director, being around family, but like the president, his work never stops. There was always someone not willing to make an assessment in the office without verifying first. Today had been different; he got through breakfast with his wife and daughter with no calls. Now approaching lunch and still no calls, 'this day might be perfect, until Beatriss and her mother spring on me what their hiding' he thought. He spent a lifetime analysing people and places. He knew when something was coming, and it was no different with his family. He knew at breakfast that they either wanted to tell him something or wanted him to do something, but weren't game enough to ask. Then, his train of thought was broken by a knock at the door. "I'll get it," he yells out.

As he opens the door, a young pizza delivery man greets him.

"Spelling?" the young man asked.

"Ay, yes, that's right," the director said.

"Pizza, sir," the young man said.

Just as the young man was handing the pizza box over, a ringing sound came from inside the box, and the box started pulsating. Startled, the director drew a pistol from the belt of his trousers and pointed it at the now terrified delivery man.

"What is in the box?" the director asked the young man while pointing his pistol at his head.

"I don't know... a phone?" he said, shaking, nearly dropping the pizza.

"A phone... who's phone?"

"I don't know."

"Is it your phone?" the director kept up his interrogation.

"It's not mine."

"Are you in the habit of delivering phones with your pizzas?" he pressed.

"No... I don't know."

"You don't know much, son, do you," He was sure the boy was telling the truth.

"So, are you going to answer it?" the director asked.

"NO, it's your pizza," the boy stated, just wanting to get the hell out of there.

Lowering his pistol, he used the tip of the barrel to lift the lid of the pizza box, and yes, there was a phone taped to the inside cover of the box, and it was still ringing. Damien ripped the phone from the lid, hit the answer button, and put it to his ear.

"Yes," he said warily.

"Give the boy a tip. You've scared him half to death... and don't be cheap," a familiar and annoying voice said over the phone.

"Damani," Damien said.

Damien only had $20 on him and reluctantly handed it over.

"What do you want?" Damien asked angrily.

"We need to talk, now; give your daughter her pizza; I ordered her favourite. Grab your work phone, and I'll send coordinates to it," Art said.

"First, you don't tell me what to do. Second, how would you know what pizza my daughter likes, and third, and I don't have a work phone."

Suddenly, his secure phone to the Whitehouse and Pentagon started ringing.

"Are you going to answer it? Or do you want me to set off the alarm system in your house?" Art threatened.

"What do you want?" he asked gruffly.

"We have to talk, face to face; I've secured an area. I have something bigger than both of us, and I need your help. It is also connected to the assassination attempt." Art said, concerned.

"When?" Spelling asked.

"Now," Art said.

Spelling hung up, grabbed his coat off the rack, and tucked his pistol into his belt again. Then, he walked over and grabbed his phone off the floor, his 'work' phone. Then, he headed into the dining room, where Beatriss and her mother were chatting at the end of the table.

"I ordered some pizza for lunch, but I just got a call and have to pop out for a little while, work stuff. So, when I get back, we will talk about whatever it is you've been trying to tell me all morning," Damien said.

His wife got up and kissed him on the cheek. "That's what I get for marrying a spy."

"That's what you get. Won't be long," Damien smiled and turned for the doors; when he gets home, he will have the most arduous 6 months of his career.

Damien Spelling headed east. From the coordinates sent to his secure work phone, driving in his sensible, plain family SUV, he would attract little attention. Still, he needn't have worried as overhead one of AZTECKs most sophisticated drones was following his every move; the drone wasn't tailing Spelling but tracking anyone tracking him. The drone could search for any signals of digital tracking. As Spelling exited the highway, a conflict of thoughts went through his head. 'This prick demeaned me and the CIA last year with his larking about. He's dangerous with that much power, but... he must know I don't trust him, and he still needs my help with something imperative,' we'll see, he thought. The GPS led him to a rural area and said there were 5 kilometres to go. He had been watching every car, every person; he didn't believe he was being followed. Up ahead, he saw a diner; by the GPS, that's the spot. As he was pulling into the parking lot, two cars were parked outside, neither standing out at all. His work phone rang. "Come inside, everything is secure," Art's voice told him. As he was about to close his driver's door, he paused, took his pistol out of his belt, and put it in the glove compartment; this guy sees everything, so he must know I'd be armed, a show of faith.

As he walked into the room, he was being a good spy, checking all the exits and checking all the people in the diner. Well, all two of them, Art Damani and a lady dressed as a worker behind the counter.

"Come sit, Damien; we have a lot to discuss,"

Never devoid of manners, Damien stuck out his hand in greeting, which Art accepted.

As they sat, Art spoke, "I see you noticed the exits; we have a 5-kilometre free zone around the diner; nothing digital can track or hear us. However, in the event of someone armed coming in to stop us or kidnap you or me. There is a pistol taped on the underside of your table, and Helen has some heavier ordinance behind the counter; there are only us three and some robotic friends here to protect us. Do you feel safe enough?"

"I wouldn't be here If I thought there would be a problem," Damien answered.

"Ok, I'll just rattle off everything we've found out, and you step in where you want clarification."

Art began with a recap of the assassination attempt on the president at the Ark. The effort to kill him and shut down the ARK. The Australian SAS team that helped save him. Then the retaliation of the Water Tiger at Mike Maddens home. He was sure to emphasise the hatred and fear of the Water Tiger to everyone. Then he went into the tracking of the Water Tiger to Estonia and the mission to bring him in. Damien sat there unflinching, taking in every word and analysing Art simultaneously. The only time Art saw any muscle movement in his face was when he told him the information came from the Water Tiger and he wanted to work with us. Art continued with the meeting at the HUB and finished with their theories of how to continue. Damien sat there thinking for a moment.

"What's the coffee like here?" Damien asked.

"The Lattes good," Art said, surprised.

"Ask Helen to make a big pot of it," Damien asked.

The CIA director sat there gathering his thoughts and words before he spoke.

"I have worked my craft in a lot of countries; I have been there when wars start, wars finish, and constantly there to prevent them from happening. This Water Tiger is your smoking gun; he has been involved in some pretty hideous things that most don't know about. If he doesn't like it, you better sit up and listen. This could be the biggest thing since the Cuban missile crisis with JFK. I will tell you this, and you better take this on board quickly. Everyone you have talked to about this, and everyone you've asked to help, is on a hit list. Also, their families are all in danger; many people will die before this is over. You better make sure they know it and prepare for it."

"I will; I will make sure and take all precautions." Art said intently.

"Now that I'm involved, more will happen, but more will be at risk. I have the contacts to look into the Russian connection. The money is obviously being filtered through the Saudis. So, we need to concentrate on the American connection and the Russian connection. I know you can contact me, but how do I contact you? Damien asked.

Art slides one of his unique phones across the table to the director.

"With this, anywhere outside of your work headquarters is secure." Art informed him.

"What about the Whitehouse?"

"Yes, it's fine there; their security is not very up to date," Art informed him.

"Oh, great," Damien sounded discouraged.

"To pull this off, the calls have to be coming from high up, and since they wanted the president gone and you dead, then they see you both as major threats. This UN sanction is just a credibility attack to see if they can make anything stick and push your stocks down," Damien informed Art with a clinical no thrills voice.

"That's what I was thinking. Am I in danger?" Art queried

"Yes, definitely, you and your son. If they bring you both down, AZTECK collapses. No more talk of peace and harmony for all. In Africa, it will turn into a bloodbath overnight."

"Oh My God!" Art said, horrified.

"We may need all gods on our side before this is over. How deep are your pockets, Mr. Damani?"

"I will fund whatever you need, Damien."

"Keep it secret, but record every cent. We all may be on the chopping block in the end, and we need a trail to show who's side we are on. Blood will spill by the end if we succeed and congressional enquiries will then start. They may arrest us both as traitors before we can finally clear our names." the director said seriously.

"I will need someone close to the President to work with us, and I know just the right person, and he hates my guts... perfect."

CHAPTER 12

"LEXI??? YOU'RE DEAD"

The ARK was operating as usual. Mrs. Sanders, the kitchen manager, was up early, as was customary, getting everything ready for her staff. The cleaners were buffing the floor, and supervisors set up individual eating areas. Security guards were having a coffee during a break in their shift. Everything progressed as a typical day should. Yet, it was like a different dimension in the HUB, an altered reality. Life and death decisions for millions of people in the world. What would Mrs. Sanders think if she knew a World War could start soon? Would she still be willing to cook the risotto for the ARK staff lunches?

Ab was feeling alert this morning, some exercise outside the ARK with Loki and Thor, nutritious breakfast, now up to the HUB. 'He was thinking about the three superpowers going head-to-head. This could be the biggest event of my lifetime, horrible... but good. Now he has something to challenge his intellect'. Ab didn't think of himself as being some kind of Einstein but lately he has had to take up Tia Chi and meditate to calm his mind. Thinking, constantly analysing, being the HUB central connection kept him busy, but the enquiries and complications were not perplexing. Simple mathematics and keeping up with global markets gave most of the answers, but now, to stop a World War. Currently, there are so many working pieces, world chess. Ab was waiting to exit the elevator, ding, 'time to process,' he thought. He walked down the hallway and entered the HUB. The distress of what he saw shocked him to his core; this is the HUB, the most secure building in the ARK; how could this happen here? As Ab looked over to the conference table. Here were Lexi and Doby getting freaky on the table. Lexi's long legs were stuck up in the air while she laid flat on her back, as Doby had his pants down, inward bound, from the edge of the table.

"WHAT THE HELL! Get a room, you two," Ab said, shocked

Doby pulled up his pants so fast that he whacked his testicles hard. "Awww," he groaned as Lexi was pulling up her G-string.

"Are you alright?" She asked, concerned.

"Yeah… I'm fine, just had a little calamity."

"Don't you damage them; this is to be continued," she said cheekily.

"Well, not in here, it isn't. What were you two thinking? Anybody could have walked in," Ab said, exasperated.

"Ab, I'm so sorry, it was my fau…." Doby said before Lexi cut in.

"Oh, stop being chivalrous, my love, sorry Ab, it was all my fault; I woke up in a mood and took it out on Doby when I got here," she explained.

"Well, this isn't the place for your MOODS; you have rooms," he said, still irritated, "We have a potential World War coming, and you're doing THAT!" He explained, pointing to the table.

"Why do you think I was in a MOOD! You all want me to make it known to all my old friends I abandoned, OH HEY, I'm still alive, so sorry you've worried about me, and I didn't let you know I was ok," she said, getting irritated herself.

"Yes, I realise that the request would have horrible consequences for you. That's why I sat up last night trying to work out different ways, so you don't have to contact them."

"You did that for me," Lexi said warmly.

"Yes, I came up with a few workable options … but none of them have the efficiency that you contacting Anonymous would have, but I am prepared to put the options to the meeting this morning," he said.

"Thank you, Ab, for thinking of me," Lexi said genuinely. "I have spent the night going over it too, there really isn't any other way… and I'm really sorry, you came in too early before we really got freaky on the conference table," she ended cheekily.

"Geez, Lexi, you couldn't have been doing much more than that anyway," Ab said

"OH, yes, I could… do you want to see?" Lexi said in a sexy voice.

"NO!" Ab and Doby said instantly

"What's no?" Art said from the HUB doorway

"NOTHING," Ab and Doby said straight away.

Art turned and looked at Lexi. "Have you been naughty again, dear girl?"

"Always," Lexi said with a cheeky smile.

There was a ding of the elevator as the rest of the team started appearing. Mike and Seb appeared through the exit door from outside, obviously doing early morning training.

As they all gathered and sat around the table, strangely, they were all waiting for Mike to start. Mike eventually got the hint. "I think we should start with the report from Art and Director Spellings meeting."

"When you think you have a grip on how the world works and then you meet Director Spelling, I sat there opposite to him for half an hour, laying out everything that had happened and how we thought they were linked. He didn't flinch; the whole scenario seemed normal to him. He reviewed and then, for the next 2 hours, went through what we needed to do and what the potential outcomes would be; he said blood will spill before this is over. Oh, he told me now that he's involved, and that we are taking steps to stop them, our lives are all in danger, including our families. This is the most significant event since the Cuban missile crisis. He is contacting someone who is close to the President to see if anyone is pressuring him. Cause to make this happen, it's all top end decisions." Art said.

"I totally agree," Colonel Briggs said.

"We need to work out how best to protect our families, and by the way, my lawyers accepted an invitation to 'please explain' before a committee of the UN charter. Director Spelling is also using his contacts to look into the Russian connection. He said the Saudi link is just money, but they need to be trailed digitally to see who contacts them for more links in the chain. So that leaves us with Anonymous; Lexi, do we leave contacting them until we have more leads or do it now?" Art asked.

"Now, before I lose my nerve," she said timidly, which Art noted, but didn't bring up. Because Lexi is never timid.

"1 pm, we'll all meet again to draw up our first moves, review all the information. Many heads make light work, my father always said." Art ended his update.

Mike stood. "1 pm then. Team, we have a meeting in an hour, in the ballroom. Ab, I would like your input if you have the time?"

"I will be there," Ab responded.

They all got up and dispersed from the room. Ab and Doby went to their consoles, while Lexi just sat there at the conference table. "Are you alright, Lexi?" Art asked.

"Yes, nothing that a carton of scotch won't fix," she said.

Art laughed, "What brand?"

"Glenfiddich 20yr old," Lexi suggested

"Good taste," Art said, patting Lexi on the back. As she clawed her way back to her room that night, after an arduous day, there at her door was a carton of 20yr Glenfiddich. On top of the carton was a note, in Art's own handwriting, on it said, "never has one given so much for so many… except maybe spiderman, but you will have to ask Doby about that. XXX"

Earlier on, in the HUB,

"Do you want me to hang around while you contact your friends?" Doby asked Lexi.

"Thanks, sweety, but no, I best do this myself," Lexi said.

"Ok, well, if you get into trouble, just hit the alarms; I know how you like doing that," Doby said as he bent over and kissed Lexi on the forehead.

Doby and Ab packed up and left the room. They left Lexi with an empty HUB with her thoughts and a mission. Lexi was thinking, 'What if they changed the protocols? Stands to reason. She had written them, so if she disappeared, it would be best to change the system. Well, only one way to find out. Lexi started hitting the keys. Then, up on the screen came a message 'ARE YOU LOST,' Lexi typed 'NO I WaNt 2 B FOUNd', 'Follow friend you know the way,' Lexi was amazed everything was still the same. It was time to enter the algorism, the actual test. The dates were coordinates, longitude, and latitude; Lexi pulled up a map, nearest capital city, weather the last three days there, pages in the local newspaper. The keyword is Christmas, fitting, Lexi thought. She typed Christmas on the screen. Now, let's see what happens… nothing… nothing… then,

'WHO ARE YOU???',

"Well, that's new," Lexi said out loud. 'Friend,' Lexi typed,

'WHO ARE YOU,' Lexi sat there thinking, then typed, Gidgit.

Almost immediately, 'BULLSHIT! GIDGITS DEAD,' 'where did you learn that algorism?'

'I wrote it.'

Lexi wrote on a hunch, 'who's my best friend?'

'I am,'

'Marcy?'

'Lexi?'

'Yep,'

'WTF! You're alive; where the hell have you been?' Then, for the next 10 minutes, Marcy went on a rant about being abandoned, the pain of thinking she's dead, and a million other things. Lexi just sat there and let her type. She had a lot to get off her chest. Then finally, the writing stopped.

'Are you coming home?' Marcy typed.

'Not just yet. I was offered a hand to leave the country before the FBI nabbed me because of my ex.'

'Lol, well, it didn't do him any good. Didn't you hear, about a month after you disappeared, he was arrested by the FBI cyber unit for fabricating government documents? He's doing 7 years.'

'Lol, good to hear, scumbag he was... Marcy, I need your help.'

'Anything girlfriend,'

'I need you to contact the council; I have a mission pretext for you guys, government and private enterprises.'

'Lol, are you kidding? That's never going to happen, you know that.'

'It has too, to stop a potential World War, Marcy; we always said we did this for the people, it doesn't get any bigger. So, call the council and let them hear me out. At least give me that much. This has to happen to save millions of lives.'

'My God, you're serious.'

'Deadly serious! This time tomorrow, I'll call back. So, did you find me?'

'What do you mean?'

'I know you, Marcy. You have used this time to track me down, so where am I?'

'Bitch! Are you with the government? I can't even get a solid hit,'

'No, private, more powerful than any government.'

'No way, who?'

'Lol, see you tomorrow this time; love you, Marcy. Oh, by the way, I have a man....'

'NO WAY!' Marcy replied.

Lexi signed off smiling that went better than she could have ever hoped, getting her best friend/sister in arms on the line. Now, all we have to do is sell the story tomorrow. Lexi picked up her phone. One last thing to do before the meeting later. She started texting.

Doby's phone started playing the spiderman theme; he had a message. He looked at it. It was from Lexi.

"I'm still horny, see you in 5," Doby sighed.

CHAPTER 13

MOVING CAMP

"Exceedingly disastrous, Ji-tae Jin. Those lapses with the security could have cost us dearly." Fredrick Nessler said.

"I believe the security team's focus has been readjusted. I know my men got the message, as did the prince." Jin replied.

"Why did prince Mashur need a lesson?" Nessler asked.

"He walked around here like he was in command; he is just a money launderer, nothing else. It would be best to inform me of these visits in the future. We don't know who is watching, and the least leads, the better. The Americans and Russians have the money to pull this off; they only use the prince's family to hide the money trail. When do you want me to finish here?" Jin asked.

"You are perceptive, Ji-tae, and correct; I should have given more thought to the 'What ifs.' I would like you to finish up here in the week, and the cover of the renovations to the castle will begin. Your next assignment is on the island of Navassa in Haiti; pack warm. It should be a lot easier to protect."

"There is no such thing, mark my words, Nessler. Every step we take forward is another step towards something happening, many moving pieces. Are we sure this disease is secure? Do I need to get my teams inoculated?" Jin asked.

"Not yet; it is only a variant of Covid-19."

"COVID-19, this is the world-ending disease you're planning on!" Water Tiger said fiercely, as if he had wasted his time with this operation, hoping to get Nessler to divulge more of the operation.

"We do as requested... the disease isn't meant to destroy China...." Nessler paused, about to tell more than thought better of it.

"Your word is good enough, Nessler; you have never led me astray before; I will follow their instructions.

"As will I, as will I."

"I will cease operations here at the end of the week; it will take me another week to get my squads there quietly." Water tiger informed him.

"That is fine; we will start moving the operations after then. There will be a large reward for all of us on completion," Nessler assured him.

"They already negotiated my fee; that is all I require," Water Tiger finished.

"Then I shall be off and start the proceedings at the next site. Success to you, Jin," Nessler said.

"And to you too, Nessler," Ji-tae Jin responded.

After Nessler had left, Water Tiger sat; he had to process. Covid? Not to destroy? The clues seem to be elusive. He did a security walk around the grounds; he knew he wouldn't be detected using the phone, as the tech security packed up and left yesterday. He would pass what he had on, little as it was. He grabbed the phone out of his pocket and dialled.

CHAPTER 14

"PEEK-A-BOO, I SEE OMG!"

Lexi had just finished breakfast at the food mall, Eggs benedict, passionfruit yogurt, and a pot of coffee. She now feels revved up and ready to start the day. A few "Good mornings" and men attempting to attract her attention, as she walked to the elevator, brightened her morning. She doesn't feel she's an attention-seeker, but a girl does like to get noticed.

As she walks down the hallway from the elevator, as she approaches the Hub door, she hears cackling, a lot of cackling. Wondering what all the light-heartedness is about, Lexi enters the Hub. After being excited about spending the day with her, Innamorato working together. It's incredible how a couple of steps in your day can make. Lexi entered the Hub to find another woman all over her man, laughing and carrying on. Lexi, a woman of class and refinement, reacted to the situation, coolly and with sophistication.

"What the fuck's going on here?!" she bellows out.

Rosi Jensen was startled so much by Lexi's outburst she fell into Doby's lap on his computer chair. Laying there in Doby's lap, her skirt flicked up and what Lexi saw stunned her to no end. She was wearing superhero unmentionables like Doby.

Moments before, Doby shared a video clip from a DC animated movie, where Harley Quinn was singing on stage to the Blonde hit song, 'Hanging on the telephone' with Batman and Robin watching in the crowd. It was one of Doby's all-time favourites, and thought to share it with Rosi, who too was a huge fan of animated movies and graphic novels. Rosi was leaning over Doby's shoulder watching the clip when 'BOOM' Lexi screamed out. Now Lexi is standing over them with the greenest eyes either of them had ever seen and Wonder Woman staring at Lexi from between Rosi's legs.

"I believe you have somewhere to be... Miss Wonder Woman," Lexi said snootily.

Rosi twigged to where Lexi got the Wonder Woman line from; she jumped out of Doby's lap, pulled the front of her skirt down, and ran for the door before there was bloodshed. Doby sat there like a deer in headlights.

"I can explain," Doby gets out.

"Oh, this should be a good story," Lexi said disparagingly.

"You know, I don't make stories up. I was just showing Rosi a clip from a Batman movie."

"It must have been funny the way you two were carrying on and the way she was hanging all over you," Lexi continued.

"She was just leaning over my shoulder," Doby protested.

"If she was any closer, you'd be wearing the same clothes, and I don't think the Wonder Woman undies would suit you."

"Yes, that was just rude. You're trying to make something out of nothing. I won't apologise for sharing an interest with somebody," Doby said, fighting back in the conversation.

"Well, you haven't shared your interests with me like that."

"The only thing you're interested in is sex!" Doby regretted saying it as soon as it left his mouth.

"Is that right... I haven't heard you complaining," Lexi says as she turns her back to him and goes to her consol.

The day passed with an unnerving silence.

The following day, Lexi was heading to the food mall for breakfast, and here were Doby and Rosi watching something on Doby's laptop, laughing again. She had already lost sleep the night before with guilt for carrying on being so jealous. Plus, not having spent more time getting to know Doby's world... BUT, what male complains about sex? Now coming into eye contact with Rosi and seeing the scared look in her eyes as she gets up and leaves quickly to go to her lab, Lexi has to add shame to her list.

Another day in the Hub passes with unnatural silence as both go about their work. The atmosphere is thick with...? No one that came into the Hub could put their finger on it. There was apparent discord between the two, but they still worked together effortlessly. They maintained everything working in the park and worked on the info that came from Mike's team on their last mission.

The following day, everyone gathered in the Hub to hash out what they thought should be their next move. They had all agreed on contacting Lexi's old group Anonymous, but what else? They had to move fast but carefully because they didn't know who else was involved. The communication from Water Tiger was valuable, but not enough; he couldn't press his hand; otherwise, he would come under suspicion.

They gathered in groups, some in idle chitchat, others bouncing ideas off each other. They were all waiting for Lexi, who was the last to arrive, and she didn't disappoint with her entrance. As she walked through the door, Art never saw such a diverse number of reactions in a single room, to a single event. As Lexi entered the room, the Earth moved on its axis. In walked 'The New Lexi,' no more Goth makeup with dark eyeshadow and black lipstick. No more black clothes with the ripped t/shirt with ample cleavage showing. No more long black studded boots with spikes and studs. This Lexi was Miss America suburbia 2025. Subtle makeup, long sleeve shirt, business length skirt, sensible shoes with sensible length heel, her hair up in a bun. Lexi still looked dazzling. She could wear a potato sack and still run for Miss America. It was the complete reversal overnight of who she was and the things that made her unique.

The looks ranged from WOW, to OMG, to What the? But it was Doby's expression that said it all; he looked like he saw his best friend's soul ripped out of their body. He was devastated.

"What?" was the only thing she had to say to everyone staring at her.

Katelyn thought it best to say something before she got a complex.

"I hate you!" she said to Lexi.

Lexi looked stunned. "Why, what did I do?"

"Girl, you can wear anything and still look like a supermodel."

Lexi smiled back at Katelyn; she thought this girl was definitely my new BFF. "Well, it's not too late to give the boss the flick and marry me."

"Are you a billionaire, girlfriend?" Katelyn threw back.

"Ah, no,"

"Sorry, this girl needs new shoes... and knives". Everyone in the office burst out laughing, which broke the ice.

As Lexi walked past Doby, "Here, Lexi, I got you your latte."

"Thanks Doby" and she ruffled his hair like you do a child.

Katelyn stood there and made an up and down gesture over Lexi's new attire. "It was time to grow up," she said loud enough for Doby to hear.

The meeting was fruitful; they all agreed that the first thing to do was to get more information. Navassa Island had to be monitored for all ins and outs to find out as much as possible, then backtrack who was paying the bills. Nessler was the key; they had to learn more about him and who pulls his strings. They had to move fast because they needed to secure surveillance at all the local ports. After all, Navassa was only approachable by the sea. They also agreed that if Anonymous came on board, they would let them have Nessler as their goal to hack and trace everything he says and does, especially his money.

This was a world event, and they felt like the 300 Spartans they had to prevail, as the result of failure would be catastrophic.

CHAPTER 15

UNLIKELY ALLIES

The HUB was filled with light chatter as they awaited the conference with the council of ANONYMOUS. The stakes were high, but there was sanguinity in the air and hope of possible new allies.

Lexi typed on the keys and soon came a reply, "Hi Lexi, it's Marcy."

"Hi Marcy, are they all there?" Lexi asked.

"Yes, some are on video chat."

"Ok great, I would like this on a conference call, so I can communicate to you all," Lexi asked.

"Ok, I'll send a link, done" Lexi hit some keys and connected to the Anonymous council.

"Ok, do you all know who I am?" Lexi asked.

"Yes," was the multi-voice response.

"Do you wish to do a trace to see if you are being compromised?"

Marcy jumped in, "don't bother, I tried yesterday and couldn't even get a solid link to trace; her tech is imposing," Marcy said to anyone listening.

"Our ...council, for want of a better word, is all here. The outline of what we are suggesting is what Marcy has told you. I wish you to take a vote on whether you will join us. I will give you the skeleton framework; if you all vote to join, I will fill in the names and places. It has to be unanimous, or else we can't continue. First, if you vote to work with us, you need to know the importance of what you will do; it will put you and your families in significant danger. The people behind this pending disaster will stop at nothing, including murder, to stop anyone who opposes them. Ok, the outline is there are three influential world superpowers; two are working together to attack the other and split up the country's resources. They are planning a biological attack to cripple them. We have the evidence. A man on the inside is helping with information. There are several sites. We're tracking the first and started moving pieces into play to monitor the second. We need your help with computer power and tracking; we are prepared to give you all the backing you need; we just don't have the numbers to survey everything and everyone. Questions?" Lexi finished.

"Why not go to the authorities with what you have?" a voice said.

"They are the authorities; to achieve such a massive move, this would be choreographed at the highest level of government," Colonel Briggs said.

"Then my point would be, what makes you think anything we all can do could make a difference?" the voice said again.

"We don't," Art said as he entered the discussion, "But we need to try. From what we can analyse, it is a small group with significant influence, orchestrating everything. That's why we need your help to dig up more info." Art said.

"Well, that's the outline; I now need you to vote on whether you want to join us," Lexi informed them.

"I'm in," came several voices over the speakers. "Count me in too," came Marcy's voice.

"Is that all of you, Marcy?" Lexi asked.

"No, there is still one who hasn't said anything yet, Kent; what is your vote?"

"World Wars, spies, biological war? It all seems implausible to me?" Kent said.

"How's your history Kent?" 2 Planks spoke up.

"Very good," Kent replied.

"Then, you already know those things have been done repeatedly over the last 70 years, actually a lot more than people know. We have first-hand knowledge. This is just the latest attempt." 2 Planks said.

"Fine, it is against my better judgment, but my vote is yes." Kent agreed.

"Then it is agreed. Here is the information as we have it so far." Lexi went on for 5 minutes, outlaying everything that had happened so far and all the information they had gathered. Lexi withheld the name of their man on the inside and the name of Mike and his team.

Several comments came across the speaker. Wow, holy shit, is this possible? Then a voice said, "AZTECK is the high-security mob you're working for; I've hacked them heaps of times; they are not very secure," Kent said.

"Clark, you only got through to places they will allow you to get into," Lexi said.

"We have received a message from our man inside; the next biological site is on Navassa, in the Haiti Islands...." Mike paused before he read the next part of the message. "He says the disease they're working on is a variant of COVID-19". That news sparked a torrid of conversation, mostly confusion, covid-19. It's been restrained with worldwide immunisation. Even a variant wouldn't have a massive impact on China. They threw theories around on how they could use it and why and what impact it would have. This went on for 10 minutes before a voice spoke up. "I believe you may all be missing the point."

"Please identify yourself and explain." A female voice from the council spoke with authority.

"My name is Ab Thoyana; I believe you are all correct but may be missing the point. You all agree that a covid-19 variant would have little effect. My hypothesis is that it won't be released in China but the rest of the world and that the test labs are for an antidote for the United States and Russia, too... save the day. Getting war approval in either country is difficult, so they have to convince others it is necessary, including allies. How easy would it be to go to war if everyone in the country was screaming WAR! So, I believe they will set up China as the scapegoat of the instigator of COVID. This means they would need a smoking gun, like biological labs, like the ones set up. I think you will find the virus is being manufactured in China somewhere."

They all went silent; it was so correct, obvious, and simple that it was downright terrifying. Mike was the first to speak. "I think Ab is on to something; all the tech personnel we saw in Alatskivi Castle were Asians."

"We need to move; what would you have of us?" the lady with the authoritative voice said.

"We need you to find anything you can about Fredrick Nessler and his involvement with ILLUMIUN Corp; he is their coordinator, but be careful around him, particularly with surveillance; this man would kill or have you killed with no hesitation. We need to know everyone he speaks or communicates to." Art said.

"We will need to crack Illumiun security first," Kent said

"We can give you that," Art said

"Can we communicate through this channel?" the lady said.

"Yes," Art replied

"We seem to have a lot of work to do; we will be in contact." on that, the line went dead.

They all looked at Lexi. "Who is she?" Art asked

Lexi shrugged her shoulders, "I have no idea."

CHAPTER 16

"ARE YOU WATERPROOF?"

'Waiting, I hate waiting,' Art thought to himself, while scratching Loki's head. His life for years now has been fast-paced, always decisions to make, always things to fix. Finally, he decided he needed fresh air, so he headed up to the Hub and went through to make his way to the Ark's helo pad, with Thor and Loki in tow. As he passes through the Hub, Doby and Lexi are working away furiously, giving info back and forward, working like one brain, but there's still that something in the air between them.

Now, as he looks out over the rails at the beauty and wonders he has created, he can't help but wonder why? With all this beauty, why do people want a World War? When the alternative is this? A gentle breeze surrounded him, and he breathed deep the smell of Jasmine. There was a gentle roar of a lion in the distance and an elephant answering the call. Hopefully, they're saying... thank God for this man.

A gentle voice from behind broke his euphoria. "Is all well with you, father?"

"Yes, Ab, just thinking," his father replies.

"I don't think so; you looked like you were trying to readjust."

"A chip of the old block, very perceptive of you," Art says.

"You realise all you can do is try. All the good men are not standing around doing nothing, as the saying goes."

"World War, Lexi changing her style. Has the world gone mad, Ab?" Loki let out a whine as if to agree with Art.

Ab laughed; he has readjusted. "Good news. All the pieces are in place on the docks; we have tracked everything and everyone going to the island. So at least we will have information to make further decisions. Now come inside; the animals already think you're a great man for saving them." Art took a deep breath and let it out slowly. "Ok, let's Kick-Ass; it's time to help Mike plan their next mission, anyway."

The Hub was full again within the hour with a few extras: Rosi Jensen and Tyson Lumming. Tyson and Rosi were updated and brought up to speed. Plus, given the time to get over the shock of it all. The small number trying to save the world, Tyson and Rosi, were brought in because they needed every devious ploy in the book to conceal the surveillance of the key players on the island.

"First, I get it. I see what you're trying to do, but maybe you should have brought us in earlier, and maybe we could have worked something out, but all we can do right now! Is give you what we have around the ARK already. Personally, I think a rhino sitting on the docks might attract attention, so best we stick with the birds. They will give you video feeds, sound, GPS tracking, and satellite connections if they get close enough. We could use bats for anyone sneaking around at night." Tyson informed them.

"Captain Mike, are you guys like navy seals? Can you go in the water?" Rosi asked.

"Yes, Rosi, we are waterproof," Everyone started laughing. "And call me Mike."

"You know what I mean," Rosi said, embarrassed.

"Yes, I know. I was only teasing; why, what did you have in mind?" Mike asked.

"Well, satellite tracking is spasmodic, even if we highjacked the CIA satellites too. I believe I could make a high-powered underwater tracker from the tech from one of Art's monsters, the Creature from the Black Lagoon, but how to attach it to a bottom of a boat is above my skill set, so I'd leave that to you."

"You have a brilliant young lady working with you, Tyson; that would be an enormous help, Rosi."

"Lexi and I can write a program to track all the information, when, where, etc.," Doby added.

"Ok, great plan. Now the hard part, we need more info on what's going on inside the building." Art added.

Zikmund joined the conversation. "Well, going from their last operation, we can't get close with any tech; they can detect it. Looking at the photos of the building, it's covered with surveillance cameras around the entire building..."

"You did homework! Oh My God," Katelyn threw in. Everyone had a laugh.

"Ha ha ha, as I was saying, before I was rudely interrupted; I couldn't see an entrance to even go in old school."

"Smith is right, the building is covered. There should be an exit from the cellar as this island is in a hurricane area, but I couldn't see anything in the photos we have. I hate to say it, but we need the Water Tigers' help to get in. Either he has to get us the info or help us get in," Colonel Briggs said.

"Tyson, can you hack their feeds?" Mike asked.

"Yes, but not without them knowing. Colonel Briggs is right; we would need Water Tigers' help."

"Then we wait; the phone link to him must be monitored 24/7." Art said.

CHAPTER 17

"DEAD IN 3 MINUTES"

The smell of sweat, disinfectant, and some other odour Damien couldn't put his finger on, lingered in the air of the Whitehouse gym. Damien Spelling, head of the CIA, had studied the work and personal file from a private investigator he hired to track his target. This was the only time apart from breaking into his house at night that he could get to say something to him. Damien looked in the mirror at the gym and saw what he had become ...physically. He looked gaunt, pale, and oh my god, I have an old man's baggy arms. He wanted to blend in, look natural, so he started working on an arm-exercise machine to work on those baggy arms, then his target walked in. Chad Langdon, Head of the Secret Service and the President's personal bodyguard.

Chad walked in and looked at everyone who was in the room. Interesting, a lady from the press group and ... Spelling, director of the CIA.

To Damien's surprise, Chad came and set up on the machine beside him, putting his water bottle in the holder and putting his towel over the seat. "Good morning, Director, new to the gym?" Chad greeted him.

"Yes, Langdon. My wife finally saw me naked and said she refused to retire with a man that looks that old." Damien let out a little chuckle, which Chad didn't respond to.

"This is my quiet time; I sweat, process, and work out the kinks in my body and mind. So, when and where?" Chad asked him.

"Sorry, what?" Damien tried to fain that he didn't know what he meant.

"When and where did you want to meet? I'll be there. And stop exercising before you kill yourself. Just an FYI, choose lighter weights and do more repetitions.

Damien sat up soaked in sweat and heart racing from 5 minutes on the machine. "You're not surprised that I want to speak with you?" Damien sounded confused.

"You're the director of the CIA; I assume you wouldn't want to talk unless it was imperative."

Damien passed on the time and place of the meeting. The same place he met Art Damani; it is secure.

Damien picked up his towel and drank most of his water bottle in one go. "Thanks for catching on so quick; I think I would have been dead in 10 more minutes," Damien joked.

"I'd say more like 3," Chad said with a straight face.

"Smart arse," Damien said, then walked off.

Chad smirked and started on his routine.

Two days later, Chad followed the instructions and was driving up to a diner in the middle of nowhere. 'Who would eat here? There's nothing around for 50 miles. Maybe it's a CIA safe house'. As he pulled into the driveway, three cars were in the parking lot. Deciding to stay armed, he walked into the café. Inside three people were sitting in a far booth and a woman was behind the counter. The lady greeted him with a "Good morning," and Chad wished her the same. Director Spelling got out of his seat to greet him, then so did the other two gentlemen who had their backs to him. To his surprise, it was Art Damani and Mike Madden.

"I see you brought, The Cheat. This can't be good then; trouble follows him," Chad and Mike stared off at each other, leaving an awkward silence, then smiled and greeted each other warmly.

"I meant it; if you two are here, it can't be good," Chad said.

"Where's the President? Is he locked in your trunk? You don't normally leave home without him?" Mike jibbed.

"I got a hall pass."

"When you two have finished joking, we have some serious issues to address," Spelling said, frustrated.

"With what you're about to drag him into, this might be the last joke he hears for a while," Mike said.

Chad turns and gives Spelling a serious look. "Drag me into what?"

"It's best if Mr. Damani tells you what he has found before I tell you what I need." Spelling said.

"Do you remember your time at the Ark last year?" Art asked.

"Oh, you mean dragging the American President around a jungle, while being chased by a horde of terrorists hell-bent on killing us all, before being saved at the last minute by a man I couldn't stand to be in the same room with two hours earlier? Yes,

Mr. Damani, I don't think I will forget that... ever!" Chad said cynically.

"Well, when you put it like that. But what I meant is that those events, the assassination attempt on the President and myself, were part of a bigger plot". Art continued and pieced it all together, working with the Water Tiger, the mission at Altaskivi castle, everything. Chad sat there stunned and let it soak in; these were not the men to make up stories. "So, where do I fit in?"

"We need you to spy on the President, and whoever speaks to him, anything related to China and Russia," Spelling said.

"So, you want me to commit treason!" Chad puts to them.

"You're treading a fine line there, but yes," Art injected.

"Well, as I see it, I have three options. One, you let me go and hope that I don't say anything to anyone. Two, you kill me and dispose of the body. Three, I join you in this mad quest, save the world and probably end up in jail and losing my career. I should have let you keep working in the gym and killed you off then; I'm in."

"Fantastic," Spelling said.

Art gave them details of how they all can communicate.

After Director Spelling and Chad Langdon left, Art turned to Mike. "Do you think he will pass on any information?"

"Yes, he's a straight shooter, plus I think he was more in because he will want to protect the President," Mike answered.

"You don't think the President's involved, Mike?"

"No way. You saw how much they wanted him dead, but it's someone close to him, and Chad will find out who. He has too, because we have nothing at the moment till Water Tiger rings back." Mike said.

The trip back to the Ark in a luxury private jet made Mike uncomfortable because it was too comfortable. To pass the time, he went over all their plans for Navassa. Have they done all they could? Will it be enough? One thing still stuck in his mind: Sam and the boys. Does he send them home? Can they stay? Would they want to stay? That's the first conversation for when he gets back.

CHAPTER 18

"MYYY BOOBIES"

"I feel bad doing this; we should be back at the Ark helping," Katelyn protested.

"Nonsense. We have a life even when we're saving the world," Lexi said.

"Anyway, if girls don't shop, the economy would crash," Sam added. All three started laughing.

Travelling through Mogadishu in Art's BMW iX Xdrive with bulletproof windows. The day was muggy, with light showers blowing through all day, but that didn't dampen the spirits of this wedding shop day. Lexi had it all planned: shop, stop for drinks, shop, stop for drinks, drinks, and stop for more drinks.

The trip nearly didn't happen. There was a standoff between Katelyn and Art, both as hard-headed as the other. Art wanted to send a troop carrier with 20 Ark soldiers with them as an escort. Katelyn said, "no way." The battle raged on for hours, neither wanting to give up ground. Finally, cooperative negotiating started. Katelyn wants one guard, Art 18. After another hour, they got down to an amicable solution. 4 guards and Katelyn must go packed. Katelyn thought it was a good deal because she always went packed anyway, and this time, Sam and Lexi were too.

"So, where to first?" asked Katelyn.

"Cake! I'm hungry; I could go with some samples before 1st drinks," Lexi says cheekily.

"What do you mean first drinks? How many are we having?"

"I lost count... I was drinking at the time," The girls burst into a fit of laughter. After spending so many years being one of 'the boys,' Katelyn enjoyed having girlfriends.

As their car pulled into the curb, the escort car swung in behind, and four of the Majors' top men jumped out and formed a guard on either side of the lady's door. Katelyn looked at them and walked off to one side,

"Team huddle." Katelyn bent over, as did the guards, thinking they were getting their instructions for the day. "Now, I don't care what Art told you to do today, but you are not following us around." Katelyn swiftly pulled out one of her knives in the middle of the huddle, "Bertha here doesn't like to be shadowed; it makes her crotchety." Katelyn hands one guard a credit card, "Book your drinks and food on this today. It's on me, no alcohol! Stay around close but not in the same store, OK?" the men nodded. "As well. If you behave yourself, I will give the Major raving reviews for you... If you don't, I will tell him you followed us into the ladies' toilets... are we clear?" the men nodded nervously and went on their way.

"What did you say to them? They look ill?" Sam asked.

"I just reminded them of a legend."

"Did you just give them your credit card?" Lexi asked, confused.

"No, that was Art's. He won't be needing it today," Katelyn says with a wry smile. "Let's go eat cake; I'm starving now."

Five shops and seven bars later, the guards herded the women back into the car. Sam was a little 'Merry,' she asked the driver to open the sunroof in the BMW and climbed up and start waving to all the traffic and pedestrians. Everything was fine till a busload of young police cadets started whistling at her and asking her to take off her top... which she began to do before Lexi and Katelyn pulled her back in the car.

"Woo, what a great day. We should do this again for my birthday," Sam said, a little slurred.

"When's your birthday, Sam?" Lexi asked.

"3 days,"

"Party Time," Lexi and Katelyn said in unison.

As Lexi and Katelyn chaperoned Sam back to her unit, they found Mike inside having a coffee. Aidan and Oliver were on their iPads with headphones on slouched in unique positions over the lounge chairs.

"So, what do we have here?" Mike asked suspiciously.

"Sam's not feeling well; I think it was something she ate?" Lexi said.

"Something she ate, you say, hmm," Mike tried to keep from laughing.

"Should I call the doctor, Katelyn? It could be serious, maybe even food poisoning?"

"Oh, ha ha ha, yes, she's a little tipsy," Katelyn blurted out.

"Who's tipsy? I'm fine. We have just been out drinking for wedding cakes and dresses. But, Sherlock, did you know Art's got a giant pussy that disappears? See, Katelyn, I didn't even mention the busload of coppers." Sam said, while swaying around. Katelyn and Lexi dropped their heads.

"Bus load of police?" Mike looked at Lexi.

"They wanted to see my boobies," Sam blurted. "Myyy boobies," she added.

"It's alright, Mike, we stopped her in time from humiliating herself," Katelyn said.

"It's fine, ladies; she's going to have a grand hangover in the morning. Did you get what you wanted, Katelyn?"

"Yes, I did. The shopping isn't too bad here. I had to get the dress altered. Just have to set a date... before the world ends."

"Ok, I'll get this one to bed before she pukes everywhere," Mike said.

"Ok, see you later, Mike," Katelyn says.

"Oh Mike, we are throwing Sam a party on her birthday. So, we will need some input from you for that."

"No worries, Lexi. She should be sober by then," Mike joked.

"Party Time!" Sam yelled as she tried to dance and nearly fell on her arse.

"Ok, shower time for you, young lady," Mike said.

"Ooow, are you going to take me to bed? You big stud," Sam slurred while giggling.

"She's all yours," Lexi said as she turned for the door.

"Bye Mike, you big stud," Katelyn threw in, laughing, as she went out the door.

Mike decided just to take Sam's shoes and dress off and lay her on the bed to sleep. "Sweet dreams... rest those boobies" Mike kissed her head and smiled. He thought, 'I can't wait to tease her in the morning with that.' As Mike walked out the door, he turned off the light and looked back at her. "Finally, something normal going on," he said to himself; he sighed and walked out to spend time with the boys.

CHAPTER 19

"IN HONOUR OF SERVICE ABOVE AND BEYOND"

Finally, the weather had cleared, and it gave a shiny, clean appearance to the Ark's grounds. The pungent smell of flowers and vegetation gave everything a new feeling, to the start of another day at the Ark. There was a roar of hungry animals from the pens from the veterinary hospital.

There was a sense of electricity in the air as the boys were trying to shovel their breakfast in their mouths as quickly as possible. Today was a workday. Their mum wasn't sharing breakfast with them as their dad told them she wasn't well. "Something she ate," he said. They had dressed in their AZTECK uniforms, including their new boots and safety jackets. They had been on morning patrol before with the Major, but they were actually working today. Art and Tyson had agreed to put Aidan and Ollie in charge of the robot raptors on patrol, under the supervision of the Major.

The boys had made their way to the loading docks for the Major to pick them up. They had said their goodbyes to their father as the Major waved and called out "good morning" from the jeep. Then off they went on another day of Christmas in Santa land. Mike thought, 'I can't see them wanting to go home, and it's not as if I can talk to Sam this morning or maybe even tomorrow,' he had a laugh and turned and headed back to the unit to check on Sam.

Mike made his way through the food mall, grabbing a coffee and heading to his unit. He grabbed his keys and gently turned them slowly, hoping to sneak in and not wake Sam. As Mike slowly opened the door. Like some SAS ninja, not being heard, not being seen, he enters the unit... and Sam is sitting at the dining table drinking a coffee. "What are you doing?" she asked, confused.

"Trying not to wake you up," Mike answered.

"Ah, I'm awake,"

"I can see that; how do you feel?" Mike asked.

"I'm fine; why?" Sam said, still confused.

"You came home a little unwell; I thought you might be... not feeling your best this morning," Mike said, feeling confused himself.

"No, I'm fine; I woke up, had a shower, and made a coffee," she insisted.

"What do you remember about yesterday?" Mike persisted.

"We went shopping, had a few drinks, and came home. So, what's with the Spanish Inquisition?" Sam said, concerned.

"Oh nothing, so you're fine?",

"Yes!",

"And your boobies?" Mike asked.

"My boobies, what has that got to do with anything?" she said, concerned.

"Oh, no reason, and do you still think I'm a stud?"

"What are you talking about?".

"Oh, nothing."

"Where are the boys?" Sam asked, getting off the confusing conversation.

"They're on patrol with the Major this morning."

"I would have liked to have seen them off."

"You seemed... exhausted after your day out," Mike smirked. "We have things to talk about though,"

"Such as,"

"You, the boys, here, now. I want to know your thoughts on our immediate future," Mike asked.

"Gee, so serious this hour of the morning. Well, we stay here, find the boy's tutors. Mum and Dad might like to move into the house for a while!"

"NO! Nobody at the house. I'll have it locked up." Mike said firmly.

"You don't think someone will come to the house again? I thought Jin was on our side now?" Sam said, worried.

"He is... sort of, but we can't say the same for the people he works for. There are trillions of dollars at stake here; they will not take it kindly to us trying to stop them."

"Then here is the safest place for them at the moment till they sort this out," Sam said with conviction.

"And if it's not?"

"We'll worry about that then. We are safe. You concentrate on what you do best, Sherlock!" Mike smiled with an immense weight lifted off his shoulders. Then, suddenly, his phone started buzzing, a message.

"Sweety, we have to go; Colonel Briggs wants us at the Hub asap."

"Both of us?"

"Both of us!" Mike reaffirmed.

In the Hub, all of Mike's team were called to attend, including Sam, Art, Lexi, Ab, Doby, Tyson, and Rosi, the entire gang. As the Colonel stood on the other side of the conference table, he waited till all were in attendance. "Sergeant, call your team to attention."

"Team, form up, attention!" 2 Planks command was law as if he was a General, and the team responded thus.

"In response to hostilities at the moment and the team being on permanent watch away from the base. I am awarding these medals as a field command. Captain Michael Madden, step forward." Mike steps forward like he is on dress parade.

"For years of service and duties above and beyond, I now promote you to the rank of Major. Congratulations," the Colonel saluted Mike.

Mike returned the salute. "Thank you, sir." Sam put her hand over her mouth in surprise while Lexi gave her a big hug.

"Sergeant Sebastian Morrison, step forward. In the line of years served and duties above and beyond, I now promote you to Warrant Office Class One. Congratulations." "Thank you, Sir," Seb replied as he saluted.

"Corporal Katelyn Gouw, step forward. In line with years served and service above and beyond, I now promote you to the rank of Sergeant. Congratulations,"

"Thank you, sir." Art was trying to act mature and not to bounce around like an excited school kid.

"Corporal Zikmund Chvalat, step forward. In line with years served and duties above and beyond, I now promote you to the rank of Sergeant. Congratulations.",

"Thank you, sir."

"Corporal Thomas Ash, step forward. In line with years served and duties above and beyond, I now promote you to the rank of Sergeant. Congratulations,"

"Thank you, Sir," Thomas saluted and moved back into line, while Rosi jumped up and down like a schoolgirl.

"In a soldier's career," the Colonel continued, "whether it be commissioned or non-Commissioned, it is a great privilege to be there for the awarding of special medals. I have only attended one, and it wasn't a soldier in my command. Now, I have the absolute pleasure of awarding two special medals to soldiers under my command. Sergeant Zikmund Chvalat Sergeant Thomas Ash, step forward. In duties performed in saving the President of the United States and sacrificing yourself to save the lives of your team and other allied forces. I now award you both with the Victoria Cross medal for bravery."

The room lost all military decorum at that moment. With a round of applause and cheering from the supports, even Thor and Loki sensed the importance of the moment and let out a roar.

"Thank you, Sir," Zikmund and Thomas said together.

"Warrant officer Morrison, dismiss your team."

"Team attention! Dismiss!" Immediately, everyone flocked on to Zik and Thomas to congratulate them on their awards. Sam then went to Mike, giving him a big kiss on his promotion. Next, she approached Seb and gave him a big hug and kiss. "You're forgiven now for getting my husband into two bar fights," she said with a smile.

"Thank God, I didn't know how much longer I could go on being reminded every second day about it," he joked.

"Just don't do it again, Warrant Officer, or no more kisses,"

"Well, we can't have that, can we?" Seb laughed.

Ab had to step in and pull Rosi off Thomas, as she wouldn't stop kissing him. But, he thought, 'that's all I do these days is stop everyone from bonking on the furniture. He still dreams of Lexi naked on the conference table, pleasant dreams, but still dreams that won't disappear.'

They all had a celebration dinner arranged by Art in the food mall that evening. Low key, just 20 staff waiting on them. The boys were entertaining every one of their exploits of using the raptors to herd Buttercup, the female rhino, away from a damaged fence for repairs.

"I still have a huge scar from that cow; Art, did you ever get anger management for your animals?"

"No, I couldn't afford it after replacing 20 baboons you killed," he joked back.

A shiver went up Katelyn's spine. She hadn't told anyone, but she was having night terrors from her run-in with the baboons.

CHAPTER 20

BIRTHDAY BASH

The music blazed and echoed through the food hall, mixed with the sound of laughter and people enjoying life at the moment. Sam's birthday was a tremendous hit and just the distraction they all needed. 170 workers 43 soldiers were protecting the Ark inside and out. And only a handful of them knew of the threat that lingers over the world at the moment. For now, there's music, and not just any music, Tyson, as his effort towards a splendid party, hooked The Wolfman robot to a jukebox and had Wolfy lip-syncing to everyone's favourite hits.

Everyone was up dancing, and Art showed he was more than just money by 'cutting a fine rug' while dancing with Katelyn. The boys had crashed early and went back to their unit to sleep. Doby elected to phone sit during the party, waiting on that elusive call from the Water Tiger to go to the next stage of their plan. But, for now, all that was forgotten. Music, fine food, good friends were all that was needed.

Sam was sitting chatting with Mike, Seb, Katelyn, and Lexi. "Lexi, I have to ask you something?" Sam said coyly.

"Anything, birthday girl," Lexi replied.

"On our shopping trip the other day, did something happen involving me?" Sam said while staring at her.

"You, gee no… umm not that I, hang on I just remember there's something I forgot to tell Art, I'll be right back." Katelyn tried to slither away from the table as well.

"Both you girls, SIT!" Katelyn and Lexi sat down.

"Spill it," Sam said firmly. If the boys were here, they would quote that mum was using 'Face 12, last chance before imminent reprisal.' But both girls sat there umming and ahhing and twiddling their thumbs when Mike spoke up.

"Well, so the story goes, you needed fresh air because you were feeling unwell. So, you asked the driver to open the sunroof; you then climbed up and started waving to the cars passing by, most likely to tell them you were ok. Then, a busload of cadet police officers came past and requested something from you,"

Sam butted in, "requested what?"

"To see your boobies," Mike said with a sheepish grin.

"Oh My God! I didn't?" Sam said, horrified.

Mike hadn't finished with her yet. "Don't worry, you were an enormous hit, to the point where they were throwing pieces of paper out the window with their phone numbers on."

"Nooo," Sam said in a small voice, folding her arms over her breasts.

"Don't worry, Sam. We pulled you back in before you got your bra unclipped. Thank God you struggled with that," Lexi said, reassuring her.

"Why didn't you pull me in earlier?"

"You seemed like you were having a great time, and we didn't want to spoil it for you," Katelyn said

"And the fact, Katelyn was pouring another glass of champagne, and we didn't want to spill any," Lexi added.

Sam sat there, stunned, with her mouth open.

"Don't worry, if you had, big deal, it would have made their day. How many strawberry blondes with perky boobies are they ever going to see in their lifetime?" The comment didn't reassure Sam.

"Mmmm boobies," Seb added with bad timing as Sam threw him a 'face #4, death by staring', just as she was about to tell Seb 'Not to give her breasts a second thought,' a phone rang, no, THE phone rang. Doby jumped on the phone so fast he forgot everything he was supposed to say.

"Ark," he got out.

"I have information for you," the Water Tiger says.

Doby trying to remember everything started rambling, saying, "we need your help."

"Is the captain there?"

"Ah, yes, he is. Oh, he's a Major now," Doby informs him.

"A Major, isn't he a lucky man?"

"Here he is" Doby hands Mike the phone.

"Madden here,"

"I hear congratulations are in order, Major," Water Tiger says in a dull tone.

"You don't give a shit about my rank any more than I do; what have you got?"

"I will be at the Island tomorrow. Are you ready?"

"Yes and no, security was up before we could set up inside. We will need your help to find out what's going on inside."

"What do you need?" Water Tiger asked.

Mike explained the options available to get the information out uncompromised. The conversation was short, tactical. Neither side giving too much away because of the lack of trust of each other.

Everyone gathered around to hear what was said. Mike outlaid what Water Tiger said, what he said they needed, and his reply.

"Then it's done; I suggest we all get some sleep tonight. Tomorrow, we plan our next operation," Colonel Briggs stated. On that, everyone grabbed their things and headed off to their rooms. Tomorrow was coming fast.

CHAPTER 21

THE TEA-LADY JOINS THE TEAM

The HUBS energy was like that of the allied base before any SAS teams went on a mission. Everyone was mobile; everyone knew their roles and went around with gusto to get it done.

They set the meeting for 8am, but it was 7am, and everyone was already here, and the ambience was charged. Everyone had prepared and had brought every bit of information they had that might help. Tyson and Rosi bought the schematics for their underwater tracker and some sample robotic birds. Doby and the 'new soccer mum look' Lexi were busy linking up all the latest satellite and spy cam footage they had to a laptop. Mike and the team were there looking fresh, showering after an early morning drill session, and were talking about gear changes depending on how Colonel Briggs thinks we should play it out. Art and Ab were discussing something in the corner that looked a little heated, and Sam brought a trolley of coffees, cold drinks, and cakes. She had never been to an operation meeting before and wondered all night what her purpose would be. She felt like an unskilled labourer standing in the corner awaiting instructions. Now, walking into Hub and seeing everyone working setting up folders, photos, and charts, she felt like a right twit, the old tea lady, like in the movies.

As Sam dropped her head and was just about to turn around before someone saw her, a gentle voice spoke up beside her.

"You're a lifesaver; no one's had time to grab anything this morning... What, no croissants? Pick up your act, lady, or you'll be dropped from the team." Sam giggled, and Lexi gave her a kiss on the cheek. As Lexi was walking back to her console, she caught the eye of Mike, and she nodded her head towards Sam in the doorway. He had seen that 'deer in the headlights look before,' Sam was feeling out of place.

"Coffee, thank god someone's switched on this morning!" Mike races over to the trolley to grab a coffee and cake. Then, taking Mike's cue, the team came over and started helping themselves and thanking Sam for bringing some food. Sam felt relieved at the response, even though she knew Mike had instigated it.

Seb was there, leaning over the trolley, looking for something but not seeing what he was looking for. "Have I forgotten something, Seb?" Sam asked.

"Yeah, I can't see any booobies" He started laughing, and Sam pushed the tea trolley into his leg. "Oow, geez, you're a cranky tea lady,"

"Serve yourself right, cheeky shit," Sam joked.

"Let's get started," Colonel Briggs said.

"Now, the plan will be a 3 phase move operation. First, Sherlock, Smith, and Jedi will infiltrate the island at night by the sea."

"Second, they will hand off a miniature video cam and unique sleep canister to the Water tiger. He has informed us we cannot get inside, as it is a biohazard sealed room. The best we can do is to film the surveillance monitors. He will knock out the guard on monitors with Jedi's new canister and set up the video recorder."

"Since they detected the surveillance eagle on the last mission, we can't afford a Wi-Fi signal, so the device will just record. Water Tiger will wake up the guard 10 minutes before the next guard comes on duty, chastise him for sleeping on the job, and retrieve the recorder. He will then make a handoff to Sherlock, and they will all extract to the pickup LZ by sea."

"Third, the second team of 2 Planks, Steel, and Miss Lexi will be aboard a boat, obtained by Mr. Damani for the mission. They will fain motor trouble and request permission to tie up to the doc to make repairs. If allowed, they will stay tied to the doc a few hours while Tyson and Rosie's birds wander the grounds being monitored by Lexi aboard the boat. They then will retrieve the birds, then extract to the pickup LZ."

"All the intel we have is in the folders in front of you; you have today to review it all and make suggestions. The teams leave tomorrow. Are there questions?" Colonel Briggs asks.

Sam put up her hand. "I have a request, Colonel."

"And what is that, Samantha?"

"I wish to go on the boat also," Sam said.

"NO way!" Mike said emphatically.

"Samantha, what tactical purpose would there be by having you on board?"

"None," Mike said again.

"Quite a few. I also have medical training, so having 2 medics on board is a bonus. Two, I believe that Lexi and Katelyn will be in bikinis to attract attention away from the surveillance birds, so six boobs are better than 4."

Seb butted in with "Mmmm booobies," Mike, Colonel Briggs, and Sam gave him an angry look.

Sam continued, "Three, I have weapons training, thanks to my husband."

"Yeah, but not combat training," Mike protested.

"Who saved your life from the Water Tiger, who here has shot the Water Tiger... hmmm, anyone, no, I rest my case."

Mike sighed and put his head in his hands.

"I know you're concerned for me, but if I'm reading this right, the boat won't even go to the dock if it's fired at or not given permission. I also am a great scuba diver for any other emergencies, like saving yours and Zikmund's ass."

"Mike, she has a lot of excellent points," the Colonel said.

"Fine, but if you get killed, don't come crying to me," Mike said, finally giving in to the onslaught.

"Ok, that's settled; 2 Planks, you have another team member, work it out how best to use her."

"Ok, anyone else, no one. We will reconvene tonight at 1800 hours to finalise."

Ab walks over to Mike and Sam before the in-depth husband and wife conversation starts. "Excuse me, Mike, Sam. I believe you will have concerns for the boys while you're on this mission. The boys are becoming a big part of the security team. I am sure the Major will gladly have them on patrol with him during the day, and it would honour me to stay with them at night." Tyson leans over and joins the conversation, "the boys will be busy the next few days, anyway. We are field-testing two new raptors, and I would like them to train the new operatives if that's ok with you both. They will spend a couple of days with Rosi and the new raptor operatives."

"Wow, they will love that," Sam says.

"Ab, Tyson, that is very nice of you both. Thank you for that," Mike says kindly.

"Great, all settled, and Mike, Sam will be fine; she is a competent lady," Ab pats Mike on the shoulder and walks off.

"Seems you have everyone convinced," Mike says, still not happy with the situation.

"What can I say? I have friends in high places; my husband is a Major; did you know that? Come on, let's go back to the room and have mission sex!"

"You've been hanging around Lexi too much!"

"I didn't hear a no!" Sam said as she walked off with a wiggle on her hips.

That night after the final Op meeting, they all had their choirs. Sam, who didn't have much to pack, went and helped Katelyn stock a Medi bag, or bags, so it seemed. The boat is stocked for all medical emergencies and hopefully wouldn't be needed.

"Nervous?" Katelyn asked Sam.

"No, is that normal?"

"No, it's not; I was terrified before my first Op. I remember it was in Kenya, a peacekeeping force, and we got ambushed."

"Oh my god, hopefully, that will not happen to us," Sam said, now worried.

"Just remember your surroundings, study where your weapons caches are, check them when you go on the boat, and follow instructions immediately from either 2 Planks or I, and you'll be fine."

A few hours later, Mike came home and found Sam studying photos of the boat and the island.

"You're coming in here, right?" Sam pointed to a spot on the map.

"Correct,"

"Won't they see your underwater scooter thingy, sitting on the water's edge?"

"No, my scooter thingy will be 50 meters out, underwater, tied to an underwater weighted thingy."

"Oh, clever boy," Sam praised.

"That's why I'm a Major, because I'm good with my thingy's," Mike joked.

"Oh, are you just?" Sam flirted.

"Time for bed team member, early start. The boys know what's going on?" Mike asked.

"Yes, I explained what was happening, that I was going on a secret mission with dad; they seemed worried at first. Then I told them they're training other security personnel on the new raptors. After that, they forgot I even mentioned a mission."

"That's our boys," Mike said, laughing.

CHAPTER 22

ALTERED VIRUS. W.H.O CAN WE TRUST?

'The drone,' that's what Chad Langdon calls it, to stay invisible in a room when people are asking the leader of the free world about whether we should rename male and female toilets and just call them toilets. Just once, maybe on my birthday, just let me pistol-whip one person who comes in with dribble like that, just one.

The Oval office is an exquisitely decorated room; the President is always courteous, especially after our near-death experience at the ARK last year. 'Most people think the hardest part of being the President's shadow is taking a bullet for him. No, it's the standing in the corner of the room and listening to 'the drone' for hour after hour. But then, sometimes, you get to hear the juicy bits of what's happening around the world. Then at the end of my shift, I can race home and tell my wife, "Hey honey, guess what I heard today?". Well, I could say that if I was still married. Secret Service life is hard on families and partners, especially when you can't share the 'Juicy bits' you hear.'

'Now, I'm asked to spy on the best President that the United States has had in decades. Possibly lose my career and end up in Guantanamo Bay prison for treason.' Chad sighs.

"Are you right their champ? I thought I heard you sigh?" the President asked Chad.

"Sorry, thinking about last night's game," Chad replied.

"Yeah, Oh My God, they were horrible; it was like the opposition had covid, and no one wanted to block them."

"Accurate analogy, sir," Chad said, agreeing.

"I know what will cheer you up?"

"Sir?"

"Your favourite person is coming in later," the President said cheerily.

"Good god no, not Director Spelling," Chad said, exasperated.

"Yep, old blood and guts Spelling, probably wants me to bomb a day-care centre somewhere," Chad, and the President laughed.

"I suppose I shouldn't laugh; he would go to any lengths to protect this country. Well, back to work, more papers to rubber stamp."

'Any lengths,' Chad said under his voice.

There was a knock on the side door. "Come in," the President greeted.

"Excuse me, Sir, do you have a moment?" Secretary of State Linwood Cashdon sticks his head through the door.

"Certainly, Linwood, come in, have a seat."

Linwood seemed concerned about what he was about to tell the President as they both sat. "Mr. President, I have received the initial reports from the village in Southern Africa with the fresh outbreak of covid. WHO's report says they are trying to keep it contained, but it is an impoverished region, and people need to travel to find food for their families."

"Send relief, Linwood; we must support WHO to contain this outbreak."

"Good move, Mr. President. They have confirmed that it is a new strain. It hasn't been named as yet. However, the initial report says it has a lot of the same factors as the first COVID-19 outbreak." Linwood was reading from a folder.

"Well, that's good, isn't it? So, a lot of the world has been vaccinated against that strain?"

"Normally, I would say yes, but this one has been altered," Linwood said.

"Altered, you mean it's mutated, mutated again?" the President said, astonished.

"No, Sir, not mutated but altered... by someone,"

The President sat there stunned, "Oh My God, do you have proof of this? Who on God's earth would do such a thing? This has ravaged every country around the world."

"It's only a theory at the moment. WHO are redoing all their tests and breaking down the virus, cell by cell, to confirm? Sir, I suggest once they finish their tests, we should test it as well." Linwood advised.

"Don't we trust WHO?" the President asked.

"Well, there have been issues before, but I believe we need to see the results ourselves. Can you imagine if their theory is right? The ramifications of such a threat are catastrophic? We would need to find out who it is."

"Your right, God Linwood. I hope you're wrong, for the world's sake." A knot the size of a basketball set in the President's stomach with concern chiselled all over his face.

The hairs stood up on the back of Chad's neck. 'Well, there it is,' he thought. 'The virus has been let out of the bag. Now to let Spelling know.'

Hours later, the thunderous arrival of CIA Director Spelling as he crashes past the Secret Service officer on the door, "Don't worry, son, he always wants to hear what I have to say."

"Good afternoon, Damien. Are you working on your stealth techniques?" the President asks.

The question threw the director. "Sir?"

"Oh, I didn't hear the screams and yelling in the hallway like your usual entrances," the President joked.

"Humour, ah-ha, I'm glad someone is having a good day. I'm not!"

Director Spelling informed the President, though it sounded more like ranting. He went on about the bloody Chinese spying, the blasted Russians near a border, and the usual whine about the FBI not sharing information. After the President listened intently to Spellings' report, he offered advice on some issues and said he would look into others.

"Thank you, Damien. Keep me up to date."

"My pleasure, Mr. President. That's what they pay me for."

Director Spelling looked over at Chad, "Langdon,"

"Director," Chad replied. Spelling made no reaction to the code that Chad had just passed on. 'Director Spelling' when he had no new info, or 'Director' if he had further information. Damien knew he had to make a pickup at a drop-off site tonight.

Later that night, in his private office at his house. The room that is tamper-proof and spy-proof, Damien Spelling opens the communique from Chad Langdon. Deciphering the message, a name jumps out at him, Linwood Cashdon. He holds all judgment until he has deciphered the full note. Luckily for him, Langdon has an eye for detail and issues notes with every turn of phrase and mannerism. Years of training, years and years of listening to tapes of people doing the wrong thing. Spelling closed his eyes and replayed the conversation in his mind as Langdon described it, right down to the voices. At the end of the conversation, he opened his eyes. "You prick! You were selling it to him," he gets up and calmly walks over to a whiteboard, takes a deep breath, then begins.

2 hours later, there's a knock on the door, and it breaks his concentration. He opens the door to find his lovely wife Kylie with a pot of coffee and two choc chip cookies. "Thought this might help," as she walks in and places the tray on the side table. He doesn't bother to try to cover the board up; they both knew many years ago that they could kill her for the things her husband knows, or they think he knows. Yet she stayed. 'Write that up in your romance novels,' he thought. "Thank you, dearest. As usual, you're a lifesaver,"

"And you're a country savour, don't stay up too late, remember you're older now and can't keep it up that long anymore."

"Oh, but there are pills for that these days," Damien joked.

"Good lord Damien, wash your mouth out; you're not at the barracks anymore." The director gives his wife a hug and a kiss on the cheek.

"I won't be long; the next phase is going to take a bit of planning. Best left to daytime planning,"

"So, you don't want the cookies?"

Damien turned on a serious face, "touch those cookies, and I'll have you assassinated,"

"Ha! You know you can't operate in this country, so bring it on," at that, Kylie turned and walked off, laughing.

Damien looks at his whiteboard; he knows the chain of command and who can do what. If Cashdon is in on this, he can't do it alone; he needs... more mouths crying wolf, 'more mouths' he thinks to himself. Spelling walks over to the board in a trance-like state, lets his mind control his hand, places three circles on his three most likely scenarios, and then steps back to look at what has been circled. He put the circle around the same group on each plan, military command, without realising it! Well, I finally have a starting point. Now, cookies and bed, I have gym in the morning.

CHAPTER 23

THE BELLS OF WAR RING

The room was a monument of 'the glory days' with medals, models, and photos lining the walls. 4 star General and head of the armed forces, General Roger Hagart, has had a colourful career. Tank commander, then shooting up through the ranks during Desert Storm and Afghanistan and now hundreds of drone strikes, Hagart is not afraid of recommending action. Now he's looking forward to his biggest battle yet, CHINA. Possibly even a World War. Most of these things would horrify an ordinary person, even an average military person, but General Hagart saw the end game. Even with the millions of lives lost, the world will be a better place with a cowed Chinese government. It sends the power back to Russia and the United States and would stop countries like North Korea from flexing any muscle. 'The world would be safer and more manageable,' he thought.

There was a knock on his door. "Come in, Linwood." As Linwood Cashdon entered, the General stood and offered his hand.

"Good morning, Roger, a lovely morning for freedom," Linwood said cheerily.

"Morning Linwood, yes, a beautiful sunny day, but don't get ahead of yourself. There's a lot to happen before we can achieve peace."

"Yes, so very true, but we have finally struck an agreement with Russia over the spoils of China."

"Excellent, and their military?"

"Scrapped down to a defensive stand-point, but left under communism. We will offer China a position in the free trade agreement worldwide. That way, we can keep them on the market for manufacturing and appoint a friendly administration."

"Sounds impressive, so long as they no longer will be a Super Power. There is a lot to be done before they fold; I have my Generals working on scenarios of battle plans to encompass any response from China, including nuclear."

"Nuclear! You don't think China would launch nukes?"

"I know they will; once they're backed into a corner, they will not care who gets hurt. It is definitely possible that the United States will get hit by 2 nukes before bringing China to its knees. You have nothing to worry about, Linwood; you will be locked up in NORAD with the President and I."

"I have family and friends also?"

"Tell them to stay out of the big cities and military areas. Linwood, we discussed this at the start with the Russians; you were there. You heard about the estimations of people dead and collateral damage. It's too late now to put your tail between your legs and run!"

"Yes, yes, I know. Sometimes it's a lot to take in, the military side, that is."

"What about Nessler?"

"All is well; he says everything is on schedule, with no interruptions that couldn't be dealt with."

"And the terrorist?"

"Doing his part, having him there and being recorded on surveillance, adds all the credentials we will need when it becomes time to push the two Presidents."

"Remember, he is a liability; make sure Nessler has it covered when the time comes to eliminate him." General Hagart stated emphatically.

"I will, General. I have informed the President of a human intervention with the virus. The Russians also, and they have passed it up the chain as well. Once the WHO rechecks its findings, we will do our checks, and so the Russians and the results will be legit. We will then be ready for the final phase, and the world will see China as the aggressor. What if the President refuses to move on them?"

"Don't worry, China will provoke them into it. Ok, we are set then. I will ready the troops and have training drills set in the right areas."

"I will make sure everything stays on target and keep the President hyped on the issue," Cashdon assured him.

"Excellent, excellent."

CHAPTER 24

"MAN DOWN, MAN DOWN!"

'A perfect day, warm sunshine, crystal clear waters, barely a cloud in the sky, and the people on the docs are exceedingly polite and helpful. So, what's wrong with this picture? We are heading off to save the world from itself and possibly get shot,' Sam was thinking as she was loading equipment onto the boat. 'Do your job, listen and trust the others, was what Mike said. Sorry, it's Sherlock. We're on assignment now, and we must use our code names. What was mine ah... Redster and Lexi's was Humpster. Got it?'

As the boat pulled out of the docks, 2 Planks was at the helm, and Steel was in the co-captain seat. Sam was helping Lexi set up the reconnaissance birds on the deck to do a test fly. It would be two hours before they released the birds onto the Island and headed for the dock on Navassa Island. Navassa Island was a little pimple of dirt between Haiti and the Bahamas. On this pimple was a lighthouse being refurbished by the United States government as a gift to the Haitian people. Unbeknown to everyone, they had constructed a portable medical laboratory in the basement to develop and produce an antidote for the new virus. That's sure to be a tourist attraction. "Come see where the antidote for the Xvirus that killed millions of people was made. Don't touch anything, or you will be left on the Island".

'Keep busy,' that's another thing Sherlock said. Sam was going through all the advice given to her by the team. 'Stay busy, be relaxed, double-check the equipment, familiarise yourself with the position of the firearms, and Smith's advice: just rock that bikini. Trust Smith to keep it real,' Sam smiled to herself. 2 Planks pulled up fifty meters offshore, and Lexi released the birds. She programmed them to go to predetermined GPS coordinates, and then Lexi would fly them in the rest of the way till she found the best spots. It didn't take Lexi long; she had done her homework on the Island and knew precisely where she wanted them to be to get the best coverage.

"All set?" 2 Planks asked.

"Hang on, ladies battle gear," Steel called out. On that, Steel, Lexi, and Sam took off the shirts and dropped the shorts to just their bikinis. 2 Planks was stunned. Each woman was different from the other in shape and style, but they all had one thing in common; they were stunning! 2 Planks noticed Sam felt awkward beside the other two women; for all her hard-ass exterior at home, she still thinks she doesn't cut it in beauty. "Sam! You look gorgeous," he yelled. Sam started blushing and said,

"Thank you, 2 Planks."

"Come on, Captain, show us some skin; we don't know which way the guards on the dock will swing; you might have to do the flirting." 2 Planks undid his shirt and showed off his sixpack.

"Damn boy, you give me a boner!" Lexi yelled. It was 2 Planks' turn to blush as Sam and Steel laughed.

"Lexi's right, Seb; you look like a hunk," Sam said. 2 Planks blushed again, even redder than before.

"Are you blushing?" Steel teased.

"No!" was 2 Planks' firm reply.

"Everyone ready," 2 Planks asked again.

"Yep, Redster ready, you ready, Humpster," Sam said jokingly.

"Yep, Humpster ready, you ready, Redster," Lexi joked back.

"Yep, Humpster, I'm packin' my pea shooter, just in case we get attacked by them injuns Humpster," Sam said in an awful cowboy voice.

"You two know, by carrying on like that, you're making fun of what we do." Steel said while looking at Sam seriously. Sam wasn't quite ready to give it up just yet.

"Well, doggone it. Aren't I lucky I have you as the captain instead Ol' starched pants Admiral Sherlock Bli! So, shiver me timbers, ladies, stay busy, check those firearms, suck in those boobies' women, if you can't do it yourself, get the team to help you," Sam was in fine form strutting around the deck acting like her husband as the boat broke out in laughter.

"Why aren't you like this at home?" 2 Planks asked.

"Who says I'm not funny at home?" Sam said, queering 2 Planks.

"Ah, nobody," 2 Planks returned quickly.

Steel walked over to Sam and grabbed her hands. "You're scared, aren't you?"

"Terrified," Sam said in a small voice. Her hands were shaking. Steel grabbed her hands firmly. "You know your job, so just go and do it, and you'll be fine."

"Ok, let's move," Steel yelled, and off they went. As the boat was about to come around the last bend before the dock, 2 Planks stopped the boat and went to the engine compartment and grabbed an oily rag and wiped some grease on his hands, and flipped a switch Art had put on the boat to imitate a blocked fuel line. The boat rounded the corner with a spitting and spluttering motor. The ladies were all positioned near the weapons, ready for anything. Surprised; there was only one guard on duty at the dock. 2 Planks puttered to the end of the doc, and Steel threw a line over a pillion as the guard made his way down the doc.

The guard started calling out in Chinese, and 2 Planks and Steel pretended they didn't understand a word. Finally, the guard's voice became louder as he waved his hand for them to leave. As he approached the end of the dock, they could see that he was only a young man in his mid-twenties. 2 Planks decided it was time to converse with him.

"Do you speak English?" 2 Planks said. The guard just looked at him and said nothing.

"Do you speak English?" he repeated.

"Yes, I do. You can't be here; move on!" the guard ordered.

"We are having engine trouble; I just need a steady dock to tie her to, so I can make repairs; it shouldn't take long. I have to have these ladies back by dark."

"This is a private dock; you can't be here, now move on," the guard issued again.

Steel knew it was time to bounce the boobies; she gave Lexi a little tap on the leg. "Oh please, can we tie off here for a little while? We won't leave the boat, please," Steel said in a sweet country girl voice. Then Lexi joined in with an excited schoolgirl voice,

"Oh pleeease," bouncing up and down, making her boobies wobble madly that nearly sent the young man cross-eyed. They thought they had him, when in an almost apologetic voice, he said, "Sorry, it is not allowed." Sam threw in but using a different tack, reverse psychology.

"Oh, come on, ladies, you can see he will get in trouble with his employer if we dock here. He looks like a nice young man; he wouldn't stop three women from sunning on the deck for a few hours while the captain makes repairs if he was allowed to." She said, smiling.

"You will stay on the boat?" the guard asked.

"Yes, no one will leave the boat," 2 Planks replied.

"Make your repairs quickly," the guard said and walked off back down the dock to continue his patrol.

"Thank you," the ladies all yelled.

Steel gave Sam a thumbs up, and as Sam was walking off, Lexi gave her a cheeky slap on a bare arse. "Woo," Sam let out a surprised yip. Lexi leaned over her shoulder. "Smart and hot! You give me a boner, too," Lexi said in an alluring voice. Sam turned and gave Lexi a gentle shove.

"Naughty girl!" she said, giggling. Lexi looked down at Sam's crutch, "I see you took my advice on shaving her." Sam looked stunned and placed both hands over her the front of her bikini. "Very naughty girl! Stay out of my crutch"

Lexi looked at her cheekily, "Why?" and turned to walk off to check her monitors. Sam stood there with her mouth open; she hadn't been hit on by a woman before, she didn't know what to say. Finally, she decided to work, do her checks, and focus on the mission.

An hour later, Sam comes back on the boat after a dip to cool off and goes to head below deck. She feels radiant; the water was a pleasant temperature; she feels cleansed and glowing from the sun. As she goes down the steps to the quarters, 2 Planks is heading up the stairs to go on deck. The pair try to squeeze past each other and nearly wedge themselves together in the stairwell.

"Hang on, I'll move down," 2 Planks says. As he squeezes himself past Sam, she could feel something firm rub across her lower stomach. She takes a quick glimpse as 2 Planks reaches the bottom step, and woo, she was right. To add to her thoughts of acting classy, she opens up a conversation to show that nothing was noticed, but then she looks down, and her nipples have given up the ruse.

"So how long before we shove off Captain Seb?" she says, trying to add humour into the mix.

"Probably only half an hour or so, then we head out," Seb said.

Sam tried so hard, so very hard, not to try to have a glimpse of Seb's excitement. He was muscular, handsome, intelligent, and funny, great to be around, but don't look at his ... but she did... and Seb saw her looking.

What happened next was a comedy of embarrassing errors; Seb, feeling incredibly embarrassed, tried to push it down and hold it between his legs. Then Sam said, "It's alright, I didn't see it," at the same time watching Seb trying to keep it between his legs. When Seb couldn't hold it, it popped up like a jumping jack, and Sam flinched as if it was going to poke her in the eye. Now they were both embarrassed and blushing wildly.

"I think I better head up and start getting ready," Seb said.

"Yeah, I better do what I came down here to do," but for the life of her, she couldn't remember why she came down below deck. So, the comedy dance continued as they both tried to pass each other and went the same way.

"Oh, stuff it!" Seb stood still, placed his hand on Sam's cheek, leaned down, and kissed her. To Sam's surprise, she let him. Time blurred, and she couldn't tell how long they were kissing when Seb ran his hand over her bikini top and started caressing her nipples. Sam was on fire. There was a tingling sensation up her body. Sam knew what had to be done. It wasn't what she wanted to do, but she knew she had to do it.

Sam gently grabbed Seb's hand and pulled it off her breast. She looked him in the eyes and said, "It would be wonderful, but there are a million reasons we can't." Then she slowly pulled away.

"I'll head back upstairs," Sam said gently, but she was still on fire, blazing. She thought, 'best get out of the room before her knees buckle.' As she was walking up the stairs. Seb calls out, "Sam I ..."

Sam turns, "Yeah, me too, but that's not how our cards played out." As she comes out on the deck, she passes Lexi,

"You alright, girl?",

"Yeah, it's just hot below deck," Sam answers. 2 Planks came up just then, and Lexi noticed the sweat on the glistening muscles.

'Wow, I bet it was hot downstairs,' she thought. She continues to go below deck when Steel calls out, "more guards, it may be trouble."

"Ladies, you know your positions," Seb commands, with a notable change in his voice.

These additional guards' storm past the young dock guard as if he isn't there. They were heading for the boat. 2 Planks calmly walked over to the motor, flipped the switch, and headed back to the driver's chair. They are too close now to make a run; they have to play it out. Steel and 2 Planks noticed they were carrying AK47's, no pistols but a knife each.

"What are you doing here?" the self-appointed leader of the group says in excellent English. Their appearance was Chinese, but these guys are Americans.

"We are just leaving; we had to stop to repair our engine," Steel informs them.

"Why, in such a hurry to leave? We could party a bit," the leader said as he eyed up Sam and Lexi.

Steel steps forward. "There won't be any raping and pillaging on my boat."

"Oh, you think you are in charge" the leader shoves the barrel of the rifle under Steel's chin. "I'll do as I fucking please."

2 Planks goes to move forward. "Move, and you have her brains all over your pretty shirt," he snarls at 2 Planks. The other two men have their rifles pointed at Sam and Lexi. The leader turns and looks Sam up and down.

"You look like a good place to start." Just then, Steel rips off her top; standing there bare breasted, she calls the leader.

"I thought you wanted to party. Come try me first," she said, to lure the leader over to her to keep him away from Sam.

"Wow, you really want it, don't you?" as he grabs Steel's breast.

"Hang on, that's not fair! You do this every time. As soon as we meet guys, you flash your bits, so you get laid first, and we get the leftovers. Not this time," Lexi rips off her bikini top. "What do you think of these babies?" Lexi says, jiggling her breasts.

"Very nice, but you will have to wait your turn; this one is waiting for it," the leader looks down at Steel's crutch and points the barrel of the rifle at it. Lexi's distraction of the leader and his men looking between her legs was all the time Steel needed. As he looked up, Steel had a knife on his jugular.

"One flinch from me and your toast," Steel says, looking straight into the leader's eyes.

"You will all die; we have the guns," the leader said, shaking.

"It won't matter to you; you'll already be dead, and then I will kill another of your men before they can even pull the trigger," Steel said in a cold dead voice. "Now tell your friends to drop their rifles and step to the side, and you can walk away... alive."

"Drop your weapons. Do it!" the leader yelled. Seb stepped forward and grabbed the leader's rifle. 2 Planks took the magazine and the bullet out of the chamber and gave him his rifle back. Sam and Lexi did the same with the other soldiers.

"I told you there will be no raping and pillaging today. Now leave, peacefully."

The three soldiers exited the boat and stormed down the dock to the young guard. The young guard was getting extremely worried. The men coming back weren't happy, and he saw a half-naked woman on the boat. He knows what the Water Tiger does to people who don't follow the rule. What did these men do?

Seb bent down and through Steel her bikini; she appreciated the sentiment towards her modesty. "Grab the wheel, I'll get the line," 2 Planks commands. As 2 Planks was making his way to the back of the boat, everything from then happened in microseconds. First, he saw the leader grab the rifle off the young guard and aim it at the back of the boat. 2 Planks screamed and made a dive for Sam to protect her. The sound of automatic fire filled the air. Bullets ripped into the boat, and 2 Planks was hit twice, once in the head and once in the back. Blood was pouring over Sam from 2 Planks' body as she screamed.

Lexi had a different view of things; she heard 2 Planks scream Sam's name and tackle her to the ground; she listened to the shots and then looked up and saw the young dock guard pull a pistol and shoot the leader in the head and watching him fall in a heap to the ground. Then she saw the young man pick up the rifle and force the other two men to the ground at gunpoint. Lexi was confused by what she saw. Broken out of her shock by Steel screaming at her to get the line for the boat. She ran over, slipped the post line, and Steel hit the accelerator.

Sam was crying for Seb to wake up; she was in shock. Steel got on their comm and called to Art, "Boat to base, boat to base!",

"Base here," Art replied. "Team member down, gunshots, require immediate Medi evac," Steel informs them, trying to keep her emotions intact. "Head to these coordinates. A medical team will be there waiting." Art informs them. 'Thank god for Art; he has always got everything covered.' Steel turns her head and sees Sam still crying over 2 Planks. She takes control! "Lexi, come here!" Lexi jumps to the command. "Take the wheel; just keep it on that heading." Steel runs to 2 Planks and Sam; she grabs Sam and slaps her. That worked. "Get a grip, Sam; we need to save Seb. Get the Medi kit!" Sam was alert now; she races and brought the kit back.

"I see two wounds, head and back. Help me roll him over to see if there's an exit wound." They roll Seb over and found no exit wound. "No exit, patch the wound on the back and keep the pressure on. I'll check the head wound." Sam applies the wound kit and applies pressure. "The wounds are deep, but I don't see an entrance. It may be what knocked him out. I'll apply a bandage to stem the bleeding. Sam, make him comfortable and monitor his vitals,"

"Will do," Sam responds. Steel races to the wheel and checks the bearings and looks at her watch. "Around 10 minutes to the evac," Steel says.

"How is he?" Lexi asks. Steel turns her head towards her and says nothing. That look says it all.

CHAPTER 25

THE HAND-OFF

Smith, Sherlock, and Jedi moved silently through the crystal-clear waters with their submersibles. Sherlock knew the key was to get from the tie-off point to land, which is where they're most vulnerable. So far, so good, with the jets tied off, they made their way to the shore, 50 meters away. Their gear was in tow in equipment bags. As they reached the shore, they poke their heads above water to check the surrounding landscape. This was challenging; they were vulnerable, and their senses dimmed from the time underwater, but they have assessed the area quickly. Sensing no danger, they moved quickly, stealthily, to a heavy clump of trees. Well trained, they don't need to talk; each knows their job. Dressing in their Gilly suits, Smith puts a GPS beacon in his bag so they can make their way back if they get disorientated during a firefight.

An hour later, both Sherlock and Steel were in position, while Jedi was looking for the best spot to hide and cover the exit area in case of a quick retreat. Sherlock took the forward position to make the hand-off to the Water Tiger, and Smith took a covering position to protect Sherlock. So far, there have been four crisscrossing patrols. Each guard carries an AK47 and a knife. Sherlock thought, 'A lot of patrols for a lighthouse.' They obviously wanted to cover a large area effectively, but the downside is it's complicated for the guards, so they form a path and stick to it. Then the next shift just follows that same worn path. That makes it easier to plot their course and time for Sherlock and Smith.

Another hour passes quickly as Sherlock and Smith fight the usual adrenaline from hiding so close to patrol paths. You have to be on guard every second, not knowing if your cover will be blown. But, armed with silenced 9mm pistols and knives, their mission is to not be detected. It's saving the integrity of the information they collect, and Sherlock's team was the best at what they do.

½ hour to hand-off. Suddenly, Sherlock hears faint gunfire from what sounds like an AK47, but on the other side of the island. The patrol moving in front of Sherlock stops; this was obviously not something that should occur. 'The boat, god, I hope not' the thought passes through his mind quickly. He has a job to do. He can't help the boat, and 2 Planks and Steel are there. They know how to handle situations. 'Everything will be fine' was the next thought that passed through. Then suddenly, Water Tiger comes out ½ hour before hand-off, heads to a jeep, and leaves toward the docks.

The Water Tiger arrived at the docks to find one of his guards standing over three other guards, one obviously dead.

"What is going on here, report?" Water Tiger snapped.

"Sir, I was patrolling the dock, and these three came down and boarded a boat that was docked here."

"What boat? There is not supposed to be any boats here!" Water Tiger asked, already knowing.

"A boat struggled in, wanting to use the dock while they made repairs to their engine. I allowed it on the proviso that no one on board left the boat; no one did. So, these three came down and boarded the vessel. I don't know what happened, but they sped off fast; I noticed one woman was naked. This one snatched my rifle off me and fired at the boat; I shot him for breaking your rules," the young guard reported.

"Was anyone hurt on the boat?"

"I am not sure; I saw the captain, then he wasn't there, and the boat sped off."

Another incident did not impress the Water Tiger, more to cover-up. "You two, where are the magazines for your rifles?"

"The woman disarmed us. The naked woman; we didn't touch her." the guard pleaded.

"A naked woman disarmed, three armed guards!"

"She had a knife!" One guard pleaded.

"Where was she hiding the knife? Up her bum!" With lightning speed, the Water Tiger drew his pistol and fired a shot in the back of the head of the two kneeling guards. He turned and faced the young guard.

"Why did you not contact me about the boat?"

"It was my decision; you are the leader. If your men can't make the right decisions based on your parameters, we aren't much good to you." The young guard said, not backing down.

"Yes, that is true. I will send some men down to hang these three by their feet outside the barracks. Then maybe the rest will start thinking like you." The Water Tiger praised the young man.

"Thank you, Sir," the young guard stood to attention.

As the Water Tiger walked to the Jeep, he thought to himself, 'the young man has potential; I should offer him a spot with me if we live through this daily horror show.'

Back at the lighthouse, Sherlock and Smith were on edge. It was time for the hand-off, and they just heard another two shots. Then around the corner came Water Tiger in his Jeep; he pulled up abruptly. He seemed agitated, pissed off! He jumps from the Jeep, yelling and mumbling to himself, then unleashes an attack on a set of metal rubbish bins. The three guards in the vicinity looked terrified.

"You three!" he pointed to the guards in the area. "Come here, take my Jeep to the dock and grab the three bodies there. Then bring them back and hang them by their feet from those trees outside your barracks."

"Yes, Sir!" the three men couldn't get in the Jeep fast enough to get away. Water tiger roamed the area as if he was thinking, knowing he was on the cameras. He was looking for the sign, a little arrow in the dirt to show where the recording device was; he found it. Knowing one of the team was nearby for the hand-off, he bends down to pretend he was tightening his bootlaces, grabs the recorder, and says, "Your boat was fired upon."

'Why did he say that?' Sherlock thought, 'I can't do anything, I'm stuck here till the hand-off, on radio silence. Maybe it's another way to torture me.' Sherlock thought.

As Water Tiger walked into the security room and addresses the guard. "Did you tell three guards about the boat on the dock?"

"No sir, number 13 was hanging around this room and saw the boat and the women on it. Then he left."

"From now on, only you, myself, and Nessler are allowed in here; this is your room now. If anyone comes in here, you direct them to leave. If they don't, you have my permission to shoot them. Now go help hang up Lucky 13 and his friends. I will stay here until you are back."

"Yes Sir," 'hang up, Oh my god!' the guard thought.

The Water Tiger set up the miniature device, amazed at the technology. 'So small, I bet this is Damani's.' he thought.

He waited for the guard to come back; he was covered in blood and in shock when he did. 'Good, he won't be looking for a device in his state,' he thought.

The following 2 hours passed, so slow for Sherlock as he waited for the hand-off. 'Did someone get hurt? I have to maintain control. Get the info, evac carefully. We were not here,' he thought.

After the hand-off, Sherlock moved ever so slowly to get out of the patrol area. It was killing him, 'was anyone hurt?'.

He couldn't even talk to Smith and Jedi at the Water edge as they put on their scuba gear. So instead, he made simple hand gestures. BOAT, SHOT AT, DON'T KNOW? Smith turned as he sprinted to the water and dived in with Jedi close behind, obviously wanting to get back and find out if they were all alright.

They reached the pickup boat and grabbed the comm. "Scuba team to base," "Base here," "What happened to the boat?"

CHAPTER 26

THE RESCUE

As Steel rammed the throttle forward, the boat sped at full speed to the coordinates that Art had given her. The team was lucky in one regard; that the weather was good, and the sea was calm. She saw ahead a tiny Island, more like a small dirt outcrop than an Island, that had a helicopter on it. She thought, 'What the hell, how am I supposed to get him off the boat?' She slowed, as the water depth was not as deep. On her approach, she saw an old timber dock that looked like it was ready to collapse. While pulling up alongside the Paramedics and what looked like a doctor waiting to board. After tying off, she saw the dock had recently been shored up. "Art, you're a lifesaver," she said out loud.

The doctor and medics jumped on board while Steel tied up the boat. "Excuse us," the doctor said as he pushed Sam out of the way. Sam wasn't about to be pushed out of saving Seb's life. "Excuse me!" Sam snaps at the doctor.

"I'm sorry, but we are trying to save his life," the doctor angrily returns.

"If you want to save his life, then shut up and listen! Here are his vitals," Sam showed them her arm; it had all Seb's vitals on it, only taken a minute ago. "He has a bullet through his left Rhomboid at an angle moving across his spine; there's no exit wound. The second wound to the head doesn't look like it has penetrated, but I believe it has caused a concussion, as I haven't been able to wake him." The doctor looked at Sam and smiled, knowing she had just saved 4 minutes of this man's life; now it was his turn.

"You heard the lady, no exit wound; we need to get him on the chopper so I can use the ultrasound to find the bullet." The doctor issued his instructions. Sam was amazed.

"You have an ultrasound machine on the helicopter?"

"We do now, thanks to Mr. Damani." The doctor replied.

"Where will you take him?" Sam asked.

"If we can stabilise him, we will fly to the Bahamas where a jet is waiting to fly him to the States. If we can't, I will take him to a private hospital in Nassau, and we will have to operate there.",

"Can I go with him?"

"Are you family?" the doctor asked.

"Yes!" Sam lied.

"Fine, we have room for one more; just stay out of our way."

Sam turned to Katelyn, tears in her eyes. Katelyn thought she saw something else, but it just could be the whole emotion of what had happened. "Tell Mike where I am" she turned away and ran to the helicopter as Seb was being loaded. Katelyn ran to the helicopter just as it was taking off. They opened the door, and Sam stuck her head out.

"Here, our comm and some money, keep us informed," Katelyn handed her the package and turned and got out of the range of the blades. As the blades spun and the helicopter turned and headed off on this glorious summer day, she wondered for the first time, 'What the hell are we doing?'.

****

"What the hell has happened?" Mike asked.

"They fired on the boat; Sam is alright, but Seb has been hit. He is in the ICU in Nassau private hospital. The last we heard from Sam; he was in surgery."

"Sam's there with him?"

"Yes, she opted to go with him."

"Your mission Mike?" Art asked.

"Successful, we retrieved the recording, but at what cost?".

"We have received new intel of conspirators in the Whitehouse," Art said,

"Ok, is Sam safe where she is?"

"Yes, Katelyn gave her some money and a comm set. I'm arranging a credit card to be given to her tomorrow by a local banker for her needs.,"

"Thank you, Art, keep me informed." Mike hung up and looked at Smith and Jedi, who listened to the conversation.

"You know, we should be there," Smith stated.

"Yes, I'd like to, but we have to report back; there's a lot more at stake than just Seb; we can fly back after we've reviewed the intel."

"Why did Sam go with him?"

"Family, someone has to be there in times of need; I'll ring his family once he is out of surgery."

CHAPTER 27

MOMENTUM

(Momentum: The quantity of motion of a moving body…)

Another day in suburbia in the Washington suburb of Bethesda North, as a totally unremarkable car, with a totally unremarkable colour, pulls into the driveway of a home that looks like 100 others in the suburb.

Lorri Stapleton greets a repairman on her driveway as she is watering her Leyland cypress hedge. Her hedges are the envy of the street, so high and lush. Lorri calls to her husband Roger that the repairman is here.

A voice calls out from the yard next door. "Having trouble again, Lorri?" Lorri turns to greet the friendly, if not a somewhat nosy neighbour.

"Hi! Yes, Janice, it's that pesty security system again. I swear, if it wasn't covered by warranty, I'd throw it in the trash," Lorri adds with a bit of a chuckle at the end of her statement.

"Well, you're our neighbourhood watch president, so if you're not safe, none of us are." Janice and Lorri had a good chuckle at that one.

"Janice, I have to supervise Roger; otherwise, they'll talk him into a more expensive system; bye now," Lorri said cheerily as she turned off her hose and walked inside.

Lorri walks inside the house and looks at the repairman.

"We should hire her, I swear to god, every person who comes to the house, she's there to watch me greet them!".

Roger walks over to see what was going on.

"Are you banging her?" Lorri asks.

"Who?" Roger asks, confused.

"Janice, next door. Is she watching to see when I'm not home so she can come over to show you her cookies?"

"What! Hell no, I'd rather Sally from the P&C meetings", Roger says while making out he is giving it lots of thought.

"What, the skank with the boobs hanging out and skirt so short when she bends over you can see what she had for breakfast?" Lorri asked, shocked.

"Yeah, she likes muffins," Roger added.

"No, you like muffins!" Lorri said, exasperated.

The repairman just stood there, not saying a word, head going side to side until he thought it would unscrew and fall on the floor at his feet. He finally joins the conversation as he takes off his hat and sunglasses.

"Did you ever think she may be a Russian plant?". Roger and Lorri looked at each other with an 'Oh my god, we hadn't thought of that look.'

"Is everyone here?",

"Yes, Director." Damien Spelling took off his workman's coat and hung it on the hook. He loved visiting Roger and Lorri, but swears he doesn't know how they stay happily married.

He entered the kitchen, and here, feeding their faces on the cookies Lorri baked this morning, was the rest of his Black Ops team. The team comprising ex-CIA operatives working off the books, typically in very sticky situations like they're in now. Technically speaking, the CIA has no mandate to operate inside the United States, but sometimes, rules need to be broken; this time, they need to be shattered.

"So, update me." Spelling asks.

Roger, the husband who has the hots for Sally in the short skirt, does the update since he is the team leader.

"Well, Sir, we cloned Secretary of State Cashdon's phone this morning at a breakfast bar. We couldn't tag his car in fear of it being detected as he goes through security at the Whitehouse. Thanks to your friend Damani, we cloned his home, internet, and house security system. Sir, his gear is off this planet. Has he offered to share his toys?",

"No, he hasn't! and he's not my friend," Damien said, annoyed. "The sneaky little bastard won't share his tech," Damien added. He continued, "Ok, keep me updated on everyone he comes in contact with, especially military, and keep an eye out for Nessler."

"Yes, Sir."

"Now, is everybody covered? This will get dirty, increase your home surveillance, go into buddy watch until this is over. You need to keep a diary of everything you do and record?".

"Sir, you've told us to never keep records?" Roger asked.

"Yes, I know, but the shit is going to hit the fan no matter which way this pans out. But, on the other hand, the records this time may keep us out of prison for 20 years charged with treason."

"Sir, what about you and your family?" Roger asks. "We'll keep on guard. If it gets too hairy, I'll call in the Ghost team."

Roger looked shocked. "Are we going into the bowels of hell?"

"We certainly are, team; make no mistake on that."

CHAPTER 28

A PICTURE PAINTS A THOUSAND WORDS

As the Korean Airline flight A643 touches down on a wet, miserable day in Pyongyang. Ji-tai-Jin reflects on all the places he won't be visiting. It's been 6 years since his last visit home, and like this one, it's all business. With no friendships here and little family left living, he has no reason to visit or sight-see. He was a ghost; he had to be to stay off the grid and stay alive with every law enforcement agency in the world looking for him.

Upon disembarking, two soldiers greet him, dressed in Nth Korean military uniforms before he enters the terminal.

"Mr. Ahn?" one soldier asks as he approaches.

"Yes,"

"Come with us," the soldier orders.

The soldiers led Ji-tai-Jin through a back service entry. This is not new for him; as represented by the status of his reputation, it is customary to usher him to a vehicle through areas with no security cameras.

On the front passenger seat of the vehicle will be all the papers required to cross the border into China. A top priority status card that gives him easy access in China.

His two-hour drive to the Sino-Korean friendship bridge was uneventful, even to a point where Ji-Tai-Jin didn't even notice the scenery. He was so engrossed in the job at hand. It had been six weeks since the boating incident on Navassa Island. Even though they have said they are tracking everything and everyone they know so far that is involved. It seems a little too late. The organisation he is working with seems to have the upper hand and is progressing unimpeded.

His next destination is an old cannery building near the Chinese/Nth Korean border in south Dandong. He is to meet Nessler there to outline the project further.

Passing through the border, security woke Ji-tai-Jin out of his daydream drive. The seriousness of the guards, no one comes into China or North Korea without the proper papers, no one.

The drive to the cannery was an eye-opener. China had put a lot of time and money into the town since he was last here. Dandong is China's most southern seaport and one that ships to North Korea. It was on the Yalu River, and the city shone like a new beacon of China's growing wealth. But for every newly rebuilt province, there was one that was left to rot.

Reaching the address, it surprised him to find workers painting and repairing structures. What was most surprising was the Chinese soldiers on guard on the outside. The Water Tiger parked his vehicle and made his way towards the soldiers.

"Papers," the Chinese guard demanded.

The Water Tiger handed over the documents to the soldier, who studied them carefully. Looking at the papers and his passport as if they could tell the difference between a fake or real one. After a minute, the soldier hands back the documents and says, "Please go inside; you are expected."

Upon entry to the front office, Fredrick Nessler and a Chinese captain greet him.

"Good afternoon, Water Tiger; I hope your trip was pleasant," Nessler asked cheerily.

"Uneventful, which is how I like it," the Water Tiger responds.

Nessler turned to the captain. "Thank you, captain; we will finish this later."

"Well, what do you think of our troops, Tiger?"

"I assume they are, our troops."

"Yes, they are," Nessler said.

"What happens if the real troops stop in?"

"We have sentries on all the major roads that let us know when the patrols come through. Then the soldiers make themselves scarce. They have papers to be here that will hold up, so long as there not looked into too deep."

"So, the uniforms are for the locals?"

"Exactly, with the workers fixing up the plant, it looks like a government-sanctioned operation," Nessler explained. "Come, I have much to tell you, away from prying ears."

As the two men entered the main office on the first floor, it reeked of fresh paint from the renovations. Kessler looked around outside to check that no workers or security were nearby.

"Ok, there is a lot to tell you. First, I need you to survey the surrounding area and tell me what you need to protect this building. This will be the staging ground for the world to see that the Chinese are behind the new virus."

"We are attributing the virus to the Chinese, not infecting them?" asked the Water Tiger inquisitively.

"That is correct. Did you think we were going to poison China?"

"Yes, you hadn't said otherwise. It is not my job to ask questions, just to do my job as efficiently as possible," the Water Tiger added.

"Ok, then. No, we are releasing the virus in different parts of the world and blaming the Chinese. This strain of COVID-19 will be diagnosed as being manmade, and all the evidence will point to China."

"I see. The world then will demand retaliation, and they will force China into conflict. Genius strategy. I hate to throw in something that's probably already been thought of, but there isn't a superpower strong enough to take on China by itself without going into a nuclear confrontation." Stated Water Tiger, hoping to pry every bit of information out of Nessler while he is so chatty.

"What about two superpowers?" Nessler added with a twist of I know something you don't.

"Never! You will never get Russia and the United States to work together, especially in a war of this magnitude."

"Already done. They have struck a deal; we have the right men on both sides pushing the right buttons. The press and the citizens will do the rest." Nessler said, like a proud peacock.

"Unbelievable! I assume they are relying on China to react with the military to escalate the confrontation?"

"Yes, exactly!" Nessler crowed again.

"Did you have a hand in all this, Fredrick?"

"Yes, I had a large hand in negotiating between the two and setting up a strategy.

"Congratulations! A superlative plan well thought out to meet the required goal," Water Tiger praised. "Which countries should I stay away from so I don't end up a casualty of the virus?" Water Tiger added with a laugh.

Nessler laughed with him, "I would stay away from the US and Russia, and if they react too slow, England. Nothing gets the world fired up as quickly as a whinging Brit!" both men burst out laughing. Not wanting to push his luck on this topic, Water Tiger changed tact.

"So, how long do I have here before it goes down?"

"I'd say 8 weeks; the lab will take around 2 weeks to get up and running. It has to be a fully functioning lab when they find this place. I will leave the surveillance up to you. I would suggest security outside to be soldiers or workers. Special forces gear would attract too much attention." Nessler informed him.

"Well thought out, Fredrick. Is there anything else I need to know?"

"Not that you need to know it. But a piece of information you might be happy with. When your friend Art Damani speaks at the UN hearing this week, as he addresses the press afterward, he is going to have an unfortunate mishap."

"Perilous with the security they have there!" Water Tiger stated.

"Oh, it's being done from a long way off."

"Excellent. He has been nothing but trouble."

"I thought that might make you happy. I must take your leave now. I am off back to the States to make sure all is ready. Farewell, Water Tiger, until our next meeting."

The men shook hands, and Nessler headed for the door. He stopped and turned to the Water Tiger as he was walking through. "I believe the captain of the guard wants to talk to you about your requirements for here. So long."

The Water Tiger made mental notes and observations about the conversation he just had. So, when he contacts the Captain, oh sorry, the Major. He has the answers to get things moving …8 weeks; the clocks ticking.

He goes outside, and here is the guard captain, waiting to speak to him. The captain updates him on all they are doing inside and out, plus what they planned for the future. A three-man guard marched past doing their rounds. Unnoticed by all, was the man taking photos on the other side of the road from the dilapidated old building. Not just any photos, but photos of the Water Tiger talking to a Chinese Captain as Chinese guards march past. They say a picture paints a thousand words, but can it start a war?

CHAPTER 29

ANOTHER DAY AT THE OFFICE

World wars looming, a friend in critical condition after being shot on a mission ... and still work at the Ark goes on. Floors cleaned, pastries cooked, and papers to be signed.

Art and Ab took the morning off to cruise around the ARK grounds, checking out the new enclosures and tenants.

The Ark was already huge, the size of a small city, and they were coming up to phase 2, another expansion. Phase 2 also had an expansion for the start of letting visitors into the park, including virtual tours, which Oliver and Aidan came up with. So much to do, luckily Art has great staff to make the job flow smoothly.

"Earth to Father. Come in Father." Ab said jokingly as they both bounced along the track in ARK transport.

"Hahaha, I'm here. Just thinking how big the ARK is now and we're coming up to Phase 2."

"We have drawn everything up. So, nothing to worry about." Ab assured him.

"Water,"

"We have the Desalination plant to be built which will supply us all the water we need for the future, plus the dams being proposed." Ab reassured Art.

"Being proposed. Yes, but we know there will be the first democratic elections before then. What if we don't get a favourable government and they want to take over the plant?"

"What if? Rubbish. Since you adopted me, there hasn't been a what if you haven't had 6 other ways around. Relax Father, Seb will be fine," Ab knew his father's worries weren't on money or the future of the ARK, it was Seb being injured that weighed heavily on him.

"Up ahead, look," Ab pointed to one of the ARK's many wonders. A lion's pride, all walking together across one of the grassy meadows. While at the same time a herd of gazelles grazed nearby. Balance of nature, hunt to live, that's all.

"Amazing," Art said in awe.

"They look so healthy in the short time they've been here."

"Yes, but what amazes me, the males are there too. I wonder if they're relocating?"

"Good signs Father. Good signs."

"Let's see what else is around."

Ten minutes later, after putting some challenging hypotheses together. They come into a clearing, where they come across the head veterinary surgeon for the ARK, Dr Sarah McTagash.

"Art, over here, over here," the doc said, waving her arms frantically.

Art and Ab made their way quickly over to her.

"You guys are life savers. I was just about to call Dan Hooper to send some men over. But you guys will do. Come have a look."

The doc leads them over to the edge of a creek bed. Down below was a baby African bush elephant, stuck in a bog in the creek.

"He can't get out. We need to help him."

"What do you suggest Dr. Sarah?" Art asked.

"We need to tie some ropes around him and attach them to one car, and gently pull and push him out."

"Push?"

"Yep, I need you two guys to go down there and push as we slowly pull with the vehicle." the doc said.

"I can drive," Art said excitedly.

"No, you're not!" Ab jumped in quickly. "The last time you drove one of these vehicles, you rolled it and crashed into a tree, remember?"

"I was mounting a heroic rescue to save Katelyn from the baboons." Art said with a voice full of pride and accomplishment.

"You traumatised Loki!" Ab interjected.

"A gross overstatement."

"He won't get in a vehicle if you're behind the wheel. How did you manage to traumatise a robot?" Ab reinstated.

"Hush your mouth, Loki is a living entity and is entitled to his trauma." Art said proudly, with a hint of jest.

"Abbott and Costello, are you two finished your routine? We have work to do."

Ab looked over the edge again. "Do you have ropes in your car, Doc?"

"Yes, why?"

"Go grab them. I have an idea," Ab said.

Ten minutes later, Ab had constructed a harness for the distressed baby elephant.

"Ok, this wraps around his belly and comes up the sides so we can pull him up evenly. Father and I will push and guide him up as you take up the slack in the rope and slowly drive the car forward." Ab instructed them.

"Where did you learn to make this harness, Ab?" the Doc asked.

"I learnt ropes in my village as a youngster. The harness, I just made it up." Ab said.

"Well, we're glad you came along when you did." The Doc said.

"Come on, Father, time to get dirty."

Ab checked his route, then bounced down the creek bed as surefooted as a mountain goat. Art, on the other hand, took two delicate steps, then fell on his arse and slid down the muddy creek bank, ending up beside the baby elephant.

"Well, at least I know how you got here," Art said to the elephant, laughing.

Art and Ab got the new harness attached to the baby elephant. Ab then hurled the heavy rope up to the bank top for the Doc to attach the ropes to the Ark vehicle.

Meanwhile, a concerned onlooker approached the scene. The mother of the wild African bush elephant seemed concerned for her young one, with all this human attention. Plus, there was all ropes around her baby, but she seemed to be happy to stay on the opposite bank for the moment because her baby didn't seem concerned yet.

"Take up the slack in the rope Doc," Ab yelled.

The vehicle moved slowly forward, taking the slack out of the rope and then inched forward, pulling gently on the ropes. Ab's harness was working. It was distributing the tension around the baby elephant rear instead of pulling it by the neck. Now it was just up to Ab and Art to guide him up. All was going well as the elephant moved out of the thick bog to the edge of the bank. Several attempts to help the elephant get a footing on the bank were failing as the legs of the tiny elephant fatigued, not to mention Art and Ab. They didn't want to risk just dragging the baby up the bank for fear of injuring him. As the baby elephant tired, he became vocal and started sounding distressed.

"Ab, Art. Watch your backs. Mum is coming over." The Doc yelled.

Ab looked over his shoulder and saw the mother elephant making her way down the other bank. Showing no signs of aggression, Ab and Art stood still to see what she gets up to.

Slowly the mother moves around Arts side of the baby elephant, ignoring Art and using her trunk to caress her child and calm him down. Then, without warning, she turns her attention to Art. Using her trunk, she gives Art a gentle push. Art stands there looking at her, confused. She pushes him again.

"What is she doing?" the Doc asks.

"I think she wants us to try again." Art yelled back.

"Ok, let's give it a go," the Doc replied.

Slowly, the truck moved forward, and the ropes tightened. Ab and Art started pushing as the baby elephant tried to get a grip on the surface of the bank. Several steps were made and success finally seemed achievable when the baby's strength gave way again. Suddenly, the mother let out a trumpet call, startling everyone. She moved up beside Art at the back of the baby elephant. Art was aware of her massive size, but wasn't concerned for his safety.

The mother lowered her head to the baby's bottom and placed her trunk between his legs and under his stomach. Then she thrust forward, pushing the tired calf up the bank with the help of her human friends. Ab quickly undid the harness and the young elephant ran excitedly to his mother. They all stood there watching the mother and son re-join their herd.

"Isn't nature wonderful?" Art said, euphoric.

"That wasn't nature," the Doc said in a confused manner.

"What do you mean?" Art replied.

"Art, that stuff only happens in the movies, like Hatari. It doesn't happen in real life." The Doc said assuredly.

"Are you sure you not some kind of Noah reincarnated?" the Doc asked.

"Ah no, I don't think so."

"Maybe ... the mother elephant saw Father was old like her and that he needed a hand?" Ab said, laughing.

They all started laughing. "Yep, that seems more like it." Art replied.

"It seems the day has been filled with lots of interesting things," Ab said.

"Why? What else have you seen?" the Doc asked curiously.

"We saw a full pride of lions crossing the plains before, males included."

"Where? Show me."

The Doc pulled out a map, and Ab pointed to where they saw the lions. Quickly, she grabs the truck's communications.

"Doc McTagash to base. Over,"

"Base here. What's up Doc?"

"Ab and Art saw the lion pride from sector 19 on the move. Possible relocating. Can you find and track them, please?"

"Sure Doc. Do you want me to send Scar to follow them?"

"Yes, just keep him at his maximum distance and record everything. I don't want him to interact. Put the birds on them and dig up all available footage on them from the last few days, and I'll review it tonight."

"Okey Dokey Doc. I'm on it." Doby said.

"Thanks Doby. Well, you too I suggest a return to base and a shower. You both smell like elephant shit." The Doc said laughing.

"That sounds like a plan." Art says.

"And thanks again, you both did great work today. Even you Noah,"

"Maybe it's a Tarzan thing?" Art said enquiring.

"No, you don't have the abs. Definitely a Noah thing." The Doc said joking.

The conversation home was a lot lighter; the responsibilities were still there. The injured friend was still in hospital, but the ability to deal with it all was there, too. Fresh air, helping the animals and being covered in elephant shit refreshes one's outlook and ability to deal with anything.

The day's entertainment hadn't finished as Art and Ab laughed over dinner at the videos of Loki and his new reopened AI. Loki was in the dining hall during the day trying to mimic one of Rosey's new robot monkeys. The antics were hilarious, even to the point of Mrs Flanders chasing them out of the dining area with a broom.

"Another day at the office," Art thought.

CHAPTER 30

WAKE THE HELL UP!

The sun shone radiantly as the people of the Nassau made their way to work. The tourists walked around just soaking in this beautiful tropical weather. But in one room of the Nassau General Hospital. It might as well be snowing a blizzard outside, as if Sam would notice. Sam sat by Sebastian's bed now for nearly 4 weeks. Refusing to come back to the Ark. "Someone has to be here when he wakes; I owe him that." That was what her remarks to Mike were. He understood; she felt responsible for his health since Seb took the bullets meant for her. She would be dead, or at least be the one lying here in a coma.

It's been a week since they took Seb out of the induced coma. But he still hasn't wakened. The doctors said there is no telling when he will awaken. So, Sam has been by his side this whole time, seldom going back to the apartment Art had supplied for her stay. Sending her a credit card to get anything she needed, but all she needed was for Seb to awaken. The four weeks had taken their toll on her; she hadn't eaten well or made sure she got enough sleep. The nurses found her constantly asleep in a chair, leaning on Seb's bed, holding his hand.

The only ray of sunshine she had was when Mike bought the boys to visit. Aidan had read that even though he was in a coma, they could still hear you. So, the boys just spoke to him as if he was awake. Talking for hours about the boats in the harbour at Nassau. What's happening in their latest video games. Plus, their adventures using the Ark's Raptors to herd the animals into enclosures. They even threw in some bad things, like mum was looking into tutors at the Ark so they could go back to school. The only sign of emotion came when it was time to leave. Aidan seemed fine, telling Seb he would catch up with him soon. Oliver couldn't find the words to say goodbye; he ran outside and stood at the end of the hallway, head down, trying not to cry, like a good soldier. Aidan came down and stood beside him; he put his fist out. "Raptors forever." Oliver fist pumped him and returned their battle cry,

"Raptors forever." Oliver walked back into the room and stood beside the bed, looking at the monitors and tubes. He looks down at Seb, holds his hand, and says, "Wake up, Seb, just get the hell up."

All the team had visited. The doctor's reports were very positive. The induced coma allowed the brain swelling to reduce from the hit to the head. Unfortunately, part of his left lung had to be removed due to bullet damage. But he will recover and already had by the scans. They just had to wait till he wakes up. Mike making the jest; all he does is sleep and eat, anyway.

Sam then went back to her 24/7 watch over him, only leaving when the nurses kicked her out to work with him, sending her home to shower and sleep. Not that rest was coming easy; she usually passed out from exhaustion.

Sitting there, holding Seb's hand, she was going through another low cycle; the guilt was eating at her soul. Here lays someone she loves that risked his life to save hers. Even though she was a soldier's wife, she was having difficulty coming to grips with it. His life, he never hesitated, the bravery was real. How much higher can any person reach? To be that humane. His life was more important than hers; the world needed more Seb's. This is what she said over and over for two hours through the tears.

"It was worth it for you," Seb said in a dry, throaty voice.

As Sam started screaming for a nurse, Seb tried to cover his ears to muffle the volume. Nurses and doctors on duty flurried in to see the coma patient awake. Seb had to go through all the first examinations of, what's your name, where do you live, what's the last thing you remember? He grew impatient, there was something important he had to do.

"Doc, I'm awake. I'll go through more examinations later; there's something I have to do first."

"Sam, I need your phone."

As Sam fetched her phone from her handbag, Seb started gargling some water, trying to moisten his throat. Finally, he grabs the phone and starts searching for a number in her contacts. He finds the number and dials it.

****

On the other side of the world, two boys are doing their patrols around the Ark. So far, everything is as it should be, except Buttercup the Rhino was moody today. Behind the boys were their robotic raptors, that they used for herding the animals into catchment areas. The raptors are fast and nimble and extremely efficient in the hands of these two boys.

Oliver and Aidan were standing in the back of their jeep checking the area when Oliver's phone rang. He saw who was ringing and answered with a smile.

"Hi mum,"

"Is this Private Point Break, raptor specialist?"

Immediately Oliver recognises the voice.

"Seb, Is that you? You're awake."

"Just woke up; I had to ring my partner in crime first."

"Aidan, Major, Seb's awake," Oliver started yelling in the jeep, bouncing around till he nearly fell out of the moving vehicle.

"Adi and the Major said to say hi," Oliver passes on.

"Say hi to them for me, buddy. Oh, and thanks for the wake-up call. If it wasn't for you and your mother, I'd still be asleep."

"You heard us?" Oliver asked, astonished.

"Yep, and tell Adi I can't wait to beat him in that new game you're playing. One last thing before I go. Don't knock doing schoolwork; it's the path to adult freedom, remember that."

"Ok, but I still don't understand what that means every time you say it?"

"You will one-day matey, have to go. Some hot nurses want to give me a sponge bath."

"Ooow, that's gross. See you, Uncle Seb."

"Bye, buddy,"

Seb turns to give Sam her phone back, and she's crying.

"What's up?" Seb asked.

"Nothing," Sam thought earlier that this man couldn't get any more perfect, but then he goes and adds a whole new level. "So, you heard everything I said?"

"Yep, everything" Seb put on a cheeky smile.

"Oh my god," Sam said, putting her hand over her mouth.

The nurse standing there was intrigued now. "What did she say?"

"I think she said a lot more than what she remembers," Seb said with a big smile.

The nurse and Sam looked at him, stunned.

CHAPTER 31

"I FORBID IT!"

Mike was in the Hub conference room, pacing back and forth. The new intel he received put him on edge. Now he was waiting for everyone to show. He had called this emergency meeting to pass on all the details the Water Tiger had relayed to him.

Eventually they were all sitting at the table, all with the look of 'what bad news are we receiving now.'

"Hi, I called this meeting because I just heard from Water Tiger. We have some good news and lots of bad news. Good news first; Seb is awake and responding well."

That news brought a round of cheers and whistles from his friends.

"Now all the bad news. First, Water Tiger is in a new location in China. At a coastal town called Dandong, near the Nth Korean border. Ab, you were right. They are planning to spread the virus and blame it on China. That will raise world awareness and condemnation, provoking them into a war against Russia and the United States. He doesn't have any specifics on what towns they are hitting, but he said the US, Russia, and possibly England were mentioned."

Mike paused to let it all sink in before he continued.

"He said that this is the last staging area, and we have a timeframe of 8 weeks max before it all turns into a shit show. The building is an old cannery and is being outfitted as a full-blown lab for the smoking gun effect. He has 30 guards, 20 on at any time. Everyone, the workers doing repairs, the Chinese soldiers on guard, everyone is one of his guards. The security isn't hi tech because they don't want anything to make people think it's a setup. We need to log everything that's happening and start putting it all together shortly if we are going to have any chance of stopping this."

"We need to leave immediately," Smith said.

"I agree; if we can get footage of them building the lab and the dates, we could prove that they developed the virus beforehand," Ab added.

155

"Yes, I agree. It's a brilliant strategy, Ab," Colonel Briggs agreed.

"Is there anything else, Mike?" Art asked.

"Yes, there is, something significant. Art, he has also informed me they have targeted you for assassination at the UN meeting."

That news brought an uproar from everyone. From calls, well, you're just not going. Is he sure? They wouldn't dare! But they all knew they would. They tried to assassinate the United States President.

"How, Mike. Did he say?" Art asked.

"They didn't give him details, but it sounds like a sniper from a distance. While you're giving an address to the press afterward," Mike said solemnly.

Ab stands up. "Well, that's it, I forbid it! You're just not going!"

Everyone agreed, but Katelyn and Art sat silently. Katelyn looked at Art. "You're going, aren't you?" She asked. Everyone fell silent.

"Yes, I must. Otherwise, it looks like I have something to hide; I don't wish to get shot, so I would appreciate any ideas in the next 24 hours to prevent that; it would be greatly appreciated."

CHAPTER 32

CALL TO ACTION

Linwood Cashdon paced the oval office floor as he waited for the President to get off the phone. He called this emergency meeting between himself, the Secretary of State, the Armed Forces Chief, and the President. Finally, the President hangs up the phone.

"Ok, Linwood, what's so important that we all needed to be here?"

"Sir, I have the lab reports back about the virus. It is as we feared; it has been man made to be deadlier than the other Covid variants."

All the men in the room uttered a "My God," except Chad Langdon, who stood coolly and calmly in the corner, invisible.

"But Sir, there's more. The latest from WHO is that it has broken the barrier in South Africa. Now, we have two new containment sites. One in the port of Primorsk in Russia and cases in San Francisco General Hospital. Sir, we're under attack. My contacts in WHO said the Russian government were sent the same results as us. The Russians would also know that it's manmade."

"But who? Why?" the President asked.

"The Russians wouldn't be stupid enough; they would know we would retaliate when we found out it was them. And to release it in their own port. Unlikely. A terrorist attack maybe?" the Defence Chief said.

"Are there any terrorist groups that have this kind of sophistication? It's not as if you can whip this up in your backyard kitchen." The Secretary of State questioned.

"None that we have ever been informed of. Nth Korea or even China?" the Chief of staff offered.

"China maybe, but that's not what we need to do first. Linwood issue and order to bring up all emergency plans for San Francisco, give that hospital everything it needs and lock it down. Send out all the medical data we have through the country and just call it a new variant for now. We don't want to start a panic again. Also, contact the FBI; we want every available body tracking down the first contact, and let's see where it leads before we point fingers. You all have your own assets; time to shake the trees; we need every eye on this." the President ordered.

The men all jumped to their feet and responded with a "Yes sir!" and turned and left the room. The President had spoken. That's why this man was elected; he was a doer, not a talker.

The President paced in his office. Finally, he stopped and looked at Chad.

"Want to swap jobs, Chad?"

"No, Sir, you can't shoot for shit."

The President couldn't help himself but chuckle.

"Germ warfare, it's something countries only talk about. No one's stupid enough to do it."

"A new world, Sir, but you got this,"

"I do?"

"Yes, you survived an assassination attack that lasted all night."

"That was you, not me. I'd be dead if it wasn't for you!"

"And a bunch of ballsy Australians?" Chad offered.

"Hahaha, True. How does that help me now?" The President asked.

"You survived that night because you knew who to rely on when the time came. You have a folder of reports and a bunch of maybes and innuendoes. Make the right choice on who to speak to, Sir."

"Are you sure you wouldn't like this job?" the President asked jokingly.

"No, Sir, you're too slow to take a bullet for me." Chad stood there motionless, with no expression.

"Ouch, tell me how you really feel."

The President heads to his phone. "Get me Director Spelling!"

CHAPTER 33

MISSING

The Eiffel Barista and Patisserie in Washington, DC were only a 10 minutes' walk from the capital. A busy café/Bar that serviced a lot of capital hills elite. Over the years, many deals have been struck over drinks here. Stylish décor and overpriced drinks kept the riff-raff away. White-collar snobbery flicked through the morning paper to read the shock headlines hitting the press worldwide this morning. 'Covid-19 MAN variant.' The World Press has released a statement from the Russian government that the new Covid-19 strain hitting the world is manmade. Tests from the World Health Organisation show the new strain was genetically engineered. The strain, now named MAN, spreads faster and has a higher mortality rate.

Reports say that the vaccines and boosters are ineffectual against it, as the virus has been engineered to bypass around them.

Leading WHO specialist Professor Instan Glasby says we can also construct a vaccine for this strain, but it will take time as they have to go back to square one and pull the whole virus apart again.

The paper says, Who, Is responsible? The Russian government has vowed a swift retaliation once they have identified the culprits. They have identified four sites: South Africa, the United States, Russia, and tests are being conducted in England, waiting to be confirmed.

Fredrick Nessler sat there smiling as if he was reading the funnies in the newspaper. Others, reading the same story, looked like Armageddon was coming. The café Eiffel was Nessler's favourite stop when visiting DC. Now he was waiting on Linwood Cashdon, chief of staff at the capitol hill. He didn't mind if he was a little late because he hadn't got to the funnies in his paper yet.

He enjoyed one of the outside sidewalk tables as he opened his laptop. Punching away on the keys and sipping his Chai Latte, a raised voice caught his attention.

"Where is she? Where is the whore?" a pretty woman in bland office attire was yelling.

"Who are you talking about?"

"I'm talking about the little whore you meet here; don't play stupid. I know what you've been up to!"

"I'm not meeting anyone," the man in the, 'I'm trying to climb the ladder,' suit was saying.

"Look, I found her pictures on your phone. Damn naked tramp; who is she? First, I will poke her eyes out, then yours."

Nessler enjoyed the free show with his latte, and he didn't notice the woman standing beside his table, who placed her phone down next to his laptop.

The scene raged as one threw accusations and the other useless denials. 'She had the photos.' Finally, Nessler, bored with it all, went to turn back to his computer when the lady beside his table addressed him.

"Do you think we should contact the police?" she asked

"No, she will end up with most of his money in the divorce settlement," Nessler said.

"True," the lady laughed, picked up her phone, and left.

As Nessler turned back to his computer, he thought he saw in his peripheral vision the download light flicker once, only once.

Being a man of great suspicion, he looked around and focused on the woman who was standing next to him. He saw Linwood Cashdon approaching, and it left him with the choice to go with his gut feeling or not. The woman hadn't turned around to look back.

Marcy was shaking; she hadn't done anything like this before. She did all her hacking from home on her computer. Just then, she saw a familiar face: Chief of Staff Linwood Cashdon. Could he be involved? Is he meeting with Nessler? Don't turn around, Marcy, she said to herself. You got what you came for; just keep walking. But her mind was ticking over. Just a glimpse. She turned, and she turned with her phone, ready to snap pics.

Just as Linwood came to the table, Nessler saw the woman turn with her phone.

"I think we've been made; just pretend I'm offering you my table," Nessler said in a hushed voice.

"Oh my god, I think he saw me," she said to herself. "Oh my god, oh my god," did he? Is he following me? I need to know. Marcy's mind was fighting with itself. She was really shaking now. 'Don't turn around, don't turn around.' She turned around! To her horror, Nessler had his phone on and took pictures of her. She picked up the pace and tried to weave through the crowds, but stayed out of quiet alleyways. Marcy turned again and noticed Nessler wasn't following her. Relieved but still shaking uncontrollably, she knew she was spotted. Marcy pulled out her phone and sent all the info and photos to the group. 'I am not doing this ever again,' she thought.

Nessler finds a quiet spot in the park to make a call.

"Hello, this is Nessler. I need facial recognition on the images I just sent. I want an address, and I want it now. Ready the Black team for interception."

Nessler walks off. "I must contact the others," he says to himself.

****

Hours later

"Hi Lexi, these are the files and photos we got off of Nessler's laptop. There's a lot of useful info, but we haven't cracked all the files. We thought you might have a go at them."

"Yes, I will. This is great work. How's Marcy?"

"Shaken up a bit at the moment."

"Why?" Lexi asked, concerned.

"She was the one who got the info. We created a diversion while she placed her phone in range and cloned his laptop while it was open."

"Very clever, but why is Marcy shaken?" Lexi enquired.

"Well, she thinks Nessler was on to her; when she took a picture of Nessler and Linwood Cashdon, she thinks he saw her because he ended up taking a picture of her."

"What!!! Where is she?"

"She said she was heading home; why?"

"Get someone over to her now and put her in hiding. This guy is lethal. When he finds out who she is, she's dead. Now get moving! Let me know when you have her."

Later that night

"Lexi, we can't find her; she's gone."

"Oh no... Marcy," Lexi broke down crying.

Also, that night

Director Spelling sat at his desk in his home office. He has been in this situation thousands of times in his career, and he never gets used to it. His Black ops team was connected to him via comms and helmet video feed. Tonight, they were breaking the rules again. The CIA doesn't have the mandate to operate in the United States, but sometimes, shit happens.

Tonight, it doesn't get any worse. They have to invade the house of Chief of Staff Linwood Cashdon to find evidence to prove his complicity of conspiracy and treason.

As the team moved into the house, they moved into set rooms searching for hidden files. The security was disabled; they had a small window to find something while the Chief of staff was at a staff meeting. Moving through the room in the dark, the search continued at a pace.

Chief of staff Cashdon's phone beeped as one media staff addressed the room. He quickly glances at his phone and quickly gets to his feet, and excuses himself to leave the room to make a call.

"It is, as you said; they are in my house," Cashdon says.

"I will activate our team; there is a clean-up crew on standby also," Fredrick Nessler informs him.

There were screams from a woman in the background.

"What was that?" Cashdon queries concerned.

"Just getting more information about who is following us. Don't concern yourself. I will let you know what happens in your house."

The line goes dead. 'I will have to push our schedule forward faster before it all goes pear-shaped.'

****

Spellings team reports nothing found so far. All downstairs areas cleared, and now they're heading upstairs. Once again, moving quietly, swiftly, and efficiently, they left nothing unturned.

Spelling sat in his office, watching it all unfold. Then, suddenly, a black van pulled into the driveway. Spellings team always has a camera watching the front in case someone turns up.

"Van, incoming." Spelling informs the team.

"Roger that," Roger replied.

"6 Specs, moving fast. They are after you. Evac immediately,"

"On me, team."

As the team formed in the main bedroom, Roger issued his commands.

"Toby, window exit. Lorri with me."

Lorri and Roger covered the door as the team made their exit through the window.

"We need time," Lorri says, talking to Roger.

"Yeah."

Lorri grabs a flash-bang grenade off her vest.

"Love me," Lorri asks Roger.

"Always Babe,"

Director Spelling yells over the comms. "No, Lorri, evac!"

"Sorry, boss, have to," Lorri returns.

Lorri opens the door and throws the grenade into the hallway. As soon as she hears the explosion, she moves into the hallway with speed, with Roger right on her back.

Delta forced trained the two knew each other's moves as they started firing. Taking down the first two Spec ops, coming up the stairs. The other 4 Spec ops open fire up towards Lorri and Roger, ripping through the rails and hallway walls. Lorri and Roger hit the floor as the return fire raged.

"Well, might as well piss them right off." Lorri grabs a fragment grenade off her vest.

"Really?" Roger asks.

"Cover me,"

Roger pops up and unloads his magazine at the remaining enemy soldiers. During Rogers firing, Lorri rolls the grenade down the steps. The explosion destroys the bottom steps and rails, sending wood splinters around the first-floor hallway.

Roger covers Lorri as she makes her way to the bedroom to exit. As she enters, she notices the room has been ripped apart from the firefight. She turns and covers the door as Roger comes through. Roger also sees the wrecked room, but something catches his eye. On a shelf in the room was an ash's urn. Now the urn is lying on the floor smashed, with the ashes spread all over the floor. Roger notices something shiny and makes a grab for it as he goes to the window. Grabbing the rope and hurling himself out the window, he traverses the rope quickly. Next, Lorri is at the window and goes to move down the rope. Just then, the bullets started flying through the door towards the window, and Lorri was hit in the shoulder. The bullet's force swung Lorri around, but she hangs onto the rope with one hand. She drops and to the ground as Roger grabs her, and they make their way out as the rest of the team covers the window.

In the back of the van, Roger works on Lorri's shoulder to stem the bleeding. Two streets away, they pass two police cars speeding in the house's direction.

"Well, that's going to be hard to explain if they're not out?" Max, who was driving, said.

"What did you grab?" Lorri asked through clenched teeth. Roger puts his hand in his pocket and pulls out a flash drive.

"It better be more than just porn pics of his mother," Lorri said.

"Well, that could be worth a few dollars," Roger laughs.

Next morning

"Lexi, I'm sorry. The police found Marcy this morning in an abandoned warehouse. She's dead. They believe she was tortured. They sent an anonymous tip to the police. It's a message to stay away."

Lexi's world went black. She received the news that she had been fearing. Marcy's dead. Her mind was catching fire, and the edges were burning. She will burn everyone now, everyone.

"Aaah!!" Lexi screamed, picked up her chair, and threw it through a plate-glass wall. Pieces of shatterproof glass filled the room from the implosion. Doby stood; he wanted to comfort her, but he knew she wasn't finished.

Lexi bent over, fists clenched, veins in her neck protruding; she lets out a blood-curdling scream of anguish, a sound of a soul being torn.

She collapses on the floor, crying. During this terrible time of sadness, she also found true love, her soul mate. Doby knelt on the floor and hugged her; he said the most romantic words she had ever heard.

"Don't worry, we will get revenge."

CHAPTER 34

THE SETUP

It was all over the news. The Russian government issued a press release stating that the new strain of covid-19 was contrived in a lab. Now there was no hiding; the world has ramped up.

There hasn't been a local or international sector that hasn't been affected by the announcement. Of course, it didn't help that the Russians said they would hunt the perpetrators down.

Already the President raised the DEFCON level up with Russian putting their forces on high alert. Everybody is on edge. He had the Chief of the Armed forces bringing plans for multiple scenarios of armed response depending on who they find is responsible.

Over 10 ambassadors had informed the Secretary of State about potential links to the virus. It was all building into a nightmare scenario. Now he has an urgent meeting with Chief of Staff Cashdon; it's never-ending.

As Chief of Staff Linwood Cashdon entered the Oval Office, he had the armed forces' Chief in tow for their meeting. But unexpectedly, the President had called CIA director Spelling to sit in. This international incident needed the CIA involved; this is their backyard. If any kids aren't playing nice, they usually know.

As they all sat, the President got straight to the point. "Linwood, everybody is going mad. So, what is so important that we needed to hear this straight away?"

"Well, Mr. President, this communique has come through from the Russian defence minister. It couldn't wait because it is of the gravest situation. The Russians believe they have found evidence of the perpetrators of the Man virus. It's not good, Sir; it's China."

"China!" the President and Director Spelling said in unison.

"It doesn't make sense?" Director Spelling added.

"Yes, I agree, Damien; why? To what advantage? What evidence do they have to be so certain?" The President said, not convinced of what he's hearing.

"First, they have been following the same channels that we have, but they got there first. They backtracked shipping manifests from points of origin of the outbreak centres. Then they used satellite tracking in suspected areas. There was an area in Dandong. They sent a spy in to have a look, and this is what they found." Cashdon handed the President a folder.

As the President opened the folder, inside were photographs of the Dandong site, but it was the first photo that shook him. The first was of Ji-tai-Jin, the Water Tiger, talking with a Chinese Captain. They deliberately placed the image of the Water Tiger on top to shock the President into action. After his assassination attempt on the President last year at the ARK, his was not a face he will forget for a while.

"That bastard! It doesn't surprise me he's involved." The President snapped.

As he flicked through the images, the hook had been taken. Now it had to be set.

"So, it definitely looks like some kind of lab hidden in a cannery... But it's not enough,"

"I agree, Mr. President; this is China. We can't go around accusing a superpower of infecting the world without knowing more." Director Spelling added.

"I totally agree with you both, and so does Russia. They want to hold a joint mission to check out the building." Cashdon said.

"Are you mad man! A joint mission with Russia, that's absurd," Spelling yelled.

"That's what they suggested, Sir. US Delta teams, delivered on a Russian sub." Cashdon continued.

Spelling continued his barrage. "Oh yeah, they'll drop them off and then leave them there for the Chinese. Sorry, Mr. President, but Russia finds this lab so quickly, and now they want a joint mission with us with our boots on the ground. It all sounds very convenient."

"I agree, Damien; what do you have?" the President asked.

"We're still double-checking the traces to points of origins. That's what's makes me suspicious of this intel." Spelling said.

"I agree... But I can't sit on this. If it turns out to be true and we hesitate, the country wouldn't forgive us. So, Chief, make it happen. But clarify that I don't want so much as a fingerprint left in China."

"Mr. President!" the Director protested.

"I know Damien, but we aren't going to war, just making sure who we're fighting against. Chief, if Water Tiger is at the cannery, bring him back alive. I want to know who hired him. He's just a hitman for hire. Someone's paying the bills."

"It will be done, Mr. President," The Chief replied.

"Ok, gentlemen, that's all for now; keep pushing. I want our own answers."

As Director Spelling was getting up, he glanced over to the Head of the Secret Service, Chad Langdon. Their eyes met, and both knew they had to get this information to Damani.

CHAPTER 35

HOMECOMING

'Weird' was the only way Sam could think to put it. She had an enormous sense of relief and a feeling of safety because she was home again. Back at Byron Bay with the sound of waves crashing at the beach nearby. Why was it weird? Because she was watching a nurse set up monitors and emergency equipment in her spare bedroom. Watching a close friend with tubes and wires hanging off him, and she was feeling relief. And why was she feeling safe? This was the house that 6 months ago, a group of terrorists crashed in, ready to kill her and her family. 'Weird' was the only word she could come up with.

The nurse was checking the monitors, also making sure they were all set correctly. Also making, all the tubes are inserted and functioning as they should. Her patient Sebastian seemed in good spirits as she checked his pulse. He should be off all intravenous feeds in a week and should be recovering well, so long as no infection sets in.

She thinks about how being a private nurse is far safer than working in the local hospital; with Covid around. Now they're saying they produced the new Man Covid in a lab, insane. If they had to work with wards full of infected, they wouldn't even think of doing such a thing. How long before it reaches Australia? I hope they bomb the shit out of whoever did this.

"So, doc, will I live?" Seb asked.

"Yes, and I'm not a doctor, so stop calling me that." The nurse protested in good humour.

"Sorry, Doc,"

"Ahh,"

"I know how you feel; I have had a lifetime of it," Sam says to the nurse.

"And she loved every minute of it. So, Doc, when can I surf again?"

"Never if you call me Doc again. You won't be hitting the waves for months. Even with your body healing well on the outside, the

168

damage to the insides will take a lot longer. From your charts, the surgery they did was amazing, but they had to reconstruct and reconfigure parts of your body. So, it will take time for all that to settle down." She said as she put the chart down.

"So, you're saying next week I can start paddling," Seb joked.

"Augh, why do I bother? Just consider yourself lucky to be in Samantha's home and not in some hospital. And this Art Damani, who is paying your bills, he has authorised me to get you the best rehab workers. Is he your employer?"

"No, a friend."

"Wow, you have some friends. If you don't mind me asking, how did you get shot in the back? Are you law enforcement?"

"No, just a soldier. I was protecting a member of my team."

"You didn't throw yourself in front of them to stop them from getting shot, did you?"

Seb's momentary pause told her she was right.

"Yes, their life was important."

"Wow, I'm looking after a Bona fide hero."

"I'm no hero," Seb said. Just then, Sam turned and left the room.

"You are in my book, Hero."

"No, hero, I would prefer you didn't call me that."

The nurse put on a solemn face, "I'm sorry... HERO! but until you stop calling me Doc, your name now is Hero!"

"You can't do that," Seb protested.

"Oh, yes, I can, Hero. I'll be off and see you this evening. Hero,"

The nurse turned and left the room to Seb, calling out, "Doc, Doc, Doc, Doc." She went downstairs and found Samantha sitting at her kitchen table. She had been crying.

"Everything alright," she asked Sam.

"Yeah, fine," Sam said, trying to act fine.

"I saw his charts; it is a miracle he lived." Sam's eyes watered again, and her bottom lip quivered. "But he's recovering, very well, actually. He will heal well here; he is fortunate to have friends like you willing to open their homes and let him recover in a peaceful environment. It will be good for his soul as well. He's a soldier, so PTSD is something we both have to look out for in him. So, I'm heading off. Now no more tears. It will slow his recovery. I'll be back around tonight at 7pm to monitor him till he goes to sleep."

The nurse stood up and placed her hand on Sam's shoulder. "He's going to be fine." Then, turning and heading for the door, little did she know that was Sam was suffering from PTSD and guilt. She just needed to unburden, but there was no one here, no one.

CHAPTER 36

THE HITMEN

Mike had called a meeting to outlay the next steps of what they should work on with all the new info.

As they all gathered, the mood was light, but Mike knew that was about to change. They were waiting for the last two, Doby and Lexi. Everyone heard the elevator ding at the end of the hall and heard their footsteps approaching. They weren't suspecting the change in the two as they entered. Doby came through; first, it was Doby but a 'new' Doby. He was still wearing his Marvel-style T-shirt, but it was now tucked into a pair of black jeans held up by a black leather belt with studs. But it was his swagger that completed the image. This Doby didn't seem shy or awkward; he was confident, he had a purpose.

Then Lexi walked in, after the last few months of getting used to the 'new' Lexi, business wear, clean-cut Lexi, with respectable clothes with sensible shoes. Now, the old Lexi was back. All black makeup, clothes, the works, but once again, it wasn't just the outfit; she had swagger, presence, and a steel determination.

As the pair strode into the conference room, Mike tried to find the correct label for what he was seeing in these two. That's it! Gangsters, no, Hitmen. They looked like they were about to unleash hell on someone.

'God, I hope they can keep it together. We can't afford anyone going rogue.' Mike thought.

"Thank you all for coming so quickly. First, Lexi, we are all so sorry for what has happened to your friend, and we're all here for you." Mike said sincerely.

"Thanks, Mike, thank you all. She was a great person. Loved animals, a genuine believer in what she did. She was always helping the little people. She always fought the good fight. So, on that note, Doby and I have a favour to ask you all. We would like Fredrick

Nessler to be kept alive and not killed in any of our Ops. Leave him to us!"

The room was quiet till Colonel Briggs spoke. "You know that may not always be possible, Lexi, but I'm willing to support you in this."

"Thanks, Colonel,"

Mike looked around, and all agreed. "Ok, that's fine with us, Lexi, Doby." 'God help Nessler if Lexi gets a hold of him,' Mike thought.

"Ok, next news. Seb is recovering nicely. Thanks to Art, they have transferred him to our home in Byron Bay with a full-time nurse, and Sam's looking after him."

"Poor Sam," Smith said. Everyone agreed and had a laugh, except Mike. Sam had been quiet on his last two calls to her, seeming very distant. He wished he could help get her through whatever was going on with her.

"Ok, now all the not-so-happy news. On a semi-good front, we received intelligence from Director Spelling. His team infiltrated Chief of Staff Cashdon's home, looking for information on his involvement. But they were expecting it. A battle ensued one of Spellings team got hit, but as a stroke of luck, they found a flash drive as they were exiting. It's encrypted, so Lexi and Doby, you're up."

"A pleasure," Lexi said happily.

"Next, we had our timetable of 8 weeks, but new information has sped that up again. Director Spelling was called to a meeting where Cashdon and Chief of the Armed Forces General Hagart, who we think is also involved, showed the President photos of the Dandong facility. But more incredible, the photos were of Water Tiger talking to Chinese soldiers at the lab."

"Holy shit!" Thomas had finally joined the conversation, being contented to just listen. "With what happened here last year, as soon as the President sees the Water Tiger, he would have freaked and bought into it straight away."

"That's exactly what happened, Thomas," Mike informed them.

"A very shrewd plan. In my calculations, I believe we have lost at least two weeks. Because the evidence would have to be authenticated. Then discussed, then threatened, then sanctions, then military action. It could happen in 6 weeks, but diplomacy is still the wild card here to stall." Ab informed them.

Everyone just stopped and stared at Ab. "What? It's what I do." Ab said.

"Geez, you need a hobby," Katelyn added, which got everyone laughing again.

"Ok, now the bad news."

"What? There's more, Rosi," asked astonished.

"Yes, I was saving the important stuff till last. President Edwin has authorised a joint US-Russia military op to investigate the Dandong lab."

"Holy shit, those two never work together," Smith said, shocked.

"I must agree with Zikmund; for President Edwin to authorise such a move, he either feels strongly about the evidence or has been forced into agreeing with it to save face. Either way, it means the same for us, less time." Colonel Briggs stated.

"We don't know when it is, but we need to get there first. First, we have to organise Art's trip to the UN. Director Spelling is helping with the FBI, so they are taking the threat seriously. Thomas and Ab have put together a program that shows the front of the UN building where Art will make his speech to the press. It shows every available spot for a professional sniper to shoot from and the angles. Now we can't stake out every spot. But, many of the areas have the same access points, such as the Highrise foyers. Tyson and Rosi have developed robot pigeons to reflect the sunlight and block other shooting angles as an added interference. There will be surveillance birds, the FBI, and ourselves on the ground to apprehend the shooter before he takes a shot. Immediately after the speech, we evac to Dandong to infiltrate the lab. This could be a wet job, so I will need your best out there with Seb missing. Thomas, you are promoted to 2IC for this mission. You will control all the security and are watching our backs. Also,"

"Geez, there's more," Smith whined.

"Also, Director Fleming needs the info from our raid on Dandong to him immediately. He is going to Russia to talk to an old friend about what's happening there. If we can't halt both countries, it may not stop at all."

"Has the Water Tiger been notified that they're using him?"

"Yes, I informed him. He said thank you for the heads up, but he's not leaving till we have the verification we all need." Mike added.

"Team, can you stay back? I need to pass on some training info. Oh, and Tyson, I need a word also, please."

Everyone went off on their acquired jobs. Art and Ab were discussing details of his UN trip. Then, Doby and Lexi jumped straight on the computer to decipher the files from Cashdon's flash drive.

"You wanted to see me, Mike?" Tyson asked.

"Yes, I did ...raptors, really. What's with that?"

"Just a bit of fun. They were just something for security at night, but it seems the boys have given them a whole new life," Tyson said.

"Yes, the boys. You have them on security details, their children."

"It just happened. The boy's gaming skills made them the most qualified to operate them. They are safe when they go out. The Major is with them all the time."

"And when the Major is involved in an incident?" Mike pressed.

"Oh, they're really safe. Art has a specially built cage on the truck with bulletproof glass."

"Tyson, if you need a bulletproof cage, then obviously they're not safe," Mike stated.

Tyson stood there, stunned. Mike was right. He hadn't thought of that.

"I'll talk to the Major tomorrow about it. In the future, run these kinds of things by me first, Ok?"

"Yeah, sure, Mike. Like I said, it just kind of happened. They're naturals at it. The staff and the animals love them."

"Ok, thanks, Tyson."

Mike moved over to where the team was standing.

"We have four days before we leave for the states for Arts UN address. The Major has asked if we would join him and his team at a new training facility to help with a new elite team. I think we could use this time to try out the new combo without Seb."

"What's your thinking, Mike?" Katelyn asked.

"Jedi will spot and control all the surveillance, so he's our guide. Three-man squad, in and out. It could get wet; we can't afford to sneak around this time. We need surveillance inside and out. They set it up to be a real lab, so there must be the virus there. We have to get in and out before Delta rolls in and trashes the place. Then we add it to the other intelligence we have on the other sites, and hopefully, that's enough. With the information Ab, Doby and Lexi have gained, we can then make our move on the President. So, we depart tomorrow at 06:00."

The team came back with a "roger" and then went on their way. Mike saw Tyson and Rosi over talking to Doby and Lexi.

"Tyson, Rosi. Do you have a minute?" Mike asked. They excused themselves from Lexi and Doby and came over to the conference table. "Please sit, guys; I want to throw a tech question at you."

Tyson laughed, "You Mike, Mr. I like old school; what's on your mind?"

"Do you guys know what a Ghillie suit is?" Mike asked.

"It's a camo suit that snipers wear to hide in grassy areas," Tyson asked.

"Yes, even though many soldiers wear them, but yes, correct. Ok, is it possible to make a Ghillie suit that reacts like Loki and can change to the surroundings?"

Rosi jumped in quickly, "Yes!"

"And no," Tyson added.

"Which is it?" Mike asked, confused.

"Ok, to explain it, you have to first understand, Loki. To make Loki's optic fibres change to all environments, he has to have a lot of information. That's why he has what we call feedback sensors. As he walks somewhere, he records all the information of where he just walked. So, in his data banks, he has the information of everything around him to work out a blend. He has that processing power." Tyson informed Mike.

"Now, technically, we could build a suit, but you would also have to carry enough power and a powerful enough computer processor to make it happen. You would need 360 degrees camera view as well." Rosi added.

"Mike, it's a great idea, but something that would take a long time to figure out."

"That's great, so in your spare time maybe," Mike smiled.

"Sure, we will have a look at it," Rosi said.

"Thanks, guys; it would be another item that could save lives. Ok, I'll leave you with your work." After that, Mike got up and headed back to his room. It was time to check in with Sam.

CHAPTER 37

"OLD AFRICAN SAYING"

Another day in paradise. The sun was shining brightly. The views of the surrounding mountains, the smell of flowering plants. The threat of World War 3, they nearly killed a team member on a mission. A wife away, possibly suffering from PTSD. Children running around with giant robot raptors in life-threatening situations ... just another day in paradise.

The transport that was taking Mike's team pulled into what looked like an abandoned industrial site. Five buildings scattered around the area, from office blocks to large sheds for huge vehicles. Mike's first thought was, 'awesome,' an impressive site for different drills.

The team dispersed and started unloading the crates from the back of the transport. Mike saw there were a lot of boxes with 'explosives' marked on the trunks. Obviously, Jedi has got some things to show the Majors team.

Mike saw the Major talking to one of his team and headed over to greet him.

"Major,"

"Major... this could be a Major event," the Major said, laughing.

Mike joined him in the humour.

"I see your men have excellent kit."

"Yes, Mr. Damani, spared no expense making sure they had everything they needed. Now they just need someone to show them how to use it properly."

"A couple of days of training, shooting, and blowing up shit sounds like my kind of fun," Mike said.

"Mine too," the Major added.

"Ok, gather your men in the shed, and we'll go through some safety basics first."

"Roger that," The Major and Sherlock headed back to their teams. It was time to go to work.

After a lengthy safety course, both teams geared up and started live-fire training. One hour on the shooting range told Sherlock that the Major had trained his men exceptionally well. Then next was showing them the correct procedures for clearing a building with hostages. This wasn't as easy as some thought. Frustration builds in some men as the same errors were repeated over and over. Finally, Sherlock pulled them aside to address the issue.

Both teams gathered outside and sat down together like a school assembly. Waiting intently for the principal to speak. Well, most of them, like the naughty boy in every class; Smith watched some birds singing in a tree.

"Guys, your skills are fine. Excellent for the short time you have been training. It's your mindset. You're looking at this as a drill; it's not; it's practicing life. You go about it as, ok; we have to go in and shoot all the bad guys in the building. That's NOT how you should think of it. Your team is your family; you eat, sleep and live together, so the way to look at this is, 1/ My job is to help my family and myself get through this building alive. 2/ Kill any hostiles in the building to achieve goal one. 3/ Complete the set objective after succeeding in goal one. Do you see it's all about your team? Keep each other alive. If you're here because it's a job, you are best to leave now; you will get yourself or a team member killed. Now let's try this again and see how you go."

The Majors' men went through the building without a flaw, covering each other's backs and working sharply as a team. The Major was very impressed that a mindset readjustment could have instant results; the Major was no idiot either; he listened and learned. Himself taking in everything Sherlock said and did to improve his leadership qualities.

The day flew past fast as the team broke for lunch and then split up into groups for personal training with each of Mike's team. Next, Jedi took members of the team for explosives training. That was a big hit, with everyone wanting to blow shit up. Techniques of blowing through different doors and how the room you're in can be dangerous for any explosion.

Then there was Smith and the shooting range training. He showed them how to improve their accuracy, how to set up their vests for faster reloads, and how to reload fast while rolling.

Next was Steel, another popular one with the men, hand to hand combat. None of the men seemed to care about being thrown around by her. She seemed to gain a lot more respect once she went into knives training, with the soldiers not willing to take on a woman who could throw knives that accurately. And when taking part in the self-defence drills, no matter how many times the men blocked her moves, she always seemed to pull a knife from somewhere to counter.

Sherlock took the second in commands and taught them as 2 Planks would have taught them, "you're the big brother, your job is to make sure everyone is doing their job properly, and make sure they are listening to dad, the commander. His job with the commander is to make sure the technical plans are possible with the physical abilities of the group; his job is to inform the commander that there is no point trying to take on a tank when your men have pistols." That brought a laugh from the men.

That night, the teams all bunked down in one of the large transport sheds. Sherlock and the Major went for a walk to discuss the day's training and what was on for tomorrow.

"I have a question to ask?" Mike said to the Major.

"Shoot,"

"My boys and this patrol business. I don't think it is safe for them in those situations, their only boys."

The Major laughed heartily. "Boys! I wish some of my men had the nuts of those two. I haven't come across two more confident kids in my life, and I have fought with children in battles against Somalia."

"Yes, I keep forgetting it wasn't long ago that you both were at each other's throats."

"You talk about safe Mike; what is safe? Nothing really changed. Yes, sure, we have the bigger fences now. We have a larger, more effective security team, and we deal with dangerous animals inside and out. But we still have the world's biggest target painted on us. The more we succeed, the bigger the target gets. I only assume Mr. Damani understands that, too. So, if you really want safety, send them home. But don't blame me when they run away, stow away on a boat to Africa to get back to Uncle Major and their raptors." The Major went into one of his giant toothy grins and bellowed laughter like Santa Claus.

"Don't worry, Mike, they won't run away. They would just ring Mr. Damani, and he would fly them back on his personal jet. Oh, that reminds me of something; I need your signatures on some forms."

"My signature, what for?" Mike asked, surprised.

"To open bank accounts for the boys. He wants to put them on the payroll. He said they work as hard as anyone here, and they deserve to be paid the same as any worker for their skills."

"That's unnecessary."

"Boss's orders,"

"Fine, but if they earn more than me, I'm retiring, and they can look after me." Both men started laughing.

"And what about Sam?"

"Well, there's another problem, too. Sam is going through something, but won't share it over the phone."

"Mike, let me give you some advice now. If you don't figure out how to live with both teams. You will only end up with one. Old African saying."

"Old African saying?"

"Ok, new African saying. I'm a legend now. I'm supposed to come up with philosophical shit." They both burst out laughing.

"Thanks, Major Legend, good advice."

For the rest of the walk, they went over the significant results from today's drills. After that, the Major said he wanted to continue the same exercises to strengthen the basics with the team.

As Mike returned to his room, he picked up the satellite phone and dialled. He couldn't remember what time it was there. Was it still yesterday, or was it tomorrow? The phone rings.

"Hello,"

"Hey, red, what are you up to?"

"Hi Mike, just making lunch for Seb."

"How is the patient?"

"Getting stronger and more impatient every day."

"Is there any food left?"

"No, it's a constant battle to get the nurse to bring over supplies as she comes. She can't believe he eats so much and sleeps like a baby."

Mike laughed, "Yep, that's Seb alright. Glad to hear he is recovering."

"He's been moaning like a lost baby whale to go for an ocean swim."

"Sounds like he's a hand full."

"No, the nurse and I have him covered. How's everything there?"

"We're just doing a 2-day training stint with the Major's team before we head to the states for Art's UN address."

"My God! He's still doing that, even with the assassination attempt planned?"

"Yes, he said he has to. We have done everything we can to assist. Spelling has brought in the FBI as well."

"I know you will, Mike, but it still seems an enormous risk."

"It is, but how are you?"

"I'm chugging along, still not sleeping great, but hey, you can't have everything. How's the boys?"

"Don't change the subject; it may help to talk about it?"

"That's rich coming from you."

"Yeah, but I'm beyond help," Mike joked.

"Well, now you know what I go through, and I know a little of what you go through. Is that what you do?"

"What?" Mike asked, concerned.

"Risk your own life by jumping in front of each other?"

"Yes, if we have to, but it usually doesn't come to that if we've trained well, why?"

"I understand it, and I don't understand it. Hey, it's the doorbell; the nurse is here. Give my best to the boys and everyone there. One last question, the nurse asked. Will they allow Seb to go back to the team?"

"Yes, possibly, it depends on the extent of the injury. But if Seb can't pass the medical to return. That will be it; they won't let him continue."

"That will kill him!"

"Yes, it will."

"Ok, talk later, take care... love you."

"Love you too," Mike said.

The line went dead. The weight of so much more is now on top of everything else. What did Colonel Briggs call it? ... an easy gig.

CHAPTER 38

SAVIOUR

"More apes! Seriously." Dan, the ARK's head game warden, said exasperated.

"Yes, sorry Dan, they are next on the list to move in to the ARK Hilton." Doc Mc Tavish informs Dan.

"What happened to the African jungle elephants? I thought they were next?"

"Mr Dan, I'm sorry. One has fallen ill and can't be moved until we can make sure it has no diseases." A member of the Mosh Pit crew says.

"Dan, you'll love them. They're a cute little Sumatran orangutang family."

"Stop with the cutesy voice, Doc. You know my stance on apes." Dan says.

"It was worth a go. So, you're fine with everything?" Doc Mc Tavish said.

"Yes, I will do my job, as always. Even for apes."

"Mr Dan, may I come with you to check the orangutang enclosure? I would like to get some photos and video for the park's website."

"Yes, certainly. You can help me with the placing of the gun turrets." Dan said in a straight voice.

The officer looked blankly at the Doc. "???"

"I'll explain to you on the way back to the office. You're probably the only one in the ARK who hasn't heard of the second coming of the 'Planet of the Apes' saga." The Doc said.

"Ha, Ha" Dan replied to the Doc's comment.

"Catch you later, Dan." The Doc said as she walked back to their transport.

****

As the adapted Ark van bounced along the dirt-track the boy's eyes were soaking everything in. This was something new, they liked new.

"Major, what is this area again?" Aidan asked curiously.

"It's an outside plains area. It's one of the first areas set up. It has everything, water food, shelter and an area big enough for the animals to feel free." The Major advised.

"Then why are we here, if it's all set up?" Oliver asked.

"We're here as 'Tactical support' for Mr Donohue here. Terrence, would you like to explain to the boys what you're planning on doing."

Terrence Donohue is a member of the 'Mosh Pit'. The mixed group of Wildlife rescue organisations and ARK staff. Terrence is part of the marketing/public relations group. A quiet man who has spent years behind a computer, not roaming the plains of Somalia.

"Well boys. Do you know what an Eco system is?" Terrence asked.

"Yes," the boys replied.

"The Mosh Pit is looking at introducing two new species to this area."

"Won't that unbalance the Eco system, Mr Donohue?" Oliver asked.

"We don't believe so. We've run the numbers. Checked all the scientific data. The new animals should interact fine together. We think."

"So, you're here to take a survey from the animals, to see if they would like that to happen?" Aidan said cheekily.

"Aidan! Be respectful." the Major said.

"It's alright Major. That was the same response from some in the Mosh pit. Aidan, it's more like this. The ARK doesn't have an infinite amount of money or resources. So, some species will have to learn to bunk together in peace. We will heavily monitor the test with the robotic animals."

"So, what's your role here? And why do you need tactical support from the Raptor Brothers?" The boy's fist pumped each other.

"Mr Donohue is part of the media team. He is here to take video footage of the area before the release of the new animals for a documentary show. So, if you boys behave and keep the swearing down, you may get a part in the documentary. What do you think, Mr Donohue?" the Major said.

"I don't see why not. Two young men running around with robotic raptor guards is certainly unique." Mr Donohue answered.

"Major, you know we don't swear." Aidan says.

"Not in front of your mother." The Major said, laughing.

"Hell no!" Oliver said, laughing.

The team trundled off. A camera feed on the dash collected footage for the doco, and the boys pointed out things of interest as Mr Donahue took footage with a hand-held camera. The team had been out for 3 hours getting footage. The heat was bearable, but the Major's stomach rumbled.

"How are you going Terrence, how much more footage do you need?"

"Just the plains area up ahead is the last area on my list. I would like a panoramic view of the area. Not sure what I'm going to do with it yet, but it doesn't hurt to have it."

The vehicle pulled over to an open area, giving a wondrous view of the open plains and the start of the jungle area.

"This is perfect." Mr Donohue said.

"Boy's stay in the vehicle. This is the last stop before we head back."

Doing as boys do. They took the Major literally. They stayed in the truck but let the raptors out the back to follow the Major and Mr Donohue. The Major turned, hearing something coming up behind him. Seeing the two raptors, he taps on his headset. "I thought I said stay in the truck?"

"We are. The raptors are 'Tactical support'." Aidan says.

The Major dips his head and shakes it. 'Is this what it's like to have teenage children?'

The Major suddenly jerks his head up. He senses something. He heard something? The hackles on the back of his neck rise.

"Terrence, I think it is t... Aagh." In a split second, before he could finish his sentence. A jaguar came flying out of the tall grass and crash tackled the Major. His soldier's instincts kicked in as he rolled with the collision and threw the jaguar off himself as he fell to the ground. The manoeuvre would have worked perfectly, except the Major hit his head vigorously against a protruding rock.

"MAJOR!" the boys yelled together.

Aidan was caught up in the emotion of it all, seeing the Major lying lifeless on the ground as Mr Donohue stood there frozen. Oliver, on the other hand, being his father's son, snapped into action and analysed the situation quickly.

"Mr Donohue, get to the truck. RUN!"

The jaguar was also weighing up his options quickly. Take out the scrawny animal running away or take the fallen beast that could feed his family for a month. He was greedy, take both. As he pulled back onto his hind legs, he launches himself forward towards the escaping prey. Reaching the attacking distance within seconds, he pounces into the air at the back of this fleeing animal. Claws extended, mouth open, jaws ready to snap. Then a thunderous collision from an unknown creature sent him flying off metres away.

"Yes, great work Oliver," Aidan yelled.

A well-timed body slam from Oliver's raptor, winded and sent the jaguar flying off into the dirt, saving Terrence Donohue's life.

This wasn't over yet. The jaguar still wanted his food as the great hulking beast lay still on the ground.

"Aidan, move your raptor up beside mine and defend the Major."

"Roger,"

Now there was a real standoff. Beast versus machines, as the raptors moved forward in front of the deathly still Major. The raptors let out a screech each to convince the jaguar to move on, but this was his catch and he didn't understand the sounds coming from these new creatures.

"Mr Donohue, you need to grab the Major and drag him back to the truck where we can protect him better."

"Ok." Terrence said, snapping out of his immediate shock.

The boys moved the raptors side to side with the movements of the jaguar. When the jaguar moved forward, one raptor moved forward and hissed.

"I can't move him. He's too heavy." Terrence yelled in despair.

"Aidan, protect my arse." Oliver said as he dismounted from their protective bubble.

Oliver left his raptor standing still in front of the Major. While Aidan's raptor tried to block the jaguar's path. Oliver ran to the side of Mr Donohue and grab the Major's arm.

"Ok, pull" Oliver yelled. As the Major's massive frame slid along the dirt. Oliver and Mr Donohue dragged the Major and propped him up against the front right wheel of the truck. The jaguar made his move once he saw they were taking his banquet away from his family. Taking the direct route, he dives between Oliver and Aidan's raptors in the blink of an eye. If only for the gaming skills of Aidan, there could have been a different, more bloodied result.

As the jaguar leapt, Aidan's raptor moved sideways, crushing the jaguar between each other and sending raptors and jaguar alike to the ground. The jaguar was enraged at being pinned. Head and one front leg sticking out, he thrashed and growled to be released. Bared teeth and fury in its eye's, everyone was terrified.

"Adi, keep him pinned."

Looking around for an answer, Oliver saw the Major's pistol in his holster. Grabbing it out carefully, he points it into an open area.

"Do you know how to use that?" Mr Donohue asked.

"Yeah, of course ... sort of."

"Aidan, after I shoot in the air, get the raptor up so the jaguar can get free."

"Are you sure?"

"Just do it Adi!"

Oliver moved the top chamber back of the pistol, placing a round ready to be shot. He flicked the safety off with his thumb. "Cover your ears." He yelled as he pulled the trigger.

The boom echoes across the plains area and into the forest. "Let him up Aidan". As Aidan moved the raptor up, the jaguar laid there, stunned. Oliver raised the pistol and fired again in the air. The second boom got the jaguar's legs moving as it shot out and ran for cover, having had enough of this encounter.

"Adi, watch our backs while we try to wake up the Major. Oh, and call for medical help."

"Roger, Oli,"

As Oliver and Mr Donohue poured water on the major's face to awaken him. Aidan calls through to the ARK for an ambulance. The shock and horror relayed to Doby and Lexi in the hub, hearing the story from Aidan, had them instantly worried about what would happen once Mike and Sam found out about this adventure. There was a relief when they called back and said they had awakened the Major and they were all safe in the truck.

Even if they wanted to hide this dangerous adventure, it had all played out in front of the dash mounted camera in the truck, being beamed back to the Hub.

Later that night

"Art, this is exactly the reason I didn't want the boys out in the park. There is real-life danger there in every section." Mike said, exasperated.

"I have to agree with Mike. After seeing the video footage, Aidan, the Major and Mr Donohue could have been killed by that jaguar."

"But they weren't" Ab joined in the conversation.

"By pure luck Ab, nothing more."

"I disagree." The voice of the Major came from the doorway. Standing on either side of him were Aidan and Oliver.

"Thought we'd join in, since it involves us too." The Major said.

"First, Mike, Sam. You have known me long enough to know I don't mince words. I trust Aidan and Oliver with my life out there, the same as they trust me. Oliver's choices out there were precise and executed to perfect timing. They saved our lives out there literally. Yes, Mike, you are right, they shouldn't have needed to. But we both know everything doesn't run to plan, so you adapt and learn. These boys did it on the spot and their improvisation saved lives. And their age doesn't matter. You saw Donohue out there. He froze. It wasn't his environment. The boys didn't freeze, they had our backs. Now the boys have something they want to say."

"We understand, mum and dad. It was a scary, dangerous situation. But you have your own mission tomorrow, dad, so we'll stay put till you get back. When you get back, Aidan and I would like a few things from you all. More training, first aid for one. We did not know what to do with the Major. I would like firearm's training. There are updates that are needed on the trucks and the raptors."

"Didn't the raptors work properly?" Ab asked.

"Yes, they worked well as raptors, but the jaguar didn't know what they were, so he didn't respect them. We love the raptors, but they may not be what the park needs." Oliver said.

"Do you have a suggestion for us?" Ab asked.

"Silverbacks!"

CHAPTER 39

"POPPYCOCK"

At its most splendour, the Big Apple was the city that never sleeps. Washed clean by days of rain before opening up to a glorious day for a special UN integrity meeting. The House committee issued a request to attend to Aarth Damani, CEO of Azteck Industries. It was being suggested that he used intimidation to secure permission to have Azteck build the ARK on World heritage-listed land.

The suggestion was absurd and was the invention of the Illumiun Corp board members to discredit him and his company. But Art was ready; he wasn't worried about the UN committee, but the assassin sniper hired by Illumiun had given him some loose bowel movements this morning.

As Ab checked his father for the fifth time to make sure he looked his best.

"Father, you know we can leave right now. It's not a formal hearing, just an inquiry!"

"Please don't start again, Ab; you know I have to do it. We have taken every precaution. Even Tyson's suit, untested as it is. We will get through this... now, just in case I don't, you know what you have to do."

"Now, don't you start. Everybody is in place, including all the robotics."

"Well, wish me luck," Art said.

"This is the straightforward part. You even drew a crowd."

"Really?"

"Yep, I was told 40 countries, including the US and Russia, have delegates coming to hear your address."

"Wow, almost as popular as a Bon Jovi concert."

"Not quite, but you're getting there. I'll be at the back anyway with cue cards in case you forget your lines."

"Ha, ha, ha, as if I ever forget anything... except birthdays," Art said, slightly confused.

"There's only one line I need to remember."

"I know I'm going to regret asking this, but which line?" Ab said gingerly.

"You can't handle the truth!"

Ab put his head down and groaned. "Ok, well, you better get in there and sort them out, their messing with our legacy."

"Damn straight, it should be all over in 2 hours," Art says as he walks to the officer who was taking him in.

After the initial greeting from the committee for his attendance. They asked, "Mr. Damani, do you know why you have been requested to appear today?"

"They have informed me that complaints have been raised that I used intimidation to secure the right to build the ARK in the Bale Mountain World Heritage Park."

"That is correct."

"How do you respond to these allegations of corruption?"

"Poppycock,"

"Excuse me?"

"Poppycock, Mr. chairperson," A round of laughter was heard through the gallery.

"I don't believe you are taking this seriously, Mr. Damani."

"Mr. chairperson, I was informed that I had been requested to come here to answer questions... Unfortunately, I hear no questions."

That's when it started. The barrage of questions. Why did you build there? What made you think you could influence the World Heritage Committee? Who did you approach first on the committee? Art Damani wasn't fazed; he just answered all the questions they threw at him, but it only lasted 30 minutes, and then they ran out of questions. Realising they didn't have more to ask and had been given quick, accurate responses left them looking lost.

That's when the Illumiun Corp spies kicked into gear with a personal attack on him and the Ark, but once again, Art didn't flinch. He gave them the answers they sought, or at least as much as Art was going to tell them. That lasted another 25 minutes before they ran out of puff. Then they started anew with the same questions they asked at the start, and they got the same answers once again. This lasts for 15 minutes. All up, the committee wore themselves out within 70 minutes, a lot quicker than Art or Ab predicted.

"Well, Mr. Damani, thank you for coming today and answering our questions. The committee will convene and discuss the answers you have given and get back to you with any actions. This is the time where you get to make an address to the committee."

"Thousands,"

"Pardon me. Thousands of what?" the chairperson seemed positively lost to Art's response.

"Thousands of lives have been saved since I brokered peace between Somalia and Ethiopia, stopping years of wholesale slaughter, that the UN couldn't. I saved thousands of animal species from extinction because of myself and the Ark. Now millions and millions of dollars going through those governments in revenue for businesses that I started for the Ark. Millions and Millions of lives are better off because they have a chance at a real future, like you and I have the privilege to have. Unfortunately, there has been a witch hunt today to throw mud at what we have achieved at the Ark. I can easily find out who is behind this, but really, it doesn't matter. You have your answers that you requested. You should be ashamed of yourselves. Actually, I feel pity for you and all the UN assembly. It's been two years since I brokered the peace agreement, and NOT one of you, except the United States, has ever approached me and said, "How can we help you?" Like I said, I feel sorry for you because you will now have to face your children and the world's children when you leave here today and explain to them, WHY? Why haven't you helped this man fight for peace?

"Thank you, Mr. chairperson and committee, for this opportunity to address these questions. As a parting gift," Art did, one of his magic waves the hand presentations. Then, the large screen behind the committee lit up, and a video conference call was put on the screen with all 10 members of the World Heritage Committee. "Here, if you really want to know what happened, ask them."

Art received a standing ovation from the 37 nations who attended the committee meeting out of their own time. Then, as Art was leaving, members came over to shake his hand, and the committee was left stunned, especially with the World heritage committee panel saying they weren't informed of the UN committee questioning.

It only got worse for them; somehow, the address was televised through social media, and the backlash from youth and peace groups was swift and brutal. Those who play with matches get burnt.

As Art and Ab entered the visitor's room, "Father, that was brilliant." Ab praised. "A little off-script there at the end, but a heartfelt message."

"Thank you, Ab, now the fun part. Is the team ready?"

"Yes, they're all outside, waiting."

"Well, let's not keep the sniper waiting; he has a job to do."

"Don't say that."

As Ab and Art walked off through the building. At the other end, a large contingent of the press was waiting to hear Art Damani's response to the summons to attend. They set the press conference up outside the visitor's centre of the UN complex. Ab walked out first into the bright sunlight, eyes blinking to the intense sunlight that differed from the inside lighting of the hall. He moved to the prearranged standing spot that Thomas had selected. Then Art appeared after him to the flashes of hundreds of cameras going off.

CHAPTER 40

"IT WAS ALL ABOUT ME"

Mike was informed that Art had just finished his address and that he would be out shortly. He took a deep breath and let it out slowly; he had done the 3 P's, Preparation, Preparation, Preparation. 'Now we'll see if it was enough,' Mike thought.

"Check-in," Mike spoke into his mic.

"Jedi set,"

"Smith set,"

"Steel set,"

"Spelling set." Director Spelling said he wanted to join the team's 'more hands-on-deck,' and he brought his black Op team with him. They were covering two buildings in the firing pattern that Ab had worked out. Ab had spent three sleepless nights working on an algorism that would best show the highest percentage of areas that a sniper could use from where Art was giving his media address. Based on the information he received from Thomas on snipers and their kill zones.

Director Spelling and his team covered two buildings, one that was empty and one with a sealed high-rise glass frontage. Which would mean the sniper would have to set off a minor explosion first, shattering the glass before he shot.

There were eight FBI agents covering building entrances and doing random checks of anyone entering the adjacent buildings to the UN. Jedi was on a building top with a sniper rifle covering 47% of shooter positions. Smith covered two more buildings with three of the Major's best special forces team.

Steel was beside her man. They had allocated her a position, but she said, "Screw that, Ab, I'm standing with my man." Art then went into his own rendition of Tammy Wynette's song, 'stand by your man,' which only got him clouted by Katelyn for not taking things seriously.

Sherlock had the uncomfortable job of working with local law enforcement, who were having trouble taking suggestions from someone in the military, especially one that wasn't even American.

Ab was the electronics man; he had control of over 30 AZTECK pigeons designed by Tyson and Rosi. At one push of a button at right at the exact moment, their wings would open, reflecting the sunlight to 64% of the kill zone. To help blind possible shooters or delay their shots.

Art Damani walked out to a blinding array of camera flashes as he strode to the podium set up to deliver his media address. They hurled questions at him before he said a word.

"Mr. Damani, what do you think will come out of today's questioning?"

"Today, I feel, will be a start of something new; the allegations came to nothing. Of course, certain people tried to pull down the work we achieved, but I don't believe the world will see it that way, especially the youth. They are switched on, involved, and prepared to make changes."

"Mr. Damani, who do you think handled the effort to discredit you and the Ark?"

"I believe it was my competitors and certain members of governments around the world. I will find out, and so will the world soon enough. They couldn't dispute the great work towards peace and animal conservation. And in the end, even the allegations proved false."

The questions continued at a torrid pace, as Art tried to stay focused and not think about being in someone's crosshairs. Ab was sweating heavily. Thinking to himself, 'hurry up and finish, Father, so we can get you inside.'

Director Spelling was positioned on a street corner, watching his area. There were two FBI agents walking patrol between the buildings, one at each entrance. Unexpectedly, a figure came around a corner, surprising the FBI agent. Even before the agent could address the person, he was shot with a silenced pistol.

Spelling turned and saw the agent on the ground and the perpetrator running into the empty building. Immediately he takes off running, calling in his mic.

"Officer down! Officer down! Blueberry building. Possible suspect. Proceeding on foot. All units on me. Repeat, officer down, Blueberry building."

As Spelling reached the officer, he checked his pulse. No pulse; the officer was dead. He immediately took to chasing the suspect with his pistol drawn. He didn't have time to wait for backup. With no power in the building, the only way up was the stairs. The Director tried to move with speed but with caution. He wasn't going to do anyone any good getting shot in the stairwell. The footprints in the dust on the steps told him the assassin was still going up, but he still had to move cautiously.

His Black Ops team was rolling in through the foyer fast, but the Director was already on level 4. Backup was flooding in from everywhere: ambulance, FBI, and local NYPD.

Mike's team was on alert since the call, ready to react. They're chasing down the sniper, so he shouldn't get time to shoot. Just waiting for the call, the shooter's down.

Spelling checked the door to level 5. It was open, and the footprints didn't go any higher. He opened the door, hoping the hinges were well oiled, so he wasn't heard. He could hear his team making their way up the stairwell, but he couldn't hesitate; he couldn't let the sniper get a shot off.

The door opened with a creak. "Shit!" he mumbled to himself. Pistol raised; he opened the door, expecting shots to be fired at him as he went through. Nothing; he moved around, checking all corners. At first, he saw nothing but plastic sheets hung up by builders and piles of timber and debris lying scattered everywhere. Moving around the room, he kept his back to the wall to avoid being jumped from behind. As he proceeded further to his left, he could see the window area. There were no glass panels in any of the frames, as this was an abandoned site from a company that went bankrupt before completion. Beside the window, he could see an open rifle case with the rifle still in it, but no shooter.

Just then, a blaze of shots came at him through the plastic sheets in his direction, but he got behind a pillion before being hit.

"Director, are you alright?"

Backup finally.

"Yes, he's somewhere to your left around 10 O'clock."

"Cover our entry."

"Roger, take him alive if possible."

"I'll make no promises, Director."

Spelling opened fire while the three Special Ops men moved in at speed. Training for this kind of situation was a daily event, and all three knew precisely what the others in the team would do.

Shooting, moving, covering each other, they had the sniper pinned in seconds. Then, doing as directed, the team leader told the man to throw out his weapons and come out with his hands on his head, or they would shoot him.

The team moved in, not waiting any longer; not willing to be taken alive, the assassin opened fire. In a short but furious encounter, the man was shot and fell to the ground. All the team members moved in, surrounding him. The team leader checked his pulse; he was dead.

The Director came over and had the men check him for intel. "Shooters down." That was the call that everyone was waiting for as a tremendous sigh of relief swept over Mike's team.

Steel moved over and put his hand on Art's shoulder, signalling that the threat was over. Feeling his body relax comforted her. However, standing beside him, waiting for a gunshot, was nerve-racking.

As Steel moved back into position, Director Spelling walked over to look at the sniper's weapon. It only took a couple of seconds before the Director noticed something was wrong. He grabbed the rifle and realised it was a fake!

"Second shooter!" he screamed through his mic as everyone went into instinct mode. Automatically, Steel jumped and crash tackled Art to the ground, just as they heard a shot echoing through the streets. An immediate panic hit all the press and spectators as they realised someone had fired a shot. People were running everywhere, some for cover, some in panic.

Straight after they heard the shot, Loki, Art's Panther bodyguard, appeared out of cloak mode and stood over Art and Steel to protect them from further attempts. Unfortunately, the instant appearance of a large Black Panther emerging from nowhere did nothing to calm the crowd or calm the two FBI agents flanking Art during his speech.

"He's alright; he won't hurt you," Steel yelled at the agents. "Art, Art, are you ok?" Steel yelled frantically as she checked Art for bullet wounds.

"I'm ok, I think they missed," Art said back.

An immense wave of relief hit Steel in an instant but was replaced by horror and an ice-cold chill down her spine as one of the FBI officers yelled, "man down!"

"It's Mr Thoyana, he's hit!"

From hearing those words to being back at the Ark with his Ab's body, Art doesn't remember much. Flash backs of Katelyn trying to revive Ab while he had this enormous hole in his chest. The blood, the tears from Katelyn covered in blood, saying she's sorry that she couldn't save him. The roars of Loki as he stood guardian over them. The police, ambulance, hospital, the flight home, all a blur.

Shock was the word for it. Shock, but in it all, there was shame. 2% chance a sniper's odds of getting a shot at Art, 2%. He was protected, but he gave no consideration for others, Katelyn and Ab. 'They had no protection, because it was all about me,' Art thought. "It's all about me," he said out loud.

There was a knock at the door. "Excuse me, Mr Damani. I'm very sorry to interrupt you, but there is a medicine man here to see you."

CHAPTER 41

THE GENTLENESS IN HER EYES

Sam stood stunned beside Seb's bed; it was hard to grasp what Mike was saying as they listened to his call over the phone. They both understood every word, but they couldn't or wouldn't process it. Ab, killed by an assassin at Art's UN address. Neither had any clue as they both hadn't watched any news reports as it flew through the world news with lightning speed.

It just keeps coming. The bad news, that is. First Deen last year, nearly losing Seb, now Ab.

"Are we out of our depth?" Sam asked Seb.

"Maybe, but we all bought into this, and we knew what could happen. Maybe we shouldn't have chased after the Water Tiger the way we did. Then we wouldn't have been dragged into all this. But we're here now. What troubles me is they knew to have two assassins. With one as a dummy, it means they knew that we knew, about the attempt. And that's why they had a second shooter. They've been tipped off. Most likely through Marcy."

"Doesn't that mean we are all at risk?"

"It depends on how much Marcy knew."

"Damn, more dead people in the kitchen," Sam said, trying to lighten the mood with a bit of humour.

"Only if you shot them. I need to get out of this fucking bed." Seb said, disgusted with himself.

"You're not done healing, so lay your ass down," Sam said firmly. To her surprise, Seb did precisely as he was told. The mood changed, and the conversation ended. Seb wanted time to think.

Sam spent the afternoon prepping dinner and doing some housework. She also needed time to think, now worried about everyone, Mike especially. If these people could get to Ab, we couldn't stop them. So, Mike and the team are targets now and the Ark once again.

****

The person who needed no prompting was Amari Elmi, who dropped his military title when he took over after President Abdi was killed in a car accident. Immediately upon hearing of the shooting, he called every African Television station for a formal address. Condemning the shooting of this remarkable young man as an act of cowardice and barbarism. Putting it in line with the shooting of Martin Luther King and the imprisonment of Mahatma Gandhi. Telling the world that Africa will not stand for it and will do all in its power to bring the people responsible to justice.

****

Art didn't have time to worry; he had promised his son that he would grieve later once all they had worked for is settled. "They want this' he said. 'They want grief, instability, not unity, ram your shooting down the world's throat. Make it a social media nightmare,' and so it begins. Art was on social media with the help of AZTECK staff, especially Lexi and Doby, stirring up a storm.

"Doby, Lexi. I have to leave for a while."

"What, where?" Lexi asked.

"I have to go talk to Ab,"

****

While Katelyn and the team are prepping for their trip to China.

"This is getting real," Thomas said to Mike as they loaded gear onto a transport plane.

"Are you glad you joined up now?" Mike asked.

"It hasn't stopped since I joined. Learning on the run."

"You're doing great; you have become an enormous asset to the team."

"Really?" Thomas asked, surprised.

"You tell anyone I said that, and I will come after you in your sleep," Mike said with not one drop of humour in his voice.

****

Sam went up to Seb's room to see if he needed anything before dinner. As she entered the room, to her shock, Seb's bed was empty. She ran into the ensuite to see if he was trying to go to the bathroom by himself. Nothing. Panicking, especially after their conversation about them all being at risk now. Sam searched the house at a run, lounge room, kitchen, garage, nothing. Panic had a grip on her, but an inner voice and a long-time knowledge of Seb told her there may be one place he might be.

Sam ran from the house and headed up the path to the beach. As she crested the top, there he was, dressed and standing with his crutch in the middle of the beach, looking out to sea.

Still puffing, she walks down to him as the sun sets behind them, throwing beautiful amber shades over the crashing waves.

"Leave a note next time."

"Sorry,"

"Are you alright?" Sam asks.

"No, is the honest answer."

"Want to talk?"

"Not really; you already know everything; it is just time to heal."

"Ok, just be careful; you know how treacherous this track is at night."

"Ok, will do... and Sam, thank you."

"No, thank you," Sam said sincerely, knowing that she had never said thank you for saving her life and nearly killing himself. Thank you just didn't seem enough.

"You would have done the same," Seb said.

"I wish I could really believe that," Sam said as she turned and walked away. Finally, she saw a part of humanity most never see, and now she feels inadequate. Seb returned shortly after and headed up to his room, energised and more focused. It had always been that way; the ocean spoke to him and re-energised his soul.

Seb was down in the kitchen getting a drink.

"How long till dinner, Sam?" Seb asked.

"Not for 45 minutes. Why?"

"I think I'll grab a shower before dinner."

"No, wait till the nurse comes; she will go ape shit at us if she knows you've been walking around, and especially having a shower," Sam said.

"She'll have to get used to it; I can't heal sitting in bed for 6 months. It's time to get muscles working, ready for rehab, and getting back to the team."

"Be careful, one slip, and you'll end up back in the hospital, not here."

Sam was setting the table for dinner when she heard Seb grunting and groaning going up the steps. She could understand his frustration with everything going on and wanting to heal and get back to the team. But Mike had told her it may not be possible; he may not get back.

Trying to potter around the kitchen, it got the better of her, and she went up to check on Seb. Of course, he will get cranky at babying him, but it is better than the alternative.

As she got to the bathroom, she heard banging and swearing. She stuck her head in. "Are you alright?"

He looked defeated. One of his shoes was stuck in his shorts, and he was trying to balance on his cane. His ego wouldn't let him call for help, so he would have stayed here for hours fighting it till he fell to the floor. The look in his eyes was like a baby rabbit caught in a trap. Shorts and undies trapped around his ankles, cane in one hand as he tried to reach down to pull his shoe out. Sam couldn't help but giggle.

"It's really not that funny to laugh at cripples," Seb said sulkily.

"Do you think you can hold on while I race down and get my phone? I really need to get a photo of this," Sam pretends she's making her way out the bathroom door.

"Saaaam pleeease,"

"I was only joking."

"I know; it would be funny if it was someone else."

Sam helped him unravel himself. Taking off his shoes and then his shorts. For all the trouble getting his shorts off, his t-shirt was even worse. She knew now why the nurse insisted on him wearing a hospital gown. All the damage done to his back, ribs, and lung left a massive scar from one side of his back to the other. The operations scar was healing really well, but all the trauma inside, including the repaired lung, was still recovering.

Sam helped him into the shower as he grabbed the shower door and wall for support. He looked at her and said, "Thank you"

"No, thank you," Sam replied. Like on the boat, before he got shot, he bent down and kissed Sam. This time, she didn't pull away. They kissed passionately, enjoying the moment and the feel of each other's lips. Eventually, Sam pulled away, and she stepped back. 'I have overstepped the mark again,' Seb thought. Until Sam started undressing. The curves of beautiful body were only overshadowed by the gentleness in her eyes.

Neither of them said anything; they just enjoyed lathering each other up. Seb soaped Sam up; first, he perfectly shaped curves, and the fullness of her breasts felt sublime. Then, he could feel her moving under his touch and loving it as much as he was. When he put his lathered hand down between her legs, it really affected him. It wasn't the softness of her or even the smooth, shaved curves; it was the way she spread her legs as if to say please; I want you there.

Still, neither said anything. Sam and Seb continued their shower with Sam soaping up Seb, being careful with his scarred back but not gentle with his erection. Seb thought he was going to explode; the sensation was mind-blowing. He pulled Sam off him and lifted her to her feet. He wanted to kiss her again. The passion in them both was at boiling point.

Sam turned and faced the wall and spread her legs, letting Seb know what she wanted. There was a significant height difference, and Seb had to bend down. As he did, he lifted her off her feet as he thrust himself inside her. Sam had to stand on tippy toes and grab the shower handle to maintain her balance as he moved further and further inside her. Now they were together, moving as one together. Each wrapped in the sensation as the other. Grabbing her breasts, Sam's body gave in to the pleasure, and she was overwhelmed with a flow of passion. Seb hung on; he didn't want this to end. Everything felt right, but he too was overwhelmed by the moment. She, too, didn't want it to end; her body was still tingling all over. They separated and cleaned themselves up, then hopped out of the shower. Drying and dressing like normal couples, Sam helped Seb to his room and got him into the hospital gown before the nurse came to do her nightly rounds.

Sam went down to the kitchen and finished preparing dinner... and neither said a word.

The nurse said to Sam that night that she was really pleased with Seb's progress and that they might look at getting him out of bed in the next few days. Sam brought his dinner to his room, and they watched him gulp it down.

"Well, your appetites back, I can see." The nurse said.

"I don't think my appetite will ever be a problem, Doc."

"True, very true." Sam said.

"So, coming surfing with me tomorrow, Doc?"

"No surfing, I said that. And stop calling me Doc."

After the thumbs up from the nurse, Sam sat up and watched some television before hitting the bed; no call from Mike today, except the call about Art. He would be preparing for his mission tomorrow, into China.

Sam woke up in the morning feeling refreshed; she hadn't slept like that since the boating mission. It felt good. She went into the kitchen and made a pot of coffee; sitting down, she started to think.

What is Seb going to act like when I go upstairs? We haven't spoken about what we did in the shower? Sam felt really confused, but not how she thought she would feel. Where's the guilt? Where's the throwing myself on the floor clutching my husband's photo screaming, WHAT HAVE I DONE! … nothing. She woke up feeling still madly in love with Mike, still missing her kids badly. She knew she always liked Seb; what's not to like? He is handsome, funny, charming and sweet. He has always been good to her and adores the boys as if they were his own.

But the whole no guilt thing has thrown her; she has never been one to just blindly follow society's rules, just for the hell of it. Is this what they call 'friends with benefits, cause the sex was good… no great, she enjoyed every second. 'Damn! Life should come with a handbook,' she thought. No point putting this off any further. She grabbed the coffees and headed up to Seb's room.

She opens the door, not knowing what to expect.

"God, about time; I was about to ring around to see if any coffee shops that delivered." Sam stood there, stunned. Nope, NO guilt here either.

"Quick, come over their about to talk about Ab's shooting yesterday." Sam put the coffees on the side table as Seb grabbed one of his pillows for Sam to lean up against while sitting on the bed. Just the usual kindness that she expects from Seb. They sat there intently and watched the news as they showed footage of the shooting and how the press freaked out when Loki appeared; he definitely stopped a second shot from being fired. After the news, they sat there drinking their coffee. When Seb said softly, "Sam, I have a favour to ask." 'Oh, here it comes, the belated guilt, we shouldn't have done that, it was me not you, speech.'

"After the coffee, would you help me go for a walk along the beach?"

Sam's jaw dropped. She must have looked a sight cause Seb said. "If it's asking too much, I understand; I have been a burden so much already."

"Oh, shut up. of course I'll take you for a walk. You're no burden. I would have kicked you out weeks ago when you ate me out of house and home if I wanted to get rid of you."

"Thanks, you're a legend," Sam turned and gave him a smile and left the room to grab her beach shoes. They walked gently along the beach, saying hi to all the joggers and dog walkers enjoying the cool morning at this hour.

Seb addressed the elephant in the room. "I enjoyed our shower yesterday."

"Me too; I really enjoyed it," Sam said. And that was it. Nobody added anymore. Still no guilt. We better stop before it turns into something; what if the neighbours saw us? Nothing? The sex was great; that was it. But Sam still kept thinking, 'life needs a handbook.'

CHAPTER 42

WORLD'S APART

"Hello, may I help you, Mr ...?" Art greeted the gentleman.

"Adjo, just call me Adjo, Mr Damani. I am here about Ab Thoyana." He said.

"Ab, what about Ab? I suppose you are here to offer condolences."

"No, I am here to pass on a message to you from Ab,"

The look of shock, anger, confusion must have run through Art's face as Adjo spoke to clear the confusion.

"I'm sorry. Please let me explain. I am from Bafilo in Togo. Ab's birth town. They call me their shaman, a spiritual guide. Ab contacted me in a dream to pass on a message,"

"I'm sorry," Art said. "Mr Adjo was it. I'm a very busy man and I have a funeral to prepare. So, I am sorry I do not have time for this right now. I will pass on your condolences at the funeral from your village."

"Ah yes, Ab said that you are a very practical man and wouldn't believe his message." Adjo continued.

"So, you're saying, my Ab contacted you to pass on a message. What is the message?" Art said, getting annoyed.

"He wants you to come to Bafilo to talk to him, and he wants his funeral to be in Bafilo." The shaman said proudly.

"I can understand your village would like to honour Ab, but that will not be possible as Ab is being buried here at the Ark. And, him wanting to talk to me in Bafilo... well, I'm sorry, but I'm not a great believer in the spiritual world."

"Ab said as much that he would have to convince you to come."

"Ab is going to convince me? How?"

"He said to tell you, if you have his funeral in Bafilo it would be bigger than a Bon Jovi concert,"

All the life ran out of Art in an instant. The shock, stress, confusion, guilt all hit him at once. This was a message from Ab. Art's knees buckled as he broke down and cried. He started grieving. No more walls, excuses it was time to mourn the loss of his son. Adjo placed his hand on Art's shoulder to steady him.

"He knew you would bottle it in. His final message to me was to tell you to readjust. There is shit to do."

Art looked up with tears still rolling down his face. "What do I do?"

****

Gunsan airfield South Korea

The flight to South Korea seemed to fly by as all the members had their focus elsewhere, which wasn't the most fabulous start to the most crucial mission in their lives. The only one who seemed to be focused was the Major's man, Midnight, tagged for his stealth ability. He really took to Sherlock's team's training and showed that he could learn and adapt quickly.

Sherlock decided not to roust the troops just yet as they loaded the gear quietly onto the fishing trawler. The captain was one of Spellings' CIA contacts and operated as a North Korea fishing trawler in the Yellow Seas as its cover. Sherlock greeted the captain and went over the plans. It was a simple plan, heading up the Korean coast. First, dropping the team off on rafts, and then he goes on fishing. The only problem was random boardings from either Chinese or North Korea naval boats.

Time to wake up the team.

"Get your shit together and put your baggage in the back. We won't be going home from this trip if we're worried about other things. Water Tiger has given us the times of the patrols so far, but that doesn't mean they won't change, so work on a presumption there could be new patrols. Now a last-minute update, it shouldn't affect what we're doing. But I thought you should know about it. The joint US/Russian mission is scheduled for tomorrow night. So, we have 24hr to get what we need and get out. Like I said, it doesn't affect us because our mission was to evac tomorrow night anyway, so we shouldn't be around. Jedi is our eyes; he will co-ordinate everywhere we go, and he is our angel. He will cover us from his perch if things go south. Midnight you're familiar with the monitors, so you take some of the pressure off of Jedi but mainly watch his back."

"I've got you all covered," Jedi assured them.

"We know you do; you are basically in charge, Jedi; we move in and evac on your command. Water Tiger said there is supposed to be a meeting with Nessler, that he is staying for. Once it is over, we will evac before the US troops move in. It's a Seals team, so they will come in shooting, grab what evidence they can, and leave. So, team record everything you can. This is our last chance to make a difference. Let's all get home."

So far, luck has been on their side as the team rides off from the trawler in their inflatables. However, the team still has to face border patrols along the coast as they make their way to Art's contact outside Wushi Town in China.

Later, outside a derelict building in southern Dandong industrial estate, the team moves out, heading to their starting points. Jedi and Midnight moved to their perch to see 70% of the cannery, and the other 30% will be covered by bird surveillance.

Sherlock, Smith, and Steel moved southeast of the cannery and disappeared, till Jedi was up and running. 20 minutes later, they got the call. "Watch ready, proceed to phase 1 position. All is clear." Three-man patrols on the perimeter, two mercs painting on the north wall. Two mercs on roof repairs, two mercs labouring, moving in and out of the cannery. 6 mercs missing from intel, plus Water Tiger. From then on, everything was routine for the team. Jedi watched, recorded, and informed the ground troops of what he saw. Smith and Steel moved in close enough to record the conversations of the mercs without detection. Jedi also flew surveillance birds inside the building and perched them on rafters to record what was going on inside the cannery.

All was going well; Midnight was watching the monitor from Scree, the surveillance eagle. The Chinese patrol was on time as Scree watched it roll along the highway. Midnight had the feeling something was different this time, and it wasn't long before he realised it was the vehicle. It followed the same route, same time, but the vehicle had changed from a truck to an armoured troop carrier. It didn't do anything different as it rolled past the cannery. Midnight went to see if Jedi noticed the change.

Crawling up to Jedi, Midnight says, "Did you see the patrol?"

"Yes, why. Was it on time?"

"Yes,"

"What's the problem then?" Jedi asked.

Midnight showed him the replay on the monitor. "Different vehicle"

Jedi had missed that; he noticed the truck go past but not the change. 'Could be nothing,' he thought. But he didn't like change. Deciding to inform the team of the change, he sped up the evac for one hour.

"If we don't get the go-ahead from Water Tiger, evac is now 1700 hours." Before anyone could ask why, Jedi added. "Change in the patrol vehicle, troop truck to an armoured troop carrier." 'Change, good call Jedi,' Sherlock thought. Minutes later, another call came through. "Two trucks approaching, slowing down, pulling into the front of the lab."

Just then, Jedi saw the Water Tiger finally come upstairs to greet the trucks as Nessler exited the vehicle. Men started scurrying from the back of the trucks, unloading large canisters that looked like propane cylinders. Then out of the back of the other truck came people. 12 men and women were marched out of the second truck, hands tied. Prisoners, it seemed to Jedi, and they were all in lab coats.

"Hostage situation," Jedi said over the comms.

"Stay on mission. We don't know who they are," Sherlock informed him.

"Roger, Water Tiger is talking with Nessler. He doesn't seem to know what's going on. Recording."

Water Tiger looked at all the canisters and prisoners being marched in.

"Good afternoon, Fredrick. What is all this?" Water Tiger asks.

"You'll be happy to know this is your last night here, Jin. The process has worked perfectly." Nessler informs him.

"Wonderful, and the explosive gas cylinders are a parting bang?"

"Yes, indeed."

He decided not to comment about the prisoners and keep Nessler off guard.

"Then a celebration drink is required, and I hear we can celebrate Damani's downfall by the death of his son. Surely, the grief will slow him down and make him back down."

"Yes, success all around. The change in target was a necessary one. Seems they were prepared for Damani as a target. But fortunately, he looked after himself and no one else."

The two men entered the front office. "A drink, only the finest scotch for you, my friend" Water Tiger pours Nessler a drink as they sit and chat. During the conversation, Water Tiger asks, "The prisoners, how do you want them dealt with?

"Lock them up with the others in the lab. There can be no survivors. Do it in the early morning when there are fewer people around to report the fire."

"It will be done. What do you need of me, then?"

"Nothing, for now; collect your pay and sit back and watch the show."

Jedi watched Nessler and the Water Tiger speaking; everything seemed alright, a celebration drink. He had visuals into the front office but no sound. The new workers in the two trucks were hopping back in, signifying that they were exiting. The team had what they wanted, Nessler at the site, and the conversation with Jin was also recorded. Suddenly, body language changed, tempers seemed flared, and...

"Water Tiger has been shot! Nessler's leaving. Two guards are dragging Water Tiger down to the labs."

"Standby, tell me when the two soldiers come up."

"Roger, hang on, Nessler just got a call. He's spooked, calling for the two guards, no, all the guards. They're all cramming into trucks and getting out fast. What the hell is happening? Nessler's leaving... wait, hold on, we have more movement near the river... Bugger! The Seals are here. Team, stand down, prepare to evac."

"Roger" came the call.

"We need Water Tiger," Sherlock says over the mic.

"Too late, boss, the Seals would be on you before you got out. Hold on, smoke rising from the labs."

"They are burning the place down!" Sherlock said.

"Shit!" Smith could be heard saying over the comms.

"Seals are on the East side of the cannery. Damn, time to bug out. Two armoured troop carriers heading in at speed. Guess where they're going?"

Sherlock accessed the situation and took control.

"We can't abandon Water Tiger or the Seals. Jedi, keep watch. Midnight, bring the truck up Southside for a quick exit. Steel and Smith link up on the east side for diversion measures for evac."

"Roger," came the call.

The Seals team made their way quickly from the river to the East doorway of the cannery. They were unaware that two armoured troop carriers would be on the scene in seconds. As they entered the cannery, the last member of the Seals team was spotted by the heavy machine gunner... and all hell broke loose. Both machine gunners from the armoured carriers opened fire on the doorway with their mounted 50-calibre machine guns, instantly ripping the doorway to pieces. The carriers rolled in fast and moved into position, one guarding the front door, the other the east side entrance they had just blown apart. The back of the vehicles dropped and heavily armed soldiers exited on the run, backs of the vehicles dropped, as they took up firing positions on the cannery.

The Seals team leader split his team, three defending, three gathering intel. It was a snatch and grab mission. Now the team leader wanted them out of the building within 5 minutes. The Chinese soldiers tipped off to the Seals' mission had other plans.

Three Seal members returned fire to hold the enemy back. But first, they needed to stop the Chinese soldiers from entering the building and cutting the exits off.

Sherlock entered through a back passage as the team watched, hoping to get to the Water Tiger before the Seals shot him. They overlooked him coming in behind the three Seals holding the frontal position. Without warning, an explosion at the front of the building knocked Sherlock off his feet. The carriers had opened fire with their 25mm cannons, and unluckily for the Seals, they hit the gas cylinders nearby. Sending flames and a shock wave through the inner hall of the cannery, knocking Sherlock and the Seals down.

"Sherlock, move your arse. It's getting tight out here." Smith said.

"No picnic in here either." Sherlock returned.

He got to his feet and raced down the stairwell, but kept in mind that the Seals may not be happy to see him at first. Hearing voices around the corner, Sherlock yells, "Friendly, coming in!". As he turned the corner, three rifle barrels were pointed at him. "Woo, peace, friend," Sherlock says.

"Who the fuck are you?" one Seal said.

"Major Mike Madden, Australian SAS."

"SAS! What the hell are you doing here?"

"Most likely the same as you, but for different reasons. I came for Water Tiger and to get you guys out."

"You can't have him; he's part of our mission."

Sherlock ignored them and went to the Water Tiger.

"Hey, get away from him," One Seal commanded.

"Trust me, guys shooting a Major in the back creates too much paperwork. Let's get out of here first. Let them out first," Sherlock said, pointing to the prisoners.

"Water Tigers alive, stomach wound. Light the place up." Sherlock said in his mic. Within seconds, there was a vast explosion up top.

"What the fuck was that?"

"My team and our chance to get out."

CHAPTER 43

THE NOTE

Seb heard the shower turn off, then he knocked on the door. "Yeah"

"Just me. Are you dressed?"

"Yes, you can come in."

Seb walked into the steamy bathroom as Sam was drying her hair. Sam was wrapped in an apricot towel around her waist and used another towel to dry her hair. Her breasts were swaying with her movement as she bent over, rubbing her hair to dry it.

"What's up?" Sam asked.

"I just came to see if you wanted to do a beach walk with me?"

"I'm all showered and clean now; you should have said earlier, I would have come."

"You won't get dirty going for a walk on the beach," Seb said.

"I'll get all sweaty and need another shower."

"So, you're telling me you have to be dirty to go for a walk on the beach? How dirty do you have to be?"

Sam looks up and Seb is standing there with his shirt open with his ripped chest muscles. Not an ounce of fat on him, even though he eats like a horse. She looks down and sees he is excited; she wasn't going to say anything, but couldn't help to tease him. Looking down at his excitement, she says,

"We better go now before we get too dirty."

It worked. Seb turned sideways to hide himself, but all it did was remind Sam of their encounter in the shower the other day. Feeling herself getting excited, Sam dressed quickly before they both got caught in another friends with benefits encounter. Sam dressed quickly, and they headed to the beach.

Once again, the sunset was painting beautiful colours on the water. The walkers were out, enjoying the sunset, families with small children were laughing as they watched their dogs chasing waves up and down the beach.

Sam grabbed Seb's hand, and after a few steps, she turned to Seb.

"I hate to spoil this lovely walk, but have you given any thought to what happens if you don't pass the physical to join the team?"

"Are you trying to jinx me?"

"You know there are no jinxes. Your either fit enough or not."

"I do not know; this is what I love. I live the corps, the team. I can't imagine doing anything without them."

"Yeah, but you're smart, fit, young; you could do anything?"

"Thanks, Sam. Yeah, everything but the one thing I want to do."

It went quiet between them for the rest of the walk and the rest of the night. Sam felt she may have opened up thoughts, Seb wasn't ready to face.

The following day, Sam went up to see Seb with his morning coffee. Once again, he was missing. "Out walking again, I bet," she said to herself. Heading down the stairs, she thought she heard a clank coming from her bedroom; there it was again, a clanking sound. She walks down to her room and slowly pushes open the door. Here was Seb, laying on a towel on the floor, lifting the weights Mike has beside his bed, that rarely get used.

"What are you doing?" she asks.

"Umm, lifting weights?"

"Why?"

"Because if I'm going to pass my medical, I have to make it happen."

"But what if you do too much and hurt something?"

"I'll be fine; all I have to do is concentrate."

"Concentrate, you say. Like, keep focus. Don't get distracted."

"Yes, exactly."

Sam stood there facing Seb and squatted down.

"What are you doing?" Seb asked.

"Nothing, you better keep concentrating, or you'll lose your focus."

Squatted on the floor, legs spread towards Seb. "How's your concentration going there, 2 Planks? I see one of your planks knows what to concentrate on."

"Sam, that's not funny; I could drop something on myself."

"Gee, you might have to focus on something else; your concentration isn't outstanding."

"Good timing, now that's what I call concentration." Sam stands up and turns to leave. As she is walking out the door, she turns. "I'm heading into town to grab some things. Do you need anything?"

"No, I'm all good," Seb replies, as he watches her bottom wiggle as she walks through the door.

"So, beautiful." Seb says.

Sam turns, "What was that you said?"

"Nothing, I didn't say anything" Seb lies.

Sam with a cheeky smile turns and walks out the door.

A few hours later, Sam walks in carrying two arms full of groceries. She tells herself, just going for a few things and six bags full later.

"I'm back," she calls out as she places some groceries on the floor and some on the bench. While putting groceries away in a cupboard, she notices a piece of paper on the table. She pulls a chair out and starts reading. Her stomach drops, and she lets out a wail of sorrow that tears at her heart.

Hi Sam,

This might sound like a coward's way out, but I believe this is the best way.

I tried to play the friend with benefits role, but I can't pretend anymore.

I have been in love with you for a long time, but I was happy just to be the friend that was always around.

But now, I know I won't be able to leave if I stay. Being around you is intoxicating. Your beauty, humour, and you're caring. I wouldn't have healed as fast if I didn't have you around. Making love to you is something I'll never forget.

I'm heading home, don't try to call. I have to get myself ready and join the team again.

If Mike asks, just tell him I'm heading home and don't want to impose myself on your family any longer.

Don't worry, I will keep in contact with the boys; they are family too.

Thanks for everything.

Seb x

CHAPTER 44

STRESS TILL YOU STROKE ROOM

The mission room, situation room, sometimes called the Ops room, has many names, but the one thing they all have in common is stress. So maybe the 'Stress till you stroke room' should be added to the list.

"Where the hell did they come from?" The President shouted as the armoured vehicles rolled in and started firing at his Navy Seal team.

"Looks like a setup, if you ask me," Director Spelling said.

"Sit rep captain?" General Hagart asked from the situation room. As they watch their mission go to hell from the very start.

"Two armoured troop carriers blocking two exits. I've split the team. One has gone to check for intel; we are holding them back long enough to make an exit. Just then, a massive explosion took out two of the helmet cams of one team, including the captains.

"Get them out of there, now. Contact the Russians and get them to send in the pickup now. We can't leave any men there, or we will be at war by morning, gentlemen."

"We may already be there, Mr. President." Director Spelling said, convinced.

The helmet cams on the intel team showed smoke and fire billowing from a lab setup. People were screaming in Chinese to be let out. The team suddenly spun as if hearing something from behind. Then a soul figure came around the corner.

"Sherlock. What's he doing there?" the President asked. "Who cares? I hope he has another rescue up his sleeve." Spelling said.

"You know that person, Mr. President?" General Hagart asked.

"Yes, he is the team leader who rescued me from the assassination attempt."

"Someone must have leaked the mission?" the General said.

"I think you've been set up, by the looks of it. Two armoured vehicles show up as you arrive. I think that's a given." Spelling yelled at the General.

"It doesn't matter; get them out now. Wait, who's that? The one Sherlock is trying to help. It's Water Tiger! Why is he helping him?" the President asked. The situation room saw the Seals open the door on the screen to let the civilian's escape. Then another explosion seemed to rock the building as Sherlock gave orders as they all ran up the stairs.

Sherlock started yelling in Chinese and pointing to the back door; he told them to stick to the river and head North.

Outside, Sherlock's team held their own and drew fire away from the cannery. Jedi had taken out the two machine gunners, and the explosion Steel and Smith set off made one Chinese team pull back and evacuate the carrier as it was covered in fuel and burning inside and out.

'Time to move; it won't be long before they figure where I am.' Jedi thought. "Moving." Jedi turned his back, and a 25mm cannon round hit his perch and threw him off his first-floor roost to the ground below. "Ahh, I'm hit." Jedi lay there trying to catch his breath as the wind was knocked out of him. He could feel something in the back of his neck, a large wooden shrapnel from the cannon's explosion.

"Coming to you," Midnight says over the comms.

"Roger," came the return call.

Sherlock helped Water Tiger to the back door before joining the Seals team.

The Seals team leader was patching one of his men.

"Who are you?"

"Major Madden Australian SAS,"

"Is that your mob out there?"

"Yep, they get loud at times," Mike joked.

"Louds good, your team, your call major," the captain said to Sherlock. "We won't be able to get far with them on our backs and whoever is on their way now. Time to get wet," he said.

"Time to get wet," the Seals agreed.

"Team go dark, go under," Sherlock commanded in his mic. All firing stopped.

"I don't think we will kill too many if we don't shoot back, Major," the captain said, enquiring.

"My team will lighten the load. Get in position and wait for a flare." Sherlock said.

The Seals checked their weapons and found their positions. They crouched, waiting in the silence.

They heard a scream, then silence. Then another scream, some gunfire, and another scream, then silence. Then another scream, then silence.

The captain turns to his sergeant beside him, "Who is this lot, fucking Vampires?" Then they saw the flare go up, and true to the Navy Seal's reputation, they came like a wave. Speed, precision shooting, nerves of steel, and within seconds they had taken down the last ten remaining Chinese soldiers in quick time.

Sherlock walked over to the Seals team leader.

"Time to go," Sherlock said to the captain.

"Yes, thanks for the assist. Though we didn't get what we came for. Are you going to tell me why you're here?" the captain asked Sherlock.

"The same as you, in sorts. Captain, we got the required intel. I know you are following orders, but you might want to be sure where the orders are coming from over the next month."

"What's that mean?"

"Nothing, just be safe; good luck to your team. Oh, try to steal an ashtray from the Russian sub for me."

The captain watched Sherlock walk away in the dark. "How the hell does he know how we got here?"

Back at the situation room...

"Pick up is on the way," the General told the President.

The President wasn't listening; he was processing other things. 'Ab Thoyana was assassinated. Sherlock's team is at the same site in China. It can't be a coincidence,' he thought.

"How the hell are we going to explain this?" the President asked the room.

"We don't have to; we weren't there. Well, that proves about the lab intel." the General says.

"That only proves that there was some kind of lab and that you have a leak in your network somewhere. Those boys wouldn't have got out alive if it wasn't for the SAS team." Spelling said.

"Our boys would have got out. So, what were the Australians doing there anyway?" the General countered.

At the dock near Wushi Town...

"Jedi, send all that intel to the Ark immediately; we need to get it to Director Spelling ASAP," Sherlock says.

"Already done, boss."

"Good work, all of you," Sherlock praises them.

Steel was checking Jedi's wound on the back of his neck.

"Midnight, you treated Jedi's wound?"

"Yes,"

"You did excellent work. Have you had training?"

"No, I just have a lot of brothers and sisters. One of them was always getting hurt."

Steel laughed. "Well, we might add medical training to the next set of drills with your team."

"I don't know if they would appreciate it, Steel. The rest of them just want to blow stuff up with Jedi."

Everyone started laughing as they saw their ride approaching.

CHAPTER 45

TIMES RUNNING OUT

The 'Stress till you stroke' room had entered a new phase. The infuriated stage. A mission going down the toilet, along with the intel needed to stop a war.

"Well, where do we go from here? We have no definitive proof, and we sure can't do that again. It's probably burnt to the ground now, anyway. Also, why were there prisoners there?" the President said, annoyed.

"Another sign we are on the right track; they are trying to get rid of all evidence, now that we are onto them." The General said.

"It's going to be a long night, Mr. President; I don't think we will have to wait long before China reacts." Director Spelling added.

"I agree, Damien, I totally agree."

Two hours passed with enough pacing to wear a hole in the situation floor.

"Sir, you need to see this!" a young lieutenant called. She was in charge of media, scanning world news for anything that suddenly hit the headlines.

"Russian news media across the country just rolled with this."

Chinese Man virus' site burns in Dandong. Evidence points to the Chinese Government attack, say Russian and US officials.

"Oh My God! Why would they do that? And they named us in it too!"

"Sir, Russia has released the images to the media also," the Lieutenant added.

"Crap!" Spelling said

Another voice entered the conversation. "Mr. President Chinese Naval fleet is on alert. East Sea fleet is on the move North."

"General, where's the 7th fleet at the moment?"

"In war games off of Guam, Sir."

"End the games and put them on alert. Seek clearance from the Japanese government to station them off the coast of Japan."

"Do I tell the Japanese why?"

"I'm sure they know by now, but tell them if they ask. If the Chinese air force or army mobilize, go straight to DEFCON 3."

"Mr. President, is that really necessary!" Spelling protested.

"Damien, I certainly don't want to, but I can't be caught with my pants down, either. Millions of American lives are at stake. How far away are your people with actual proof?"

"Not far, Sir."

"Then I suggest Damien, you go shake some trees quickly because this is about to get nasty really quick. And find out what's up with the Russians, too. They're acting like crazy squirrels."

"Yes, Sir, I'm on it" Damien left in a hurry to his office, hoping to have info from Sherlock's team by the time he got there.

"Sir, Russia has just upgraded their alert level," the captain yelled.

"What the hell is wrong with them? General, get me the Russian President on the line."

"Yes, Mr. President."

A line was opened between the US and Russia. An animated discussion continued for an hour, with neither side giving an inch.

"Mr. President, you're being naïve if you aren't coming to the same conclusions as us."

"There was no evidence found at the cannery site. So, nothing has really been proven beyond doubt." President Edwin insisted that they hold their ground to see what China says about being accused by Russia and the United States.

The call ended with a stalemate and a small victory for common sense. President Edwin didn't have long to wait for China's response.

CNN was giving the story prime time, and why not? In the last 24hrs, Russia has accused China of being the orchestrator of manufacturing the Covid-Man virus. Which the world is currently locking down again to stop the spread of. This manufactured strain spreads faster and has a higher fatality rate than previous strains. So now, Russia has basically accused China of declaring war on the rest of the world.

The Chinese response was severe and unrelenting. As China's President Hu Yange spoke to the world's media. It was the most anticipated news event of the decade.

"It is China's position that all evidence stated by the Russian Federation and the United States is fabricated and is a threat of war.

And all Chinese forces are now on standby to repel any aggression against the Chinese people. Yesterday in the act of war in Dandong Eastern Province, aggressors attacked but were repelled by the brave soldiers of the people's republic of China. China's allies have shown support and are now on the same footing as China. I tell the world, China had nothing to do with the Man Virus and refutes any proof to say otherwise. If these countries want war with China, then be prepared to watch their countries burn."

The whole situation room stood there in silence.

"Did he just declare nuclear war on the world?" a captain said to anybody who would listen.

"Certainly, sounded like it," General Hagart replied.

General put the whole Pacific region on alert; we are going to DEFCON 2. Get me the Secretary of State on the line.

Moments later, he was talking to the Secretary of State,

"Mr. President, how can I help?"

"Joseph, we're moving to NORAD; we're on DEFCON 2. I want all our allies on the phone by the time we get to NORAD. If I can't talk Russia and China down, we have to be prepared for the worst."

"Yes, Sir, it will be done."

"You know the drill; get everyone inside; I'll see you there."

"Yes, James, good luck."

The President turned to General Hagart. "Pack up, General, we're heading to NORAD. Get my family on the chopper. I'll see you up there."

"Yes, Mr. President," the General confirmed.

Immediately, President Edwin felt someone on his shoulder, and he turned and saw Chad, Head of the Secret Service, there with him. After all they had been through already since his election win, a strong comfort came across him. He turns to Chad.

"Here we go again, Chad. I thought last year was bad!"

"Still prefer this to fighting baboons," Chad said

"True. How the hell did that woman survive that?"

"She's SAS; I think it's part of their training."

The President looked at Chad, not a hint of humour on his face, 'He's incredible,' the President thought. But, as the President turned his back, he couldn't see the smirk on Chad's face.

CHAPTER 46

THE CEREMONY

Art's personal secretary appeared at his shoulder. Mr. Damani, I have a call for you. He claims he's the President of the United States. The surprised look on Art's face said it all. He took the phone. "Mr. President. How are you?" Art asked.

"Blood pressure is on the up at the moment. You know the threat of war with China and all. Just another day at the office. How are you, my friend?"

"Recovering, but it will take a while. Transferring Ab's body to his hometown in Bafilo for his funeral."

"Any idea who did this to him and why?"

"Yes, we do. Unfortunately, it seems we have been getting into the way of world events, and peace isn't high on the agenda."

"Can I help bring them to justice? Does the FBI know about everything going on?"

"Yes, you will meet them soon; you have already had a run-in with them before."

"Me, when? Also, do you have contact with Captain Madden's team anymore?"

"Well, the answer to your first question is here at the ARK; the second question is yes, we are working with them at the moment."

"Art, you're dancing around things. If you know something about what's going on, I need to know. A war could start any moment."

"Mr. President, a thousand people could come to your door and claim to know something about what's going on. Who would you believe?"

"The person who could prove what they're saying,"

"Exactly. So as one of the thousand, I'll tell you this. Soon you will have the proof in your hands. Your friends are very close to you, but your enemies are all around you. China is innocent."

"My God, they're about to declare war on the US and Russia."

"Mr. President, we need time. So, be the statesman and leader the world needs you to be. Play along; your enemies must not suspect that you know anything. So, react as a President would then be prepared to act when the moment comes."

"When will that be?"

"You will know when. Your friends will supply the evidence, and hopefully, old enemies may come to your aid."

"Gee Art, you should write fortune cookies. Well, I hope what you're doing works fast." The President said.

"Diplomacy is your shield; use it well?"

"Take care of yourself. I'm sorry I won't be there for Ab's funeral. He was a remarkable young man. We shall talk soon." Then the President hung up.

Art envisioned Ab standing with him. He looks over at his father and speaks.

"Diplomacy is your shield... who says that?" Ab says with a laugh.

"Well, in time of great events. Great sayings come out," Art said with a smile. They laughed and the vision of Ab disappeared.

The next day in Bafilo

"Is it just me, or does anyone else feel weirded out by this whole thing?" asked Smith.

"This is how they honour a fallen warrior," Katelyn answers.

"No, it's not the funeral. It's one day we're in China saving the world, the next we're at a funeral in Africa. No offence, but Ab would not want us sitting around while the world is crumbling."

"We've done our bit. Now it's up to the world leaders to decide whether we should burn or not. Anyway, our bags are packed just in case we have to move out quickly. Now shut up and listen to the music. This is how I want to go out when my time comes." Katelyn said. She sits there with her eyes closed, soaking in the atmosphere of the drums and singing. The town's people were celebrating the life of the warrior for peace that was Ab Thoyana. Warriors dressed in traditional outfits, bashed their spears on their shields to the beat of the drums and singing.

"And what's with the whole Zulu voodoo thing with Art? Why is he in the hut with the medicine man?"

"Augh" Katelyn was getting annoyed with all Smith's chatter.

"First off, they're not Zulu's. Second, it's not voodoo. Third, he's a shaman, not a medicine man. He is helping Ab pass on. He is a spiritual guide. Plus, he is helping Art talk to Ab." Katelyn said with her eyes shut.

"WHAT! Talk to Ab. Sounds like voodoo shit to me." Smith said confused.

Art sat cross-legged in the shamans' hut with him. Sage filled the room, but there was no sensation of the smoke.

"Soon, Mr Damani, the drums will change and you will start your journey. Time is short in the other world, so ask what needs to be asked, but mostly listen to Ab's message." Moments later, the drums outside changed and town's folk started singing a different tune. It was a sound of mourning as males sang and women wailed and cried and children yipped and screeched. It sent a shiver up the spine of Mike Maddens team. Inside the hut, Art felt himself ... phase was the best word for it. He was still in Africa. No, it was the grounds of the Ark.

"Father," a voice said behind him. He turned and there was Ab, as clear as day.

"Ab my boy. It is you?"

"Yes, in a spirit form. I couldn't pass on till I spoke to you. You must save the tears for now. There is too much to do. It seems our journey together was the ARK. In this world, the animals roar your name like a 'God of Deliverance'. They know what you are doing and praise you for it. There is another who we will continue this journey with you. Seek and you shall find." Just then, a vision of a leopard cub standing over the top of a hurt adult leopard, roaring at her adversaries to stay away. Then Art was back in the hut, feeling light-headed. A single tear rolled down his face.

"One tear," Art said. "Allow me one tear Ab,"

As Art joined his friends and members of the Ark staff outside, he felt buoyed, readjusted, but confused by the message and vision he saw.

The drums and singing changed again as Adjo exited the hut in his shaman face mask and traditional clothing. The town then, along with Ab's friends and family, joined by over 80 of the ARK staff, formed a procession to the resting place of Ab Thoyana. The music and singing were uplifting. They sang of happiness and a new journey for Ab. At the cemetery, Art looked up and there in the distance he saw, standing on top of a boulder formation, a lone girl stood in traditional clothing with a spear. The girl looked about 14 and stared at Art the whole time through the ceremony.

CHAPTER 47

NESSLER

Storm clouds built as thunder came from the North through the Bale Mountains. It looked ominous, a warning from the 'Gods of War' that all hell was about to break loose. Mike's team had been on a relentless cycle for months now. It wasn't as if they never rested between each mission; it was the continuous mental pressure of months of stressful world situations.

Mike went to check on the boys. They were with Art, giving him ideas for the ARK and trying to cheer him up after the funeral. They were their mother's children; they had good hearts.

After getting the lowdown of their tutors and the raptor team update. Mike spoke to Sam alone.

"Hello,"

"Hi gorgeous, how are you?"

"Things aren't great. Seb left and is going home. It has me worried he will overdo his fitness and ruin his recovery."

"I know, but he is an extremely intelligent soldier and has probably read ten books already on what he has to do to recover."

"He felt he was imposing. So, he left a note and left it while I was out shopping. He is emotional and probably not thinking straight."

"He has put himself on this journey now. All we can do is support him."

"He will be crushed if he fails the medical test."

"Did he say where he's going?"

"No, just home. He told me not to ring him; he can't be talked out of it. I think the rehab recovery was too slow for him."

"What did the nurse say?" Mike asked.

"That he's a madman and could end up with permanent disabilities if he pushes too hard too soon. But he's an adult, so there's nothing we can do to stop him."

"Geez, I never saw that coming."

"Me neither; I would have thrown a number 4 face if I thought it would have worked," Sam said to lighten the mood.

"You know about the number system?"

"Yeah, for a long time. They're their father's sons. How are the boys coping They'll miss him. He said he would stay in contact with the boys," Sam said.

While in the Hub.

"The trick is how we are going to keep track of him. Now that he knows someone is on to him."

"We have heaps of info on him now. We can't lose track of him. So, our best bet is to bring this net down suddenly and keep him in the United States where we can control what happens."

"Are you sure you want to do this, Lexi? It's a horrible death." Doby said.

"A lot nicer than what he did to Marcy. He has it coming. And his family as well. I want to bring his entire world down around him."

"Then, let's get started; it has to hold up to government scrutiny. It has to be airtight if you want Nessler to end up in a specific country."

"Ok, let's go, but first send the info to Director Spelling. That's stage 1."

"Done, ok, let's get Nessler."

The pair worked through the night, ending their work at 4am. They accomplished a lot of research, but it was still slow going with only two people. Next, the plan would need to be laid out. Then all the falsified documents required to pull off their story needed to be date stamped correctly, which meant a lot of computers to hack.

They created a semi-real world of horror that would overshadow Nessler's involvement in this latest conspiracy. Alfred Tennyson said, "A lie which is half a truth is ever the blackest of lies," and Lexi had plans of this being the blackest ever.

CHAPTER 48

NORAD

NORAD had turned into the Whitehouse; it was a bee-hive of activity. Politicians and their families are being moved to safety. The new situation room, tracking all military action around the globe and a President trying to stop the world from burning.

Straight into the Presidential office, President Edwin had a run of calls to the leaders of his allies. He pleaded for patience but to be ready. If talks fail. Several leaders offered to negotiate for calm since the United States was seen as an aggressor by China. The President was thrilled for their support, especially since to stall was the option Art Damani had requested.

Art said to react like a President; otherwise, his enemies might suspect something. That means my enemies are here at NORAD with him, but my friends were really close. Suddenly, he spun in his chair and faced the only other man in the room. Head of the Secret Service Chad Langdon. He got up from his chair and walked over to Chad.

"I spoke to Art Damani earlier."

"Smart move Sir, man's very switched-on," Chad replied.

"He said my friends are very close?"

"Like I said, he's very switched-on."

"Are you part of these friends?"

"I've always been that kind of friend, Sir."

"True, you have been, and I always appreciate that. So, are you going to tell me what's going on?"

"Did Art tell you what's going on?"

"No,"

"Like I said, very switched-on man."

"Geez, the world is about to burn, and everyone is quoting Confucius," the President said in frustration.

"I can give one more piece of advice; you'll need to NOT make a big deal out of Director Spelling not being here."

"He didn't come in?"

"No, Sir, He's on a mission,"

"God's speed to him, then. Ok, let's get to the situation room and see what's been happening."

The two men left the office, not knowing that the world had been amping up since they left the Whitehouse.

The situation room was a lot calmer than the rest of the ant nest, but that was their job. Stay calm, report the facts, let the President make the judgments. As the President entered, the Chief of Staff and Secretary of State tried to get an audience straight away, but the President had another itinerary in mind. So, he walked straight to the big screen, "General update me."

"Since the last report. Our Allies have gone on alert. Japan, South Korea, India, and Australia have mobilised. That brought an immediate response from Nth Korea and Pakistan, who have mobilised as well. Nth Korea has moved its Mobile Ballistic Missile launchers. China has massed troops on the Mongolian border. Russia has responded with the same. What is your response, Mr. President?"

"Keep the same levels. Have the South Korean and US air command hold a no-fly zone over South Korean waters. Also, General, I want a Stealth bombing run between Guam and South Korea initiated. I want a plane in the air at all times. Is everything running for DEFCON 2?"

"Yes, Sir."

"Outstanding,"

President Edwin turned and walked to see the Chief of Staff and Secretary of State. "Yes, gentlemen. How can I help you?"

Chief of Staff Cashdon jumped in first, "Mr. President, Director Spelling hasn't signed in."

"Yes, I know Linwood. He has informed me."

"But protocol says…."

"I know what the protocol is! He is out with his spooks trying to prevent this!" the President points to the situation screen. "Anything else?"

"No, sir, how can I help?"

"Keep everyone on task; make sure all rosters are stuck too. This is no time for sleepy staff."

"Yes, Mr. President." The Chief of Staff walks off, and the Secretary of state walks up. He looks at the situation board. "Is this all necessary?"

"This, yes. All this is standard for this type of event. They have contingencies for every move the enemy makes."

"Is China really our enemy?"

"No, but if they do something rash or stupid. We have to respond to save American lives. I have a job for you; check with the Japanese and Indian leaders to see if they have communicated with China. Find out what China wants to deescalate the situation. Then get me the Chinese ambassador on the line."

"I've tried, but he won't speak to you."

"Just make it happen! Tell him he'll be the first target at which I'll aim a missile if he doesn't get on the phone. Then, offer him something, a season ticket to the Lakers."

"Yes, Sir, I'll get it done."

"Advice, Sir?" Chad Langdon, head of the secret service, said.

"Go ahead, Chad."

"Go see your family. Go see all the families."

The President let out a big sigh. "You're right. Are you sure you wouldn't like this job? You'd be good at it."

"No, shit pay."

The President laughed. "Yeah, you're right. Shit pay."

CHAPTER 49

BITTER COLD

The bitter cold bit hard through even the best winter clothing. This was Russia; they invented cold. High winds blew through the group's vestments as they loaded the truck with their gear. Keeping one's hopes up in this weather was a momentous task.

The routine was familiar; after 42 years at the CIA, he'd done it all. Director Spelling had to make many trips to Russia in his heyday. But the bones were older and the limbs not as flexible as before, but the spirit was just as strong, and the determination that led him to the top was getting him through this last trip; he hoped it was his last trip. No journey before had been this important. They were all critical, but the stakes on this one was as high as it gets.

The Directors' Black Ops team travelled on this mission with him. He didn't know how he would be greeted, turning up on such an important man's doorstep, unannounced.

Art and the team had done their work, gathering every bit of evidence they could on the real people behind the Man virus. They linked them all together, followed the money, tapped phones and computers. Now the ultimate card was up to him to play.

There was a list of all the known collaborators in the Russian Government and military with all the intel. But, who do you give it to? Who else might be involved, and who would listen to the head of spies from America?

They travelled in a large moving van with one of their oldest assets in Russia. With Spelling in the passenger seat and the four remaining Ops in a hidden space in the back, they made their way around St. Petersburg after coming through Finland. The countryside was magnificent. Winter had a hold on Russia, but the snow only enhanced its beauty. The trip was treacherous, not from patrols but poor roads in the regional areas. It would be easy to end up in a ditch and be snowed over by morning.

5 hours later, the van pulled over beside a lake in a designated hidden area at an abandoned farm. Here, Director Spelling had a kilometre trip through the snow to the gates of a wealthy estate by

the Reka Suda. The home of the former President of Russia till 2 years ago, Vladimir Volkov. Volkov was the Russian President for 19 years and the most influential figure in Russian modern history. He retired two years ago, but Director Spelling has heard that he still controls the country from behind the scenes. For example, the new President Matvey Zaitsev was hand-chosen by Volkov and seemed to sprout the same rhetoric that came from Volkov.

In the past 10 years, Director Spelling and President Volkov have had a lot of run-ins and direct meetings to sort issues out behind the scene, mainly to save face with the Russian and US citizens. Things like captured spy swapping were an everyday event. Spelling knew if he approached the new President, he might not even give him a hearing, so he counted on Vladimir to hear him out and hopefully use his influence to stop this catastrophe. Turning up on his doorstep in the middle of a Russian snowstorm seemed the most subtle form of entry.

Damien trudged his way up to the front gate, barely seeing his hand in front of him. He looks at the brick pillars on either side of the large steel gates. No doorbell, "what!" He can see a guardhouse only metres away with a fire going, but if he yells, they probably wouldn't hear him. So, he looks around on the ground and finds a large rock. "Well, this could get me shot," he says out loud as he bashes on the steel gate. Moments later, two guards come racing out; they open the gate and march the Director into the guardhouse. The Director didn't realise how cold he was till he got inside a warm room.

In perfect Russian, the Director explained he was the CIA Director Damien Spelling. The two guards looked at each other in disbelief until Damien handed over his papers. The look of shock overtook them; Damien explained he was here to see Vladimir Volkov. One guard jumped on the landline and rang the house. Moments later, a familiar voice came on the phone.

"Director Spelling, are you here to defect?"

"Not bloody likely; how do you people live in this weather?"

"Usually indoors. No Russian is stupid enough to walk around in a snowstorm in winter. Did you want to bring your team in also?"

"I'm alone."

"Damien, I know you don't come into my country without your shadows, don't worry, they will be safe. You will be my guests; if you don't, they will be dead from the cold by morning."

"Thank you, Vladimir,"

"Not a problem; I've been waiting for you."

Damien called in the team; they left their weapons at the guardhouse and were driven to the house. The house was more like a mansion. The architecture was from the late 1800s and was a country estate of the last tsar of Russia. The timber workmanship inside was incredible, with multiple species of hardwoods used to enhance the colour scheme.

The house captain split the team up from Damien, making them very nervous. However, the nerves were eased when led to a games room. There was a roaring fireplace and food and drinks. Damien was then led into the study, where Vladimir Volkov was waiting.

"Damien, good to see you."

"Is it? You said you were expecting me."

"In all the years, we've been at each other's throat. Apart from myself, you were the one person who knew what was always going on."

"Well, I must be getting old because I fell into this one."

"Here, this is everything we have uncovered so far on this Man virus." Damien handed a thick folder to Volkov. He took the folder to a desk and started flicking through the pages.

"Captain,"

"Yes, Sir," the captain stood at attention.

"Arrange rooms for Director Spellings men; they will be our guests tonight. I will need a ream of photocopy paper. Also, bring in my Cognac, the Director, and I have a long night together."

"Yes, Sir," the captain raced off to do his commander's bidding. Once the captain returned, glasses of Cognac were poured, and Volkov had arranged his desk; he opened the file and began.

Through the night and into the morning, Damien and Vladimir Volkov, the ex-President of Russia, discussed the file's contents. Typically, the Cognac and a warm fire would have put Director Spelling asleep, but not tonight.

The conversation was intense, discussing what they believed the enemy's strategy was, how they could pull it off, then came the who would they need to pull it off. Throughout the night, Volkov made lots of notes. Damien loved the banter with him; it is rare to speak to such a great mind.

Then Volkov turned to his loyal captain again.

"I need the latest updates, please, captain."

"Yes, Sir, immediately."

Moments later, he brought in a laptop; Volkov brought up a screen with all the latest satellite images and updated positions of all the military on the planet. It was his own situation room.

"Your President appears to be a real diplomat. China has stalled its troops, most likely because of diplomatic reasons. So, I assume you would like me to talk to China and use my old influence to negotiate peace. That is why you are here, I assume."

"Well, yes, and no."

"Hahaha, the old Director Spelling, I'm about to ask for something unreasonable line."

"Spill it, Chief of spooks."

Damien laid out his plan in detail and timing. Yes, the President is stalling for time, not to slow the Chinese down but to get an answer from Volkov about his help.

"Like I said, you ask for the unreasonable. But this time, the unreasonable is the only option I have. You do know this will put my country on edge." Volkov said.

"Yes, but who better to smooth it over."

Volkov picked up his phone, "Fine, let's get this started; you better make your call, Damien."

As they both got on the phone, the earth turned, and nobody felt it. 'But with these calls, it was about to start a new horror show that would be felt around the world.' Damien thought.

CHAPTER 50

THE TAKE DOWN

The President stood like a statue in the room's corner by himself. Watching, like a chess master, he was playing out everyone's moves as they made them. He was guessing their motivation, their end game. Mostly where to cut them off before too many lives were lost. Even Director Spelling and Vladimir Volkov would have been impressed if either were here.

Chad was watching his boss as he always did. But, for some reason, he has got more engaged and more personal with this President than with any others. He could feel his stress, concern for lives, and personal disgust for hiding in this hole, but those were the rules, which were designed for the nation's good.

Chad's phone buzzed, and he jumped. 'Geez,' he thought, he's not the only one tense, it seemed. Chad grabs his phone. It's time! He moves over to the President and asks him to accompany him to his office. Both men kept their composure as they left the situation room. The concerned President and the steely eyed Secret Service Chief.

The President followed Chad to his office. "Mr. President, please take a seat. Listen carefully. I'm about to give you a folder with information about the people behind the Man Virus. You will not have time to review it all because a new ally is waiting for your call. The finer dealings can be left to the FBI. It's the players who should concern you first.

"Who put together this information? How do I know it's legit?"

"The answer to the first question will alleviate all doubt. It was first come across by Captain Madden's team, who now is Major Madden. The initial info came from The Water Tiger."

"What! You expect me to believe HIS intel can be trusted?"

"Yes, it seems even he has a conscience. Water Tiger has been helping along the way, giving us intel from within. Once Art Damani got involved, they traced everything to do with all the sites. They catalogued everything, including the money. Unfortunately, this information has come at a great personal cost to the team tracking them down. 2 Planks, Madden's Sergeant, was shot on one mission and may never return to duty. Lexi Eldridge the computer lady's friend, was tortured by the group and killed. I know you trust these people, but to bring this to a halt is going to shake your government, maybe to its own end."

"Damn my government. If my people are involved, I'll light the torches myself."

The President opened the folder and started reading. He was an intelligent man; he didn't need things spelled out; he could join the dots. Finally, President Edwin stopped and looked up at Chad.

"So, you were spying on me?"

"No, Sir, I was spying on everyone around you. My apologies; I will hand in my resignation after this is finished."

"Save it. We will probably have to do it together."

So, the tension was rising. Chad could see it in the President; he was getting angry. Continuing on, thinking something through before he read further. Reaching the page with those involved, he gave no reaction; from reading what had transpired, he knew who must have been pushing his buttons. He paused another moment. "So, Director Spelling is with my new ally to stop all this?" The President asked.

"Yes Sir."

The President reached for the phone and dialled. "Major Bracker, can you bring yourself and six of your men to Chad Langdon's office, please."

The President dialled again. "May I speak to the Director, please? This is President Edwin. Thank you. Hello Bryan, how are you? And the family? Great, excellent. Me, well, you know, a little tense, trying to stave off a nuclear war, just another day at the office. Bryan, I'm about to send you some information on Fredrick Nessler. I believe he is in the United States at the moment. This is to be your number one; he cannot get out of the country right now. The reason, treason! He is to be captured; if possible, I would like him alive. Ok, thanks, Bryan. Keep in contact."

The President looked at Chad. "Ok, who is this ally? That's going to help stop this?"

"Vladimir Volkov,"

The President stood there stunned.

"Volkov, Damien flew to Russia and got Volkov to help with getting China to step down?"

"Yes, and more. Director Spelling has convinced Volkov to come out of retirement and clean house."

"Holy shit!" the President said, stunned again.

"Volkov is waiting on a call from you."

"Me,"

"Yes, you're the President, Sir."

Chad handed the President his phone, and he dialled the number.

"President Edwin, such a pleasure to finally talk,"

"We have talked before, Geneva 2014."

"Oh yes, I remember. You were a senator then. At the arms agreement talks. You were the impertinent one who said there was no real point in signing the agreement if you weren't going to stick to it. You noticed; I stuck to it."

"Yes, but only because of what I said."

"Maybe, Mr. President, maybe. If we do this, you know President Yange will still be very upset. He still may not listen to us."

"Yes, I have bribed the Chinese ambassador to organise a call for us."

"Bribery, what will the American people say? I feel you might have a short presidency after this comes out."

"I don't really care, Vladimir; if I stop a war, I will sleep at night. What about you? There will be a backlash for you, too."

"No, not really. Once Russia sees what I do to the traitors, everyone will settle down quickly."

"What are you going to do to them?"

"Shoot them, Mr. President. Publicly,"

"Shoot them, without a trial,"

"That's how we deal with traitors in this country. What will you do, put them through the American justice system? Wasting tens of millions of dollars on fancy lawyers to let them get off on a technicality."

"Well, it's fair."

"For the rich may be, Mr. President."

"President Yange will ask for something unreasonable for his trouble. Just remember, all we have done is call China some nasty names. The main thing is to back away all military straight away. And then, as you say in America, 'eat crow' for the press for a few months. Well, maybe longer for you."

"Ok, I have the guards waiting outside; when it's done, we can call President Yange together."

"Agreed,"

"Oh, Vladimir. One last thing. Can you make sure Director Spelling and his men are returned safely?"

Volkov laughed, "Certainly, Mr. President, I might try to recruit him while he's here with me."

President Edwin laughed then, "Good luck with that, the man shits, red, white, and blue."

"Yes, he does; you better not lose him from your administration. If you survive."

"Thank you for your concern. Talk soon."

The President hung up the phone, ventured outside, spoke to the major in security, and filled him in. He was also gobsmacked, but he knew his job and who his commander was. The President made sure the situation room recording was running. He told Chad, later on, when the press had a feeding frenzy, to leak the footage to the media.

The arrests were totally different. General Hagart gave up calmly. He knew once he saw the guards entering that the gig was up. Linwood Cashdon, on the other hand, was like a scene from a soap drama. Screaming his innocence, screaming he was set up, he had names, and wanted his lawyer. You could hear him all the way to the brig.

The centre was in shock; it was a mild way of putting it. In such a confined environment, the news travelled like a bush fire. The rumour and speculation mill started instantly, not surprising considering all the politicians and their families were here. In Moscow, things went considerably differently.

After a military helicopter picked up Vladimir Volkov, it few him direct to Moscow. The Russian military surrounded the military bunker where the Russian version of the US situation room was housed. Troops jumped to attention at the sight of Vladimir Volkov; respect and fear were still prevalent in Russia for this powerful figure. The fact that 4 units of Spetsnaz special forces, over 50 KGB officers, and an armoured division turned up with him also boosted his presence.

2 Special forces teams were given names and photographs of the people to be taken into custody for treason. The fact that 2 of

them were the two highest figures in parliament made no difference to them. If Volkov said it was so, it was so.

Volkov's entrance into the bunker was as spectacular as it was terrifying. These were Russians in this room; they knew that the site of Volkov walking into the room meant, as 16 Spetsnaz soldiers stormed in from behind him, only meant misfortune for somebody.

The Spetsnaz spread out in teams, going through the room, grabbing and throwing the people on the list to the ground. Roughly handling them as per instruction, to show force. They zip-tied their hands and dragged them out, screaming, "What have I done?" The fact the President and Vice President were treated precisely the same told everyone who was in charge. Just in case anyone wasn't sure, "I am now in charge; the people who have been taken away are charged with treason against the people of Russia," Volkov looked around and made eye contact with everyone. "Contact all our forces and tell them I am now interim President and commander of the Armed forces, do it now," Furiously, officers started typing or getting on the phone. "Tell them to standby for new instructions."

The arrested parties were thrown into a transport and taken away to be... interrogated.

Volkov got on the phone with President Edwin.

"It is done, Mr. President; get President Yange on the phone."

"Ok," President Edwin agreed.

Ten minutes later, a video conference call was put through to Chinese President Yange. The three addressed what had happened with Russia and the United States, spelling out the international conspiracy. Both Russia and the US President explained that they had arrested those responsible for treason. The conversation went on then about everybody having to stand down militarily in stages. So, they all decided to do that while they were on a conference call. All nuclear sites and planes were stood down and sent back to their bases. Then the military alert levels and then the troops. All this took a few hours before they could see each other's troops returning to their bases. Finally, a safer environment again. But President Yange wasn't finished yet. "I want them all! I want all the perpetrators," President Yange said.

"Mr. President, all I can say is it won't be possible for Russia to oblige. After they have been interrogated today, they will be publicly executed tomorrow. You will be able to watch it on the news." President Volkov said.

"That is an acceptable outcome." President Yange said.

"Also, the crown Prince will be handled within his family by the King."

"Mr. President, you know I can't hand over US citizens. So, they will be tried for treason through the American justice system."

"You call that a system, years spent going through your courts, just to be let off," Yange barked.

"They won't get off; there is too much evidence against them. They are being tried for the highest-level crime there is. It has a penalty of death."

"Really, that will remain to be seen."

"Since it was your people who uncovered this heinous crime against the people of China, I will wait to see what happens."

"Believe me, Mr. President, you will have your pound of flesh." President Edwin said. "Also, President Yange, I have been notified that there was a vaccine made for this virus, and China will be sent the details as soon as we receive it, also Russia."

"Then, this meeting is concluded. On behalf of the people of China, I thank you for ending this conflict. I was prepared to do all in protecting my country; I was prepared to watch it all burn...."

The threat wasn't lost on President Edwin, and it needed a presidential response, especially with Russia listening in.

"I am glad too, President Yange, because as soon as one of your silos lit up, there would not have been any China left for you to rule. So, while I am President, it will always be a smarter option to call and talk to me."

"Then, we are concluded" President Yange ended the call, but President Volkov was still on the line.

"So, you were prepared to fire nuclear weapons against him?"

"As soon as a silo came online, I would have ended the war before it began. If I am to be criticised for launching a nuclear weapon, I might as well launch a dozen and save millions of lives from war."

"Something for me to remember."

"It is; thank you for your help, Vladimir. Good luck with finding a new replacement."

"You too, President Edwin, I will send our double agent and his men back safely."

"Thank you" Both Presidents hung up.

President Edwin turned and saw Chad, the head of the Secret Service, standing behind him with a big grin.

"So, it takes a near nuclear war to get an expression from you."

"No, Sir, I just have wind," Chad replied, wiping the grin from his face.

"You really should take your comedy show on the road. You're good."

"I might; the people would love to hear how you pissed your pants while being hunted by a leopard."

"I didn't wet myself!" the President protested.

"And your valet had to change you," Chad continued.

"I don't have a valet." The President protested again.

Chad imitated the President being electrocuted on safari the previous year. "Zzirt Zzirt."

"Maybe you're not that funny after all. Stick to the Secret Service. The President informed him with a smile.

CHAPTER 51

PAYBACK

A slightly anxious business consultant plans his next moves on the runway of a rarely used private airfield in Washington state. He feels the wolves closing in, but there is still a fight left in him.

The plane idled as the pilots did their final checks before take-off. Fredrick Nessler was on his computer sending out messages and still getting no returns. Things didn't seem right. After they tortured the girl spying on him, he found out they were close, but a little too late. Everything was already in play, but now he lost contact with the others, so the prudent thing was to exit the country expediently.

Leaving to a country with no extradition policy with the US was always on the cards. Now just to get this plane in the air and... The sound of sirens came loud and fast. Police cars and unmarked FBI cars surrounded the plane. Nessler had seconds before they entered and arrested him. He grabs his phone and makes a call.

"It looks like I will be detained. Wipe everything and send in the cleaning crew. Kill them all."

The pilots opened the door, and FBI agents stormed the plane.

"Fredrick Nessler, you are charged with treason against the government of the United States by order of President Edwin."

Nessler stood up and offered his hands and was taken away, handcuffed but smiling.

****

While back at the Ark...

"It is done. We have succeeded." Art threw his arms in the air, let out a victorious "Woo hoo,"

"Excellent. Many lives have been saved. Now maybe we can concentrate on the Ark again. We have just got a request from the President of Kenya about working with them and their reserve." Doby said.

"Excellent, that is what we have wanted, other countries, to join us. Have you arranged for Sam to come back, Mike? It is terrible news about Sebastian. Should we contact him?"

"No, give him his space. He has to fight through this part of his life alone." Art said.

"I have to ask... What happened to the Water Tiger?"

"Mike told me they took him to the pickup point for the boat. He convinced the captain to drop him in North Korea once he went to port there, then he's on his own to live or die."

"He will have to one day pay for his crimes." Art said.

"I am sure if someone really wants him, he will be found and then pay his dues."

"Congratulations, you two. Your work has led to stopping a World War." Art says to Lexi and Doby.

"We didn't give as much as Ab, Marcy," Lexi said solemnly.

"Is there something I can help you with?"

"Yes, we need your help to do this. We need to use your contacts and Director Spellings," Lexi said as she handed Art a folder.

Art read the contents of the folder and looked at them both seriously.

"Are you both sure about this? This is something you will have to live with the rest of your life?"

"Yes, we have talked it over. We think it is fitting for what Nessler did to Marcy and Ab."

"Ok, I will help. I will talk to Director Spelling, but I can't promise he will agree."

"That is fine; we can only ask," Doby said.

"Now you can start planning your wedding again," Lexi said with a smile.

"Katelyn has already got a suit designer coming in next week for measurements."

"Excellent, that's what we need is something good to happen now after all this,"

"So true, Lexi, so true," Art agreed.

The next day was filled with the start of the media circus. Both the Russian and US presidents announced to the World media what had happened; and why top officials in the Whitehouse and US military were arrested for treason.

President Volkov had a more permanent solution as he showed footage of the public execution of all those involved. The reaction of the World was that of horror. Public executions were not something for the news, and only a few countries applauded their methods, one being China. The President, although horrified, was happy for the momentary ease of media on him and his government.

All the people involved were officially charged with treason, and lawyers were called. Fredrick Nessler was surprised to find out when he transferred all his money overseas. It mysteriously disappeared, leaving him with a court-appointed attorney. Everyone was gearing up for the public trial. The President said it had to be public for the sake of peace of mind for the American people.

At the same time, the Republicans didn't waste time to organise a senate committee into President Edwin's involvement to try to start an impeachment.

That night in the Ark, after everything and everyone was settled. Sam and Mike went for a walk to the air pad for some fresh air. The air was refreshing as a slight breeze was blowing on an overcast sky, promising rain shortly.

"So, what now?" Sam asked Mike.

"About what?"

"Everything, once this is all washed up."

"Home, I guess. What would you think of me giving up the force?"

"Relieved, but that's a call for you. Could you really walk away from it?"

"I was thinking of joining Art and the ARK staff."

"The boys would be happy."

"And you?"

"Yes, me too. What about Seb?"

"He is facing his own battle at the moment; once he sits for the medical, we will be there for him, whatever the outcome. You know he wouldn't want you to feel you owe him for what he did."

"Pretty hard, not too."

"Yes, I get it, but he would want you to move on."

The missing part of her happiness was still there; for years, Seb had been a part of their lives, and not having him around felt something was missing. They stood there quietly for a while, just enjoying the night views. Mike tapped her on the shoulder and pointed below. There, walking on the path around the ARK, were Lexi and Doby, walking hand in hand in the moonlight. Sam looked at Mike; he was smiling, somehow; she knew they would work out everything together. Mike leaned in to kiss her when Lexi let out a scream, startling them both.

"Are you alright, Lexi? What's happening?" Sam yelled to them from above.

"He proposed! Sammy, I'm getting married," she yelled back excitedly.

Sam let out a girly scream only women can do when they're excited.

"Congratulations" Sam and Mike yelled down. They watched Doby continue walking along the path, with Lexi bouncing beside him like a schoolgirl.

"My god, finally some good news," Sam said.

"I'll talk to the Colonel tomorrow and see what can be done. Then, I'll check with Art to see if the offers are still there. Maybe he might think we're bad luck."

"What do you think the others will do?"

"Not sure. We'll have to wait and see," Mike said.

They walked inside to head back to their room, and the boys were still up, gaming as usual.

Lexi and Doby were just getting back in their room when eight figures dressed in night camo appeared at a section of the ARK fence.

To anyone else, the ARK fence would be impenetrable, except with an explosive charge, which would alert security. But AZTECK wasn't the only tech company in the World. There are ways around everything if you have the right connections, as these men did. They were soldiers and definitely not any of the Major's men. Two of the men lifted a section of fencing they bought with them. As it was moved closer to the ARK fence, it attached itself via magnetic pods. One by one, lights lit up around its frame. Once all the lights were working, they took to the ARK fence with a mini blow torch. The Ark defences were not alerted as the particular fencing unit kept the integrity of the electrical current and optic fibre loop built into the fence. Entering silently, they blended into the darkness and made their way towards the ARK.

Knowing their target area, they moved through one of the Ark training areas while heading to the base of the Ark. Avoiding any possible detection, they made their way up the man-made mountain parallel to the access road. Heading to the entrance to the

HUB, they were informed of the style of security system they were using. An electronic card system using AZTECK technology. They prepared to enter using a card developed to mimic an actual card in their system. For all the millions paid and tech bought, they didn't research Lexi Eldridge. There is no such thing as busting her system; you either blew your way in or knocked on the door.

As soon as the false card was used, a silent alarm went off. Since it was the HUB, the protocol was that the computers were shut down to avoid anyone being able to hack them. The controls were then sent to Art, Doby, and Lexi's room with the silent alarm. All four of the HUBS processors were still up with Doby and Lexi in certain modes of undress after Doby's proposal.

Art hit the console, sending the alarm coordinates to the Major and his special forces and getting security to put the ARK on lockdown. Since they did not know who they were dealing with yet and the fact they were already breaking into the HUB. Art phoned Mike and his team, who were on the move in seconds. Their gear was outside, so the pistols they had with them, and Katelyn's knives were all they had till they reached the security office. The officer on duty was informed immediately of the alarm going off, and since he was only one floor below the HUB, he armed himself fully and made sure all cabinets were unlocked for Mike's team, who he was he told, were on their way.

Mike and Sam sprinted to their safe and retrieved their pistols and ammunition, tipping off the boys that something was going on. Sam yelled for the boys to get to her bedroom while she took up a shooting position, watching the apartment door.

Before entering the bedroom, the boys ran and grabbed their laptops from their own bedrooms.

"Aidan, hack into the security again."

"No, if we get caught, we could be in a lot of trouble," Aidan said.

"Mum and dad just ran out of here with pistols; I don't think they're worried about what we're doing."

Aidan was the younger son of Mike and Sam, but he was the tech whiz of the family. While working with Tyson the other day, he figured out his password so they could play with the Raptors when they're in Tyson's lab having work done. Aidan realised he could access the inner areas of the Ark through Tyson's link.

Mike's team had armed and were with the security night watchmen. The plan was to hold the position till the Major's special forces arrived from behind. They had to hold the line because only one floor below were the living quarters of their families.

"I have an idea," the night watchmen said as he ran down the hallway, ducking under window panes before Mike could stop him. The watchman sat with his back against the wall beside the entrance door to the hallway and pulled two of Thomas's unique mines from his vest. He set them and turned to head back down the hallway. While passing a windowpane, he didn't crouch low enough and was seen. There was an eruption of gunfire from the other side of the window as glass and timber showered the hallway. The nightwatchman was hit in the back on his vest, which threw him up against the wall.

"Cover me,"

The team returned fire as Mike ran, then slid beside the security guard and helped him back to a covered position. Luckily, he wasn't hurt badly.

"Mike, look at his body armour," Katelyn yelled, concerned.

The guard's back body armour where the bullet had struck him was torn like tissue paper.

"Jesus, what are these guys using?" Smith said.

"This is a kill squad; they will not let us hold them up for long," Mike informed them.

No sooner had he finished speaking than two flashbangs came sailing through a broken window.

"Flashbang!" Thomas yelled as they turned their backs and covered their ears to reduce the effects. Who knows how many of them would have been killed if it wasn't for the watchmen's planting of the mines at the doorway? The kill squad came rushing through the door with precision and deadly intent, right into two of Thomas's unique mines. Not prepared for the effect of eye and lung irritation, they retreated into the room to avoid getting shot down in the hallway.

The Majors team headed up the access road, getting closer to the HUB entrance. Unfortunately, the kill squad expected resistance from the ARK security and had mounted a mini-gun just inside the Hub doorway, cutting down two of the Major's men as they rounded the corner.

"Mike, they cut us off. They have a mounted mini-gun in the HUB entrance."

"Roger that, Major. We will try to push them back to the HUB."

"Roger,"

"Smith, check the security office for a gas grenade launcher."

"Great idea" Smith turned and headed back to the office. As he reached the office, he heard an explosion. The kill squad threw a frag grenade in the hallway, which had Mike and the team diving for cover. Once again, they entered the hallway at speed, this time with some kind of special mask Mike thought must have been a new design gas mask and goggles. Unleashing fire with the special rounds they were using forced the team into cover positions. They wouldn't be able to take these guy's head-on without losing lives; he needed time to think. The kill team's lead men charged down the hallway.

From behind Mike, a figure came racing past and slid as a wall of fire erupted. Two loud shots were heard as Smith went sliding along the floor, firing a shotgun into the faces of the advancing soldiers. The heads of the soldiers disintegrated as the rounds Smith used were solid shot, and with the precision of a top rifleman that Smith was, it was lethal.

Smith grabbed one of the soldiers' rifles and made his way back to cover as the wall behind him was obliterated by fire.

"Good choice," Mike said to Smith.

"Yeah, but it will piss them right off," Smith returned.

And they didn't have to wait long before the anger was returned.

"Grenades!" Katelyn yelled as they ran further back for cover.

"Retreat to the stairwell!" Mike called as they dropped back one by one, covering each other.

Back in the apartment, things were scary as well. The boys could hear the gunfire and explosions getting closer and closer.

"Do you think this will work?" a security guard asked Oliver over their comms.

"We have to help; you said the Major can't get in to help."

On the other end of the comms were the other two guards that operate the raptor patrols in the park. Oliver's plan was simple: barge their way through the enemy, using the raptor's speed and agility. Hopefully, this would help his dad and the Major.

The boys waited till the other raptors made it up to the Majors team. They wanted to make the most impact, so they needed to work together.

The ARK was on lockdown, but everyone was awake. Doby and Lexi were underway with an evacuation of the living quarters, just in case the situation couldn't be contained.

After last year when the ARK was attacked, things had changed. Staff had been drilled better, and plans to safely evacuate were drawn up. Also, there were more reliable commanders from Somalia helping. The call had been sent out, and a division of Somalian elite was on their way. The plan is; to keep everyone alive until then.

Tyson wandered the corridors with Loki and Thor, telling everyone to get ready for a possible evacuation.

Sam told Oliver and Aidan to get ready to evacuate. She found them on her bed with laptops and comm sets as she entered.

"What are you two doing? Grab your bags; we're evacuating."

"We can't go; we are helping dad and the Major."

"What do you mean, you're helping them?"

Sam moved over to the side of the bed and looked at the laptops in front of the boys. She saw the raptors they used to help herd the animals moving down a hallway.

"Where are they?" Sam asked.

"Coming up behind dad."

"What? What are you going to do with them?" Sam was worried the boys were planning on killing people with the raptor machines.

"We're going to barge our way through the bad guys, so dad can capture them."

"OMG, seriously," Sam was invested now. "Good luck, boys."

Oliver picked up the comm. "Raptor 1 & 2, ready."

"Raptors 3 & 4 in position.

The explosions ripped the hallway apart as the kill squad started advancing down the hallway to the stairway where Mike's team was holding ground.

Mike heard the pounding on the floor; something was coming up behind him and turned to see two raptors heading straight for them. Then Sherlocks instincts kicked in. "The cavalry," he yelled.

"Make way, be prepared to follow," He yelled. The team hit the walls as the raptors took the steps in one leap, gathering speed. A determined kill squad and two robotic raptors. The immovable object meets the unstoppable force. Mike was brave enough to poke his head around the corner and see what would happen with the counterattack. The resulting display was best described later as 'human ten-pin bowling.' The reaction time of an elite army team is probably micro seconds... unless you're being charged at by raptors. Once the survival instinct kicked in, it was already too late. One member of the kill squad thought he had the raptor lined up, but the reaction speed of these creatures was incredible as it dodged the fire and bounced off a wall, cannon balling itself in the squad. With their speed and momentum, the raptors had built up, the enemy had no protection. The hallway was narrow, and the vests weren't designed for this kind of impact. Bodies are literally flying in the air.

"STRIKE," Smith yelled as the soldier ten pins flew everywhere. It wasn't lethal, but it was undoubtedly debilitating, concussions, broken legs, broken ribs. The boys, happy with their effort, got the raptors to let out one of their calls you see in the movies.

"Move-in," Mike yelled as the team pounced on the bewildered enemy soldiers, disarming them and securing their hands and feet.

The boys continued on with Sam cheering beside them. Oliver picked up the comm, "moving in behind them, be ready." The boys did their best to slowly creep up on the two soldiers with the mounted mini-gun. As they slowly crept through the HUB, they could see the soldiers ahead looking out towards the access road. They moved in. Their weight on the tiled floor gave them away, but once again, reaction times were slow, practically non-existent. The soldiers couldn't believe what they were seeing, plus the fact they had just come from where their team is supposed to have been, 'my god, have they been eaten?' one soldier thought. It was a credit to Tyson and Rosi for their craftmanship on how realistic the raptors looked and credit to the young teens on how well they appeared genuine in their movements.

The two soldiers spun around as they heard noises behind them. A look of sheer horror on their faces as two more Raptors appeared behind them, moving slowly, surrounding them. They were trapped, thinking he was dealing with live animals; one soldier slowly started moving his hand towards the handle of the mini gun.

Sam yelled, "He's going for his gun!" in a bout of over-excitement.

"We got this, mum," Aidan said calmly.

Aidan moved his controls ever so slightly, and the raptor bent down to eye level with the soldier and growled at him like only a raptor could do. Immediately the soldier pulled his hand away, and they both raised their hands slowly, hoping the animals understood surrender.

The Major's team swooped in and disarmed and secured the soldiers. The Major's blood was still boiling. He had lost two good men again, and he wanted heads to roll, literally, but he knew the boys were watching and wouldn't betray their trust with such a brutal but necessary act. So, he gave a thumbs up, knowing the boys and his team were watching as the raptors started doing their calls once again.

For the second time in just over a year, an enemy soldier had thoughts that he had entered a madhouse... and maybe they were right.

CHAPTER 52

EPILOGUE

President Yange and President Volkov were right; the US judicial system was slow and unpredictable. Lawyers for ex-general Hagart and Linwood Cashdon slowed everything done to a crawl. Filing appeals and motions to squash the charges before the case even started, but so far were having no success as the information gathered was airtight.

On the other side of the world, things were getting brutal again. Director Spelling visited the King of Saudi Arabia, Thunyayan Abdul ibn Saul and was granted an audience because of their ally agreement with the United States. At the meeting, Director Spelling handed over the evidence to the King of his nephew laundering money through the King's family trust. The following week there was endless diplomacy with the King. His first reaction was to execute his nephew and all his immediate family. Throughout the week, several people, including President Edwin and Art Damani, pleaded for the lives of all. Finally, a conciliation was reached, where he spared the immediate family but banished them from the country. The nephew was still to be executed. If he left it unattended, the King would lose his position and respect.

The world had rotated again, and the stories changed, from let's invade China to government positions like, "we were just responding to your military build-up." No, sorry for the situation we put you in, just more government rhetoric. The extra rotation of the world meant more to others, though. For example, Art and Katelyn asked Doby and Lexi if they would be interested in a double wedding at the ARK in a month, which was accepted graciously. But for one person, that rotation of the world changed everything... for the worst.

Fredrick Nessler was brought to the interrogation at Guantanamo Bay. Wondering why they still bothered with the questioning. He hasn't told them anything about who was involved, and he's not going to. As he entered the room in hand and ankle cuffs, others were in attendance. His court-appointed lawyer for one and another government worker by the looks, a federal marshal maybe. He was right; the big man was a federal marshal with news of a release.

"Well, Mr. Nessler, you'll be happy to know you'll be getting out of here today. The government has waved your chargers."

Even though he was full of excitement, Nessler was no idiot.

"What's the catch?"

"You're leaving the United States for good… you're being extradited to Saudi Arabia. I'm here to transport you."

"Saudi, what for?"

"Don't know, don't care. My job is to get you there."

"I believe it's on smuggling charges. Since I am no longer your attorney, I will wish you the best in Saudi then." Nessler's attorney said.

Later on, on the flight to Saudi Arabia, Nessler's mind was running in overtime, 'smuggling charges are a lot more lenient than treason charges, even if it is in Saudi,' Nessler thought.

The next day Fredrick Nessler was again sitting in an interrogation room waiting on the appearance of someone from the United States consulate to discuss with him the charges. Furthermore, they left him waiting two hours with no water or even a toilet break. Then, suddenly, a knock at the door; as it opened, a stunning-looking woman in a business suit walked in.

"You took your time," Nessler threw at the woman.

"Mr. Nessler, if you had a window in your cell, you would see that you are no longer in the United States. Everything here is done at the leisure of the King. Including the United States embassy."

"Yeah, ok. I want to plead a deal with the King or whoever is in charge."

"With what, for what?" the Embassy lady asked.

"I can give them names of the people who organise the smuggling."

"Mr. Nessler, I don't think you appreciate the situation you are in. The King had to execute one of his favourite nephews a few days ago because of his dealings with you and this China conspiracy. So there has to be more, something he can bargain with to our government, a trump card."

"Will that get me off?"

"Nobody knows, but it's your only chance."

"I'll send for coffee; here's some writing paper. Put down the names, the system you use, anything they can trade something for, then you might become an asset instead of a victim."

The lady left the room and brought coffees back a few minutes later.

"I'll get onto the embassy and ask the consular general to ask for a hearing with the king on your behalf."

Standing in the corner negotiating with her boss, she could be heard pleading the case for Fredrick Nessler. Minutes later, Nessler was still writing to save his life as the embassy staff member came over.

"He wasn't happy about it, but he has agreed, because you still are an American citizen."

"Excellent, I have added the Russian contacts I had too, so that should help."

"Fantastic,"

"What is the penalty for smuggling guns in and out of Saudi, anyway?"

"Guns, what guns?" the lady asked calmly.

"The guns, I'm being charged for smuggling," Nessler said, confused.

"Here, Mr. Nessler, this is what you are charged with." The embassy lady handed Nessler a folder. A look of horror came across his face.

"No. NO WAY! This is not true. I smuggled guns, not children. I'm not a human trafficker."

As you can see, Mr. Nessler, all the facts are there. Collaborated by the FBI, Interpol, and 6 other countries."

"It's all fabricated; it's all lies!"

"So, you're saying someone planted your whole history from the last ten years in some of the most encrypted sites in the world?"

"Yes, that's exactly it," Nessler protested.

"I suspected something like this. I think I know who's responsible."

"Who?"

The embassy official took a photo out of a folder and slid it across the table. Nessler went white as a ghost.

"She did! Do you know who she is?"

"No, I don't know her."

The picture was of Marcy Booking, the ANONYMOUS group member that Nessler tortured for information.

"Are you sure you don't know her? Isn't she the one you tortured to get into this position?"

"Who are you?"

"I'm the person who sent you here; I was Marcy's friend. I wanted to show you REAL power. You're sitting in a CIA holding cell until tomorrow when you will be executed."

"What!"

"Death by stoning!"

"No! no way. I'll tell them what you've done."

"You don't get a chance to speak; just scream."

Lexi was enjoying watching him squirm.

"I sent you here to watch you die screaming. The King has ordered a decree as part of your stoning; the participants aren't allowed to hit you in the head, just crush your body. There will be a religious adjudicator there to officiate. If the participants get tired, the adjudicator can call a one-hour break while you suffer and they get to rest. Isn't that nice of the King?"

"Guard! GUARD!" Lexi let out a laugh.

"They're all with us; they can't wait. I believe it will be televised. Oh, by the way, I didn't leave it there. The FBI and IRS are raiding your families and their businesses tomorrow to strip them clean. They'll most likely change their names. Especially after all the news, then your execution, then them having nothing at all. Yeah, I know, super bitch.

"Ha, nearly forgot Art Damani sends his best. You even stuffed that up. Your kill squad is dead or in custody. Actually, they were taken down by two young teenagers. Yeah, I know, kids these days."

Lexi was enjoying her rant. But, letting it all out here, like Doby said to do, bring nothing home.

"Well, the highlight for me is the stoning. Do you know I searched for days trying to find the best legal death I could get for you? No need to thank me."

"Who are you?" Nessler said, sounding totally lost for words.

"I suppose yesterday, I was Marcy's friend and an employee of Art Damani, but today I'm hell walking for you and your family...."

"Oh my god, I nearly forgot. I swear sometimes I should have been born a blonde. I have a favour to ask?"

"A favour, what?" Nessler asked.

"Tomorrow, before you die from being literally being crushed by stones. Can I take a selfie of you and me?"

Nessler just sat there, staring at her in disbelief.

"I know, it sounds tacky, but all the kids will be doing it. I just think it's impolite not to ask. I want to send it to Marcy's family and yours, of course."

Nessler had no words; he was in shock.

"See, I knew you wouldn't mind, last bit of publicity and fame. Well, I must be going now, need some sleep before the big last day. Hope you enjoyed your last coffee, which came from your executioner; life's funny sometimes."

Lexi got up and left the room. She checked that Director Spelling left instructions for Nessler to be put on suicide watch for the night, which he did.

The next evening, Lexi was flying back to Africa, where she will then catch the private jet back to the ARK. On her flight, she was sitting in her private booth crying. Looking at the selfie she took of her and Nessler before he died. Horrible, gruesome. Real-life is always more horrible than fiction. But she felt no shame; she did as she threatened and sent the pic to Marcy's family with an explanation, but decided not to send the pic to Nessler's family. Then she deleted it. Lexi flicked through mobile pics and found an old pic of her and Marcy. Then the tears really started flowing. A gentle hand was laid on her shoulder.

"Are you alright?" the flight attendant asked.

"Yes, just saying goodbye to a friend," Lexi replied.

The flight attendant walked off and came back moments later with a bottle of champagne and two glasses. "Let's say goodbye with style."

Lexi laughed through the tears. "She would have liked you."

CHAPTER 53

NEW FUTURES

The Ark was making the news today. Well, the social pages anyway. The long-awaited double wedding at the ARK is the first of many for years to come. After that, it became 'a thing' for the rich and wannabes to marry there.

The Ark had a carnival atmosphere, music, lighting, and drinks. Apart from the special guests at the weddings, there was an open invitation to staff members.

The wedding was held inside the ARK because of restrictions from the world heritage committee. Something about 'the number of human interferences in the evolution of the mountain.' Then came the debate about where in the ARK to hold the ceremony. So, a competition was held to see who could develop the best design. The vote ended up unanimous, Thomas and Rosi came up with the best plan.

It was a design that blew their minds and won the hearts of all. An African wedding shrine was built at the end of the pool, and the locker rooms were turned into Bride and Groom rooms. In addition, a unique Perspex platform was created that sat at water level in the pool, making it look like the brides and grooms were walking on water.

Everyone was in attendance, Doby and Lexi's mothers, plus their security detail. Katelyn's family flew in from Sydney on Art's private jet. Katelyn's younger sister, Tori, was a massive hit with the young men, stunning like her sister and an Australian Olympic competitor in gymnastics.

There was that light chatter and camera flashes going off as everyone wanted to remember this day, some for very different reasons. Suddenly the bridal tune was sounded as the bridal party made their way out. The men came out first in their dashing tie and tails, cream suits with vests in a jungle pattern, and desert dirt coloured bow-ties. The crowd loved it; camera flashes were going off everywhere like fireworks. As the grooms settled at the altar, they were left waiting for the traditional late arrival of their brides. Art and Doby had grins like kids at Christmas on their faces.

Then came the brides; since neither Bride had a living Father, Loki and Thor were chosen to lead them out in matching bow-ties like the men. The brides were stunning; no Paris runaway ever looked this good. They both agreed on matching dresses so as not to 'girly compete' with each other.

The dresses were more like a skin than a dress. The material was made especially for these dresses a sheer scale-like skin, with a shimmer that glistened in the lights; it also clung to every curve. It was from the company that made Katelyn's dress that she wore to the ARK ball last year, before they were all nearly killed by terrorists.

As Thor and Loki made their way up the platform, Loki did something out of the ordinary again; he recognised something, sensing danger, he stopped and lifted his paw. Everybody stopped. It wasn't till Loki and Thor turned to Katelyn and Lexi and started roaring things went a little haywire. The whole wild animal or crazy robots on the loose hysteria. Some guests began screaming, and others backed away, making for the exits. Tyson ran out of the crowd and started making his way down the platform, slipping and sliding. Art grabbed the priest's mic and asked everyone to be calm; there was nothing to worry about. Just give them a moment to sort this out.

True to form, many people had their phones out and were filming the entire episode for social media; the media contingent couldn't get enough shots. Already working on their headlines "Bride of Billionaire eaten at the altar." At the moment, the bystanders couldn't make up their minds on whether to film the man trying to run down the platform because they knew he was going to fall in the pool or film the brides that were going to be eaten by the wild animal robots.

The focus turned on Loki again as he heard someone coming down the platform. He turned and saw Tyson coming up behind him and let out a roar that couldn't be mistaken for anything but a warning. 'Don't come any closer.' Tyson didn't want to do it in front of this crowd, but he had to shut down the boys. As he reached for his wrist control, he heard a large crack underfoot. Stepping back, he saw large cracks in the Perspex, and Loki let out another softer roar to say, 'see, I told you so.'

Tyson turned to the crowd. "It's alright; the boys are warning the brides to get off the platform. It's about to break,"

Art was impressed. Never one to miss an excellent promotion opportunity. He announces that the boys just saved the girls from a faulty platform. Next, he called for three cheers for Loki and Thor. Which the crowd excitingly gave. Not to seem unappreciated, Thor and Loki let out a roar of thanks... thanks to Tyson's wrist command. Once again, the Bridal music started, the boys led the procession around the pool, and the wedding moved on with eye-watering moments.

Mike looked over to see if Sam was coping with the crying during the ceremony. He saw that her gaze was elsewhere and followed her line of sight. It went to the steps. She was watching Seb, 'Seb made it, fantastic' Mike thought. Sam looked happy he was here; she had been so miserable thinking she had babied him too much, and that's why he left. Mike was delighted that she was pleased. Mike also remembered Seb's medical for the return to work was yesterday, 'I wonder how he went, hard to tell from the expression on his face.'

With the nuptials finished and a million photos taken, Mike's face began to hurt from smiling so much. The family photos were fantastic, with everyone all dressed up. Aidan and Oliver were disappointed that the raptors weren't allowed in their pics. The reception food was set out as a buffet, there was a bridal table, but the rest was a grab a seat where you wanted.

Drinks flowed, and music blared as Tyson once again set out to wow the crowd with his Werewolf man, synced to the jukebox to sing any song requested. It was then the boy's time to shine in their suits. Disappearing off their table for over ten minutes until they reappeared with raptors in tow. The Raptors were carrying baskets of wedding cake slices and gifts from the bride and groom.

Mike noticed Seb hadn't come around to say hi, unlike him. He looked in great shape, a lot leaner than before. Art caught Mike's gaze and realised Seb hadn't come over yet to congratulate them.

Not long after, the guests were feeding their faces from the dessert table. Mike got up, went, and whispered in Tyson's ear. He turned and looked at his Werewolf, stood, and walked over to the robot. At the end of the song, Tyson paused the robot and got him to stand a few paces back as Mike grabbed the guitar out of the Werewolf's hands. Mike stood there and started tuning the guitar.

Sam was amazed the most, as she knew Mike had learned the guitar as a child but hadn't played one in over 30 years, as far as she knew. Doby popped over and asked Tyson what mike was doing, then walked over to talk with him. Doby starts strumming the guitar like a professional. Now, Lexi was amazed; she knew Doby could sing but never knew he could play the guitar. While Doby was doing some fine-tuning, Mike walked up to the mic.

"Nearly a year ago, the Ark and its staff were attacked by a group of terrorists trying to kill our friend Art and the President of the United States. Here, right where you sit now. In this battle, many good men died trying to stop it from happening. One man, an Australian SAS Elite Recon team member, died. His name was Deen Wellings; we called him Quassy. He would be here, about to sing, as was his thing. So, in this light, Doby and I are going to perform a song he often sang which seems appropriate for the occasion." Doby stepped up and started strumming some chords as they joined in singing John Denver's "My sweet Lady." The hall was silent except for the two on stage. There wasn't a dry eye in the room of 200 people. Ladies were diving in handbags for tissues as big burly men complained about the pollen in the air. As they came to the second chorus, everyone who knew the song sang with them; it was a moving experience that nearly crashed the internet the next day from social media. Sam's heard her phone buzzing and took it out of her purse; it was a message from Seb, "Life chose the right path for you."

As the song finished, to a thunderous round of applause. The boys raced up and hugged their dad, which was surprising for teenagers. Tyson reconnected the Wolfman, and the night continued.

Art felt something was amiss. As the night continued, the crowds dwindled, and the special guests retired to their rooms. But the wedding party carried on. Art had sent a message via one of the staff to Seb, saying he wanted to meet him up on the helicopter pad. He also did the same for Mike.

Mike made his way through the HUB and up to the pad. He was surprised to find Seb there.

"Hi matey, been waiting to catch up," Mike said.

"Yeah, waiting here to meet Art; he said he wanted to chat."

"Yeah, I got the same message." They looked at each other.

"I failed, can't even stay in the core, bullshit test, and doctor."

"What was the reasoning?"

"Lung damage, I passed their tests, but they said from the reports from the specialists the lung isn't as strong and could collapse again."

"I see,"

"What am I supposed to do now?"

"Well, for starters, go say hi to Sam; she thinks you're mad at her because you haven't said hello."

"Why would I be mad at her? What am I going to do, Mike?"

A voice came from behind. "Maybe I could answer that question," Art said.

"Thanks, Art, but I could never be happy with just training people."

"I didn't think you would; that's why I didn't offer. First up, are we finished with stopping World Wars?"

"There's always going to be wars while there are humans on the planet," Mike said.

"True, but otherwise extremely negative. I wanted to know if you both wanted to leave the service. Now that we have stopped chasing wars for the moment. I would like to concentrate on the Ark, the endangered animal side. How would you two like to start up a safari team? Travel the world and bring the animals in twos like Noah?" Art said.

"In two's," Seb said

"Like Noah," Mike added.

"Well, some of them there may only be one left, so we will let science do the rest. But, yes. Travelling the world through jungles finding and capturing endangered species. We received an invitation from the Kenyan government the other day to come and observe their reserve. They are interested in becoming part of the movement; it's very exciting."

"Well, I have a lot of free time on my hands now," Seb said.

"I'll talk to Colonel Briggs about it."

"You both will, and I think there are others on the list." Art said.

"Really, all of them?"

"Well, I'm still in negotiations with Zikmund. He drives a hard bargain. He wants a female companion for his Frankenstein robot I gave him." Art said.

"Are you sure the companion is for the robot?"

... They all started laughing together.

CHAPTER 54

RED IN YOUR LEDGER

The crystal-clear waters and isolation were perfect for reflecting on one's life. Mainly a small holiday island in the Philippines, Palawan was perfect. The Water Tiger ran a small boat rental charter on the Island.

It was just one of his many places to retire from the world. Here, the numbers were few, and he could blend in easily. Over the years, the hut he built had the most dynamic views of the shoreline and ocean. Even though he had enough money to buy mansions, you tend to get noticed less in a small hut in the middle of nowhere.

He still wasn't fully healed from his gunshot and hopes Nessler rots in hell wherever he is. It's been a quiet day; he even had time to go out fishing himself and catch some dinner. He was outside, fire grilling his catch of the day. When he senses something.

"Not too many people can sneak up on me" Water Tiger didn't bother to turn around. He knew why the person was here; he just didn't think they would find him this quick.

"So, my efforts towards world peace didn't wipe my previous slate?" the Water Tiger asked, already knowing the answer.

"No, you are too dangerous to be looking over one's shoulder for," the person said.

"Say hi to..." Two shots rang out from a silenced pistol. The fish kept cooking, and the night went quiet again.

****

Later at the ARK

Mike looked around the room. It was an interesting array of people. There was the fourteen-person crew of the Mosh Pit. Tyson and Rosi from bio-engineering. All Mike's crew was there with Art. They were just waiting for one more person.

"Sorry everyone, we are just waiting for one more person. Dan."

Just then, Dan walked through the door to the shock of everyone in the room. Art spoke first.

"Dan, is everything alright?" Art asked, extremely surprised.

"Yes, why?" Dan asked, confused.

"Dan, you're holding an ape?" Art asked.

"Yes. His family is giving him a hard time because he is not adapting to the new surroundings very well."

"Yes, but Dan. You hate apes. What about the 'Planet of the Apes' apocalypse?" Art asked.

"Well, Toby here can be my man on the inside. He'll tip me off if anything starts." Dan said convincingly.

"Good strategy." Art said.

"Plus, there's the fact that, if I try to get him off me, he pisses on me or sticks his tongue in my ear. So, I'm stuck with him until he settles."

"So, that's what that smell is." Art said, which brought a round of laughter from the room.

"Ok, everyone. Let me tell you about the ARK Stage 2."